"I'm dying for a taste of you, sweetheart," Nathan whispered.

Rachel tensed when his hand drifted down her spine to follow the curve of her derriere. Never had she allowed a man familiar privileges, even while she had supported herself as a singer and barmaid. Her impulse was to slap his face, but she granted him leniency because it was her fault those henchmen had beaten him up.

He opened those vivid blue eyes briefly and she got lost in them.

When he cupped his hand around the back of her head and drew her face to his, she tried to resist, but in the end gave in. Her dazed mind scolded her for permitting his familiarity. The truth was that she was enjoying the embrace of a man she didn't know....

* * *

The Kansas Lawman's Proposal
Harlequin® Historical #976—January 2010

CAROL FINCH

The Kansas Lawman's Proposal

HARLEQUIN®

TORONTO • NEW YORK • LONDON
AMSTERDAM • PARIS • SYDNEY • HAMBURG
STOCKHOLM • ATHENS • TOKYO • MILAN • MADRID
PRAGUE • WARSAW • BUDAPEST • AUCKLAND

Recycling programs
for this product may
not exist in your area.

ISBN-13: 978-0-373-29576-0

THE KANSAS LAWMAN'S PROPOSAL

Copyright © 2010 by Connie Feddersen

This edition published by arrangement with Harlequin Books S.A.

® and TM are trademarks of the publisher. Trademarks indicated with
® are registered in the United States Patent and Trademark Office, the
Canadian Trade Marks Office and in other countries.

www.eHarlequin.com

Printed in U.S.A.

This book is dedicated to my husband, Ed, and our children, Kurt, Shawnna, Jill, Jon, Christie and Durk. And to our grandchildren, Livia, Harleigh, Blake, Kennedy, Dillon and Brooklynn.
With much love.

Chapter One

Dodge City, Kansas, Late 1870s

Rachel St. Raimes muttered in annoyance as she left the boardinghouse where she lived to hurry down Front Street after dark. Loud guffaws and discharging pistols serenaded her. Texas trail drovers had arrived with their cattle herd earlier that afternoon. This evening they were celebrating the end of the trail by shooting out streetlights and gulping whiskey in more than a dozen saloons and gaming halls that lined the south side of the railroad tracks, which divided the town between rowdy and respectable.

"Well, well, lookie what we have here, boys."

Rachel tensed when she heard the man with a slow Texas drawl moving up behind her. She didn't glance back to see how many "boys" had swaggered across the tracks to wander the more civilized part of town. She quickened her step on the boardwalk when wolfish whistles filled the darkness.

"What's your hurry, darlin'?" came the second slurred voice.

When she refused to acknowledge their presence a third cowboy said, "Hey, no need to be rude to us. We just want to get to know ya, sweet thing."

Rachel clamped hold of her purse, prepared to slam it upside one of her hecklers' heads. Since the city ordinance prohibited carrying weapons on Front Street Rachel protected herself by stashing a lead weight from a cuckoo clock in her purse. Unsuspecting men hell-bent on manhandling her never knew what hit them until the five-pound weight collided with their skulls and gave new meaning to "getting clocked."

"Maybe we need to show this pretty, dark-haired chit some of our Texas charm, boys," the first cowhand declared.

Just then, Adolph Turner appeared from the darkened portal of the freight office, which sat four doors down from the boutique where Rachel worked. Although she disliked Adolph, he provided enforcement against the drunken trail hands.

"Go drink your fill on South Side and leave the woman alone," Adolph demanded sharply.

"Whoa there, friend," said the second cowboy. "We were just tryin' to be sociable."

Rachel wasn't surprised when a pistol appeared in Adolph's hand. He considered himself above the law and acted accordingly. "Be sociable on the other side of town," he growled. "There are plenty of prostitutes to go around."

Rachel gritted her teeth when Adolph snaked out his free hand to latch on to her elbow. He hauled her up beside him. All in the name of pretending to be gallant and protective, she reminded herself resentfully.

Take advantage of opportunity, that was Adolph's motto.

The instant the three unkempt cowboys raised their hands in supplication and backed off, Rachel pried

Adolph's fingers from her upper arm. "Thank you," she said stiffly.

"Say the word and you can have my full protection. Your life will become so much easier, my dear," he purred seductively.

"I have made it clear on a number of occasions that I'm not interested in your proposition." Rachel turned to leave, refusing to trade one unpleasant encounter for another.

Adolph grabbed her arm again and towed her inside the freight office. He was still wearing that charming smile she didn't trust. Having dealt with more than her fair share of manipulative men in her twenty-three years of difficult existence, she considered Adolph one of the more dangerous varieties. He had wealth and influence backing him and he didn't hesitate to use it to get his way.

"I have a package for your boss," Adolph insisted as he shepherded Rachel through the dimly lit shop.

"Hey, Mr. Turner, we took care—"

Rachel glanced over her shoulder to see the three hirelings, who worked for Adolph, enter the shop. She had no respect for the scraggly looking henchmen. The strong-arm brigade collected outstanding debts from hapless customers, who were naive enough to accept loans from Adolph.

Max Rother, Warren Lamont and Bob Hanes grinned conspiratorially when Adolph hitched his thumb toward the front door. "Make yourself scarce. I have business to conduct with Rachel this evening."

"Sure, boss." Max smirked, exposing the gap between his two front teeth.

"We have a few more accounts to collect on," Bob Hanes added as his beady-eyed gaze roamed disrespectfully over her.

Warren Lamont, the beanpole henchman with stringy

hair, didn't comment, just looked her up and down as if she were his next meal.

Rachel breathed a sigh of relief when the threesome turned on their heels and sauntered outside. The instant she was alone with Adolph, she jerked her arm abruptly from his grasp. She was wary and suspicious of men by nature and habit. It made her twitchy to have Adolph hovering close by.

"I'll tell Mrs. Grantham to pick up the package you claim to have for her tomorrow morning," she insisted.

Jennifer Grantham, owner of the boutique where Rachel worked, hadn't mentioned the arrival of an important package. She was leery of taking Adolph's word for it.

"It's a surprise gift for her daughter." Adolph pivoted to strut toward his office at the rear of the shop.

Rachel frowned skeptically while she waited at the threshold of the office. She was prepared to bolt and run at the first sign of trouble.

"It came all the way from Saint Louis on the afternoon train. I sorted it from the other goods before closing up shop for the night."

When Adolph opened the door to the storeroom and disappeared into the darkness, Rachel waited, her senses on high alert. Having good reason not to put faith in the male of the species, she didn't follow Adolph into the unlit room.

She flinched when she heard the clatter of wooden crates falling to the floor.

"Ouch! Blast it," Adolph yelped, then howled in pain.

Concern got the better of Rachel. She darted across the office to check on Adolph. She recoiled in alarm when he hooked his arm around her waist and hauled her up against him. She could feel his arousal pressing against her hip, and she elbowed him in the midsection to retaliate when he clamped his hand over her breast.

"Is that any way to treat the man who saved you from a mauling in the street?" he breathed against her neck.

Rachel shivered repulsively as she stamped—hard—on the toe of his boot. "Give me the package so I can be on my way."

His slate-gray eyes gleamed wickedly in the dim shaft of light that sprayed from the lantern in the office. "*You* are the package, love. I'm tired of chasing after you. You aren't a proper lady who has to be courted, but I can give you things that will make your life much easier and more enjoyable."

When his lips came down hard and demanding on her mouth, Rachel shoved the heels of her hands against his chest, then ducked her shoulder and plowed into his mid-section. Adolph stumbled over the crates that he had intentionally overturned to lure her into the storeroom.

With a squawk and a foul oath, the long-legged merchant went down in a graceless sprawl. Fueled by male pride and anger, he bounded up with his fist raised and his teeth bared.

"You troublesome hellion!" he snarled furiously. "I ought to turn my men loose on you after I've taken what I want. If you don't agree to become my mistress I might do just that!"

"And wind up like your previous mistress?" She smirked. "No, thank you."

Rachel had serious doubts about what really happened to his last mistress. Supposedly, she had been so over-wrought when Adolph ended their affair that she had taken a flying leap from the second-story window of Four Queens Hotel. Of course, his three henchmen *just happened* to be on hand to corroborate his story.

There had been no investigation.

"You had better consider what might happen to the Granthams if you don't accept my offer," he growled threateningly. "One way or another, I always get what I want."

"You can go to hell and take your ruffians with you," she spat furiously.

"And you need to learn subservient obedience!" Adolph snarled at her defiance as he tried to backhand her.

Rachel darted sideways to avoid being slapped in the face. She wheeled toward the office, but Adolph latched on to her trailing skirt and yanked her backward. She heard the rending of cloth and she yelped as she staggered to regain her balance. Adolph laughed cruelly as he swung her sideways and sent her sprawling inelegantly on the floor. When she bolted to her feet, Adolph lunged at her, grabbing the neckline of her gown and sending buttons popping.

Outraged, she swung her weighted purse and hit him squarely in the jaw. Howling in pain and shock, Adolph staggered back. He tripped over a crate and slammed his head against the protruding corner of a shelf. He went down like a felled tree. Blood spurted from his head wound. Several objects tumbled from the shelf and landed on his face, chest and crotch.

He lay there so motionless that Rachel wondered if he was dead—especially after the point on an anvil crashed onto his chest and forced the last gulp of air from his lungs. Frantic, she glanced around to find clothing to replace her damaged dress. When she spotted stacks of men's shirts and breeches, she grabbed two of each. She noticed a wide-brimmed hat and a small pair of boots and she grabbed them, too.

The two shiny buttons Adolph had ripped off her gown shimmered in the shaft of light, so she picked them up. Better to remove all evidence of her involvement in what might turn out to be a fatal altercation in the storeroom, she decided.

Rachel surveyed Adolph again but still he hadn't moved. Blood dribbled down his neck to stain the starched collar of his expensive white shirt. Whether Adolph was dead or alive—and she couldn't be sure which—his attack had sealed her fate in town. She had no choice but to flee town. He was influential and vengeful, and she had no doubt that his hired goons would brutalize her, corroborate whatever story he dreamed up to explain the incident in the storeroom.

She predicted he would insist the incident was her fault, just as he assumed no blame when his former mistress took the short way down to the street three months earlier.

When she noticed the pistol tucked in the waistband of his breeches, she retrieved it hurriedly. Then she took money from his wallet to compensate for her torn dress and to provide for necessary traveling expenses. Clutching the garments to her chest to cover her torn gown, Rachel dashed out the back door. She scurried down the dark alley to find a place to change into the oversize men's clothing she had taken as a disguise. When she scampered back to the street— a good distance away from the freight office—she latched on to the first horse that didn't bear recognizable markings.

While the Texans shot out a few more streetlights on South Side and provided plenty of distraction by whooping and hollering, Rachel rode away from town. She lamented leaving without a word of explanation to her boss at the boutique. Rachel had become exceptionally fond of Jennifer Grantham and her ten-year-old daughter, Sophie.

For the first time in years, she had a trusted friend and she had settled into a satisfying niche. Rachel had made a life for herself after years of trading one occupation for another. In every case, the change was the result of her dealings with a man. Damn them one and all!

Now she was on the run, forced to acquire more new skills to support herself so she could survive. She detested feeling like a weightless feather picked up and driven by the harsh winds of fate, but she accepted her destiny. She rode off into the night, carrying a stolen pistol and stolen money and wearing stolen clothing. In addition, she was riding a stolen horse.

Most likely, she had killed the domineering bastard who had pawed at her. Even if he had it coming—and he definitely did—she would be branded as a criminal and forced to remain on the run because of a situation that was beyond her control.

Her Cheyenne grandmother, Singing Bird, would have lectured her sternly for neglecting to avoid bad omens like Adolph Turner. Dead or alive, he would likely make her sorry she had ever been born.

Rachel took a moment to contemplate how many women had hanged for crimes in Kansas—and prayed to white and Indian deities alike that she wouldn't become one of them.

Three weeks later

Rachel glanced sideways while she sat on the wagon seat beside Dr. Joseph Grant. He took a swig from an embossed bottle of a patented cure-all labeled Yarrow Kidney Oil, then ignored her when she frowned in disapproval. Doc, who had saved her from disaster and uncertainty, had offered her a job in his traveling medicine show. Unfortunately, he had the bad habit of drinking his curatives—to excess—after they packed the wagon and rolled down the road each evening.

"It isn't even dark outside and already you're drinking your supper," she fussed at him—and not for the first time.

"Mind your own business, girl," Doc Grant mumbled. "I didn't pry into your past when I found you dressed in men's clothes and walking on foot in the middle of nowhere."

True, he hadn't, and she was exceptionally grateful for that.

After the fiasco with Adolph, she had ridden five miles down the road, then turned loose the horse she had commandeered for her getaway. She hoped the animal had found its owner so horse thieving wouldn't be among the list of offenses on her Wanted poster. She had walked in the darkness for hours before she heard the jangle of harnesses. She had come upon Doc, who was fast asleep on the wagon seat, while the team of horses plodded down the road on their own accord.

Rachel watched Doc tip up the bottle again to guzzle another drink. "I appreciate the fact that you didn't ask prying questions when we met, but that doesn't change the fact that fifty-proof rotgut elixirs and tonics are going to burn a hole in your stomach if you don't watch out."

"It's my stomach."

Doc smiled crookedly at her and her irritation dwindled. She couldn't stay mad at a man who was unique to the medicine-show business. He was a certified physician, not a fraudulent quack, and he preached against relying on patented cure-alls. He insisted that folks contact qualified doctors to treat their ailments. Doc was genuinely devoted to administering to patients in the small Kansas communities. Although he provided the expected entertainment, he examined dozens of injured citizens, and mixed ingredients from his stock of authentic compounds that he stored in the colorfully decorated medicine wagon he had purchased.

Unfortunately, when the sun went down he turned to the curatives he denounced and behaved as if it was his mission in life to drink all the tonics himself. He refused to tell Rachel what demons hounded him when his workday was done, so she couldn't help him fight his battles. But then, she refused to explain where she had been before she had appeared suddenly from the darkness to halt Doc's plodding team of horses.

Rachel was destined to tolerate his drinking if she wanted to remain with his unique medicine show. *Trade-offs. That's what life seemed to be about,* she mused as she took the reins from Doc's hand when he draped himself carelessly against the back of the wagon seat. She was allowed to wander the back roads, away from Adolph Turner's wrath—*if* he had survived. In return, she assisted Doc Grant while he treated patients, then she entertained the crowds by singing, accompanied by Ludy Anderson who played a banjo, harmonica or piano, if there was one available at a local saloon. She also dressed in costume to narrate Indian legends that her Cheyenne grandmother had passed along to her.

At night, she put Doc to bed to sleep off his bouts with the intoxicating tonics, though they weren't potent enough to fend off the demons that came calling from the darkness.

Doc levered himself up on the seat, then glanced this way and that. "Where's Ludy?"

"He decided to ride ahead and drum up business for us in Crossville," she replied.

"Drum up business? Ha!" Doc sniffed, then guzzled more Kidney Oil. "He's not fooling me a bit. He enjoys carousing with the ladies and he rides into every town on our circuit ahead of schedule, every chance he gets."

Rachel shrugged nonchalantly. She liked Ludy, who treated her like a sister, not a potential lover. He left her in charge of Doc more often than not, but Rachel wasn't complaining. All she wanted was to remain on the move and make enough money to support herself until whatever furor she might have caused in Dodge City died down.

"At least Ludy possesses enough talent to entertain people who show up at the wagon expecting musical acts."

"He does provide that," Doc conceded, then sipped his tonic. "While he's in town, we'll camp out as usual. We'll cover a little more ground before we stop for the night."

Having said that, Doc took another swig, then slumped beside her while she guided the team of horses down the road.

Nathan Montgomery sank down on his haunches beside a winding creek. He dipped his hat in the water, then dumped it over his head to cool off. He was hot and irritable, and the summer sun had been bearing down on him all day.

He didn't know why he hadn't opted to take the train to Dodge City. It would have been a hell of a lot easier. He supposed he'd felt the need to get back in touch with the wanderlust way of life he had known—until six months ago when he had been summoned to Kansas City to cater to his ailing father.

Nate scowled at the thought of Brody Montgomery's deceptive ruse. There had been nothing wrong with the sly old goat, who had tried to shanghai his youngest son into an arranged marriage.

"That had *disaster* written all over it," Nate muttered to his reflection in the water.

He had lived in the wilderness too long to become infatuated by the fragile, uninspiring socialite that his father had handpicked for him. Lovely though Lenora Havern was, her pasty-white skin had never seen the light of day and she had the personality of a porcelain doll that had a perpetual smile painted on her lips.

Now here he was, back where he belonged, despite his father's outraged demand to remain in Kansas City. Nate was doing what *he* preferred—and it wasn't attending the pretentious dinner parties and soirees that his older brother, Ethan, and his father enjoyed.

Casting aside his meandering thoughts, Nate submerged his hat in the water, then doused himself again. He thought he heard the crackle of twigs behind him, but with water popping in his ears he couldn't be certain. Then a snarl erupted behind him. Instincts he'd spent thirty-two years cultivating snapped to attention. He twisted on his haunches and simultaneously reached for the two ivory-handled six-shooters in his holsters.

Unfortunately, he reacted a moment too late. A shaggy-haired ruffian plowed into him like a steam-driven locomotive, launching him backward into the creek. He landed with a splat and a curse. His six-month hiatus in the city had cost him his edge. Although his reflexes were still lightning quick, the three hombres got the drop on him—and it proved disastrous.

Guffawing, two men latched on to his arms and hauled him ashore so the third man could kick him squarely in the chest. Pain slammed into his ribs and drove the breath from his lungs. Defying the pain, Nate hurled himself sideways, knocking together the two men who held his arms. Despite the lopsided odds, he landed two punishing blows on two unshaven jaws, then he barreled into the stocky scoundrel who had kicked him in the chest. His assailant hit the ground with a grunt, then groaned when Nate punched him in the jaw.

The youngest of the three men jumped on Nate's back and commenced swearing foully while he pummeled him with doubled fists. Nate tossed the young thug in the creek, then reached for a discarded pistol. Before he could turn it on the gap-toothed hombre standing in front of him, someone hit him from behind with a piece of driftwood.

Nate stumbled back, then kerplopped on the ground. Stars exploded in front of his eyes and his body vibrated like a gong. Before he could roll to his feet, the burly ruffian yanked him up and held him in a bear hug.

"Think you can take the three of us, do you? Think again," the gap-toothed scoundrel muttered in his ear.

Nate squirmed sideways to avoid another blow from the makeshift club, but he couldn't wrest loose. All three hombres commenced pounding on him. The world went out of focus as pain seared through flesh and bone and vibrated through his skull.

He collapsed on the ground, then grimaced when the toe of a boot gouged him repeatedly in the cheek and ribs.

That was the last thing Nate remembered before he blacked out.

Rachel glanced west toward the canopy of trees and underbrush that indicated there was a stream five miles down the road. "It's nearly sunset. Let's make camp up ahead," she suggested, calling Doc's attention to the trees in the distance. "It's been so hot today that I wouldn't mind a long, relaxing bath before I start supper."

Doc, who had worked his way through the Yarrow Kidney Oil, waved his bottle of Cough Balsam in the general direction of the creek. "Have right at it, princess. I'll unload the cooking utensils."

And drink himself blind, she added silently. Yet, during the time they had spent traveling across the Kansas prairies and woodlands, Doc Grant had never once mistreated her or made inappropriate advances—like Adolph and others had done the past several years. Doc was twice her age and he treated her like a daughter. He taught her to be an efficient physician's assistant and to mix the authentic medical compounds that he stashed alongside the patented tonics in the wagon. He concocted so many helpful remedies for his patients that Rachel swore she would never remember which ingredient, mixed with others, alleviated which symptoms and cured which ailments. However, she paid attention to Doc's instructions and tried her best to be the entertainer, nurse and assistant he expected.

She halted the wagon beside an oversize shade tree that sat a quarter of a mile from the dirt road. Then she stared pointedly at the half-full bottle of Cough Balsam before focusing on Doc's face, which was capped with short blond hair. A thin mustache rimmed his upper lip. His tormented hazel eyes met her concerned stare. He looked so sad it broke her heart.

"Doc, I—"

He flung up his free hand to shush her. "Go take your relaxing bath. You've worked hard and you've captivated the crowds with your performances. You've put up with me and you've earned some time to yourself." He flicked his wrist to shoo her on her way. "Go bathe now, hon. I have demons to drown before supper."

"I'll help you fight your demons if you'll tell me what they are," she offered sincerely.

He flashed a rueful smile, then he reached over to tug gently on the braid of raven hair that dangled over her shoulder. "My problems are my problems and my demons are mine to conquer. I think you have a few of your own that you keep to yourself, too. Do you plan to share them with me?"

Rachel sighed audibly. She was too ashamed to tell Doc that she was most likely wanted for murder. Or robbery. Or horse thieving. Or the combination of several offenses. He might believe her side of the story, but it was still her word against Adolph Turner's and his brigade of mean-spirited goons.

"That's what I thought," Doc guessed correctly. "You don't want to talk about your problems, either."

Resigned, Rachel climbed down from the wagon. She glanced up to see Doc take another swig from the bottle. Then he rooted around in the wagon, which boasted a colorful medicine-show logo. He twisted around, holding an armful of utensils and the makings for their supper.

She truly was curious to know what tormented Doc Grant. She'd heard snatches of mumbled utterances when he had been swimming in his cups. Something about a woman named Margie and delivering a child one dark and stormy night. She'd heard him curse God in one breath and pray for forgiveness the next. Her heart went out to Doc Grant and she hoped that one day he would trust her enough to confide his woes.

Obviously today wasn't that day.

Maybe she should confront him until he blurted out the source of his torment. Then he would demand to know who or what had her running scared.

Rachel considered herself reasonably bold and courageous, but she wasn't sure she wanted to face the condemnation and disappointment she anticipated from Doc when she admitted she was a murderess and a thief. Now, he was her best friend, and she was reluctant to lose him.

And so, they kept their secrets to themselves while they traveled from one small community to the next, treating injured patients and warning folks away from the useless patented curatives the charlatans sold.

Rachel slowed her pace as she neared the creek, which

was overgrown with underbrush and trees. She had lived with her grandmother's tribe long enough to exercise caution and to pay strict attention to her surroundings. Two-legged and four-legged predators inevitably visited rivers and creeks, so it was always wise to be alert.

The Cheyenne tribe had taught her self-reliance and survival. Her French grandfather had taught her how fickle, self-serving and unreliable men could be. As for her parents...

Her thoughts trailed off when she heard what sounded like a human groan, followed by a full-blown oath that burned her ears. Wary, Rachel crouched in the underbrush, trying to determine where the sound originated.

Several more curses erupted near the creek bank, but she didn't hear thrashing in the bushes. Cautiously, Rachel rose up to peer over the underbrush where she was hiding. She sank down when she caught sight of a man's auburn head. A thick beard and mustache concealed his facial features. Although her view was partially blocked by six-foot-tall cottonwood saplings, she noticed the man's arms were outstretched at an awkward angle. It looked as if one of his eyes was swollen shut. There were discolorations on his cheekbone, too.

When he groaned miserably again, Rachel took one step in his direction. Then she reminded herself of Adolph Turner's treachery when he pretended to fall so he could lure her into the darkened storeroom. She waited indecisively for a few more seconds, then remembered that she was packing Adolph's pistol in the pocket of her riding breeches and she had a knife tucked into her boot. After her ordeal with Adolph, she had vowed never to be unarmed again.

"Damn it to hell!" the stranger scowled loudly.

Reminding herself that she wasn't faint of heart and she wasn't about to change her ways now, Rachel clamped hold of her pistol and sidestepped around the bush. She glanced in every direction to ensure she wasn't walking into another trap. Then she approached the man who was still swearing ripely.

When she had a clear view of the stranger, she gasped in shock. She was so surprised by the unexpected scene awaiting her that the pistol tumbled from her hand and she fumbled clumsily to pick it up. Her astonished gaze fixated on the tall, muscular man. He was staked out—naked as the day he was born—and all she could do was gape at him.

Chapter Two

Although Rachel had dozens of unique life experiences to her credit, she had never seen a man in all his splendor and glory. Feminine curiosity left her gawking at the masculine parts of his anatomy. Then embarrassment turned her face candy-apple red. With a yelp, she dropped her stack of clean clothing on his abdomen so she wouldn't humiliate herself again by staring at his—

She swallowed hard and composed herself as best she could. The man was at least six feet two inches tall—or rather long, since he was lying on the ground. He was well proportioned, broad chested and covered with whipcord muscles. Try as she may, she couldn't squelch the vision of him lying completely nude from her mind.

"Who's there?" the naked man demanded, speaking out the side of his mouth that wasn't swollen twice its normal size.

When he turned his auburn head toward her, she realized that not one but both of his eyes were swollen shut. He had a knot the size of a goose egg on the side of his head and his hair was matted with dried blood. Blue and purple bruises covered his chest.

"Dear God, who did this to you?" she blurted out as she inched closer to take a better look at his injuries.

He cocked his head and tried to open one eye. "You're a woman? Well, hell! Ouch, damn it!"

He clenched his teeth and hissed out a seesaw breath.

"Untie me," he insisted hoarsely. "I want to hunt down those bast—" He dragged in a shallow breath. "Just untie me, please."

"No, I don't trust you," she said reflexively. "How do I know you aren't a wanted criminal and that a bounty hunter or lawman tied you up for safekeeping?"

Obviously, she had *wanted criminal* on the brain since she had recently become one herself.

"I'm an ex-soldier and…ex-lawman," he muttered.

His comment did nothing to reassure her, especially when she'd noticed the hesitation before he'd said, "ex-lawman." Her father had been a lawman before he'd abandoned his only child and his wife, then turned to thievery. Apparently breaking the law was more profitable than upholding it. This man might be guilty of the same corrupt thinking.

"I'm still not convinced." She stared skeptically at him and tried very hard not to become sidetracked by his washboard belly and horseman's thighs—and other body parts beneath the clothes she had tossed on him to cover him up.

"Sorry, I can't show you any sort of identification to convince you," he said sarcastically.

She glanced around, noting that whoever had staked him out had left nothing behind in the way of food, clothing or transportation.

"Look, lady, I realize this is awkward and you have no reason to trust me—"

"You can say that again."

"You have no reason to trust me," he repeated in the

same caustic tone she'd used. "But I'm pretty sure that the men who attacked me caused a concussion. I have a headache straight from hell. I'm no doctor but I'm betting I have at least one cracked rib—"

"Hold on." Rachel whirled around and dashed back to the medicine wagon.

"Don't leave me here, damn it!" he yelled, then swore when he apparently injured himself while shouting demands at her.

"Doc!" Rachel panted as she burst into the clearing near the gigantic shade tree. "Come quickly."

Doc Grant was down on bended knee, stacking fallen tree limbs on the campfire. He staggered unsteadily to his feet to follow her, and then he stumbled to a halt when he spotted the naked man she had encountered a few minutes earlier. Doc glanced speculatively from the stack of clothing draped over the man's abdomen to Rachel, who tried her best not to turn beet red with embarrassment.

"What the blazes happened here?" Doc choked out.

It was plain to see what had happened. Whether the brawny stranger had had it coming—just as Adolph Turner had—Rachel couldn't say for certain.

"I was overtaken by three scraggly-looking men," he mumbled. "I fought back, for all the good it did."

Rachel snapped to attention. Guilt hammered at her, and wary concern etched her brow. "Describe the men."

"The oldest one looked to be fortyish. Tall and thin, brown eyes and a gap between his front teeth," he reported. "One was in his middle twenties, average height, freckle faced, lean build with gangly arms and legs. The third one was short and stocky with dark, beady eyes and thick wavy brown hair. Early thirties."

"Haven't seen anyone fitting those descriptions around here," Doc Grant commented.

Rachel swallowed hard but kept her mouth shut. The naked stranger had described Adolph Turner's three henchmen. No doubt, Rother, Hanes and Lamont were out for blood—hers, to be specific. She had ruined the gravy train the goons had been riding with Adolph. Either that or Adolph had survived and had sent his brutal heathens to track her down, then drag her back to Dodge City to face his spiteful revenge.

Alarm pulsated through her veins. She had been traveling with Doc's medicine-show wagon—performing and appearing in costume to entertain the gathering crowds—thinking she was safe from discovery. Knowing those ruffians were scouting the area assured her that she needed to exercise even more caution than she was now.

When Doc strode over to untie the stranger's wrists, Rachel found herself admiring his long muscled legs, sinewy arms and broad chest. No question that his masculine physique appealed to even the most leery of women—Rachel being at the head of the list. She couldn't tell much about his facial features because they were swollen, discolored and covered with a dark beard and mustache, but she was definitely sidetracked by his body.

"Rachel, go fetch my bag from the wagon and bring a set of clothes while I examine our patient," Doc Grant requested.

She lurched around and dashed off to grab one of the sets of clothing she had swiped from Adolph's storeroom. Then she reached into the wagon to retrieve the black leather bag that contained authentic compounds and ingredients for Doc's medical concoctions.

When she returned to the creek bank, the nude stranger was sitting upright. Her clean garments were still clamped modestly over his bare hips. He was gingerly holding his arm against his ribs while Doc pried open his left eye to check the dilation of his pupil.

"Yep. Concussion. Hard to tell if your rib is cracked, bruised or strained, but I suspect it hurts all the same." Doc reached for the leather bag Rachel extended to him. "First, we'll get you into some clothes, then I'll mix up a sedative so you can rest comfortably."

"I don't need some patented elixir—"

"Listen, friend," Doc cut in sternly. "I travel around this state in a medicine-show wagon because that's what draws public interest. Nevertheless, I'm a certified physician who treats people's ailments. I am *not* a charlatan. It is my intention to undo the damage to patients on the outposts of civilization who turn to fraudulent quacks with their so-called patented medicine."

The stranger tried to smile at Doc's emotional outburst, but his puffy lips must have pained him because he grimaced.

"Fine. Sedate me," he said belatedly.

"What's your name?" Rachel questioned.

"Nathan Montgomery. I go by Nate."

"I'm Joseph Grant and this is Rachel," Doc introduced.

When Nate brushed aside the garments covering his hips, Rachel whirled around and waited for Doc to help him dress. Nate's moans, groans and muffled oaths filled the silence before Doc called her over to hoist Nate to his feet.

With Nate's arm draped over her shoulder, while Doc steadied his injured ribs, the threesome made slow progress to camp. Hurriedly, Rachel rolled out a pallet so Nate could lie down. He swore under his breath as he tried to shift into a position that didn't hurt.

Rachel knew Adolph's rough-edged henchmen were thorough when it came to strong-arm tactics of collecting overdue debts. Nate was lucky the goons hadn't broken an arm or leg.

"Drink this down and then get some rest," Doc instructed as he mixed several ingredients in a vial. "After supper I'll give you a stronger dose so you can sleep through the night."

Rachel watched Nate make an awful face when he sipped the sedative, but he didn't complain, just swallowed his medicine and waited anxiously for it to take effect.

"Go on down to the creek for your bath, hon," Doc encouraged. "I'll get supper going and you can tend to it while I bathe."

Rachel ambled off, but the moment she reached the creek her thoughts circled back to the image of Nate staked stark-bone naked. Whether he was an outlaw or ex-lawman, he was incredibly appealing to the feminine eye.

However, she didn't know Nate Montgomery from the devil. He might be using an assumed name. Whether he was honest and trustworthy was up for debate. Nonetheless, he had broadened her education of men unintentionally and the scintillating memory kept playing over and over in her mind.

"Stop it!" she muttered at herself as she peeled off her blouse and breeches, then loosened the braid of long raven hair that cascaded over her shoulder. "The sooner Nate recovers and goes his own way the better. You might have saved his life by finding him before a panther, wolves, coyotes or wild boars did, but that is the extent of your association with him. If you have any sense you'll remember that."

She knew it was best to keep an emotional distance and avoid personal entanglements while she was lying low. That was exactly what she intended to do. However, she missed her friendship with her boss at the boutique in Dodge City. Jennifer Grantham and young Sophie had always brightened mundane days. Unfortunately, Rachel couldn't contact them without putting them in jeopardy. If Adolph Turner had survived and approached Jen, demanding to know Rachel's whereabouts, she could honestly say that she knew nothing whatsoever.

Rachel sank into the creek and sighed appreciatively when cool water swirled around her. The past week had been unseasonably hot and dry. The team of horses pulling the wagon constantly kicked up dust, and insects buzzed around them, making travel uncomfortable. Doc had mixed a remedy to repel bugs but the smell was as offensive as the swarming pests.

Rachel felt her tension melt away when she submerged in the water to wash her hair. However, she was dismayed that the vision of Nate's naked body was there to greet her the instant she closed her eyes.

Nate was eternally grateful when the painkiller took effect. He mumbled a thank-you when Doc Grant dropped a cool cloth over his face to counter the swelling on his eyes, cheeks and mouth. He'd been roughed up, shot at and knifed in the line of duty the past dozen years. However, those three bastards had worked him over with fiendish delight—and he'd love to return the favor.

Obviously, Nate had lost his edge after six months of living in the lap of luxury at his father's estate—the very same estate Nate had eagerly left at eighteen to join the Army of the West. He had learned to fight and to think like the renegade Indians he'd battled, so there was no excuse for letting those three scalawags get the drop on him.

Now he was at the mercy of Doc Grant and Rachel Whoever-she-was. He couldn't stand on his own two feet without becoming dizzy and collapsing. Feeling helpless frustrated him, and lying around made him restless, but he resigned himself to making time to recuperate from his painful injuries.

He shifted slightly to take the pressure off his tender ribs, then his thoughts drifted to the woman who had happened on to him. Was she the doctor's wife? His daughter? His nurse? No one had said and Nate hadn't asked. Whatever the case, she had seen him naked and she had draped garments over his private parts to stifle her embarrassment.

Fleetingly he wondered why a certified physician would give up a private practice in the convenience of a town to wander the back roads. Had Doc Grant been run out of town on a rail because he botched a surgery? Since Nate had smelled alcohol on Doc's breath, he wondered if the physician had a problem staying sober while treating patients.

Being a U.S. marshal—not an ex-lawman as he'd told Rachel—Nate had learned to dig deep to find the answers to puzzling questions. The skill had served him well while tracking renegade Indians and ruthless outlaws—much to his father's exasperation.

"Is the pain fading?" Doc mumbled sluggishly.

"It's tolerable," Nate mumbled back, and decided the good doctor had taken a few more drinks since returning to camp.

Nate predicted he and Doc would be out cold before long. That would leave Rachel Whoever-she-was to stand guard and tend to supper. Whatever her connection to the physician, Nate hoped she had learned to handle weapons and defend herself. If those three bastards returned, they wouldn't have the slightest qualms about molesting a woman.

That was Nate's final thought before the potion sent him drifting into blessed oblivion.

Rachel emerged from her bath feeling revived and refreshed—until she returned to camp to see that Doc had passed out. An empty bottle of Stomach Bitters lay at his fingertips. He was propped awkwardly against the trunk of a sprawling shade tree. Resigned, Rachel grabbed his pillow from the wagon and walked over to ease him onto his back so she could stuff the pillow under his tousled blond head.

She pivoted to survey the bubbling pot of beans above the campfire. Then she glanced at Nate, whose breeches only extended within six inches of his ankles. The borrowed shirt—*stolen* shirt, she corrected—stretched tightly across the broad expanse of his muscled chest. He was barefoot because the boots she had confiscated—*stolen*—were too small to fit him.

Glancing east, then west, she silently prayed that no one would happen upon them while she was playing nursemaid to an injured stranger and an inebriated doctor.

Rachel had fended for herself for six years, and she had spent another six learning the ways of the Cheyenne so she could become an independent survivor. She glanced at both men, then shook her head in exasperation. Now what was that nonsense about big strapping men being the stronger sex who could protect, provide and care for women? Ha!

"Couldn't prove it by me," she mused aloud.

From personal experiences, she had learned that men were more trouble than they were worth. Her opinion wouldn't change anytime soon, either. Men were the bane of her existence.

Rachel dipped up a cup of beans and ate her evening meal. Then she tended the horses that waited impatiently to be released from the harnesses. While the horses grazed nearby, she tried to feed a cup of beans to Doc. He didn't respond to her coaxing. She was sorry to say that it wasn't the first evening that he drank his supper and conked out until his hangover greeted him midmorning.

Later, she sank down cross-legged beside Nate and removed the wet cloth Doc had placed over his swollen face. Nate stirred slightly and his mouth sagged open. Rachel fed him a spoon of broth, then covered his mouth with her hand to ensure he swallowed.

He pried open his eyes slightly and Rachel caught a glimpse of striking blue. With those vivid blue eyes, auburn hair and muscles galore, he was six feet two inches of handsome, virile man. Shave off the beard and mustache, dress him up in properly fitted clothing, and Nate Montgomery was likely every woman's fantasy come true.

Not *hers,* of course, but everybody else's. She did not intend to invest more time in Nate than it took to get him back on his feet and shoo him on his merry way.

"More," he murmured.

Rachel fed him the rest of the bean soup before he dozed off. Humming softly, she washed the utensils, then repacked them in the wagon. By that time, it was dark and the sliver of moon hung in the sky, providing very little in the way of light. She decided to bed down early.

No sooner had she pulled on her nightgown than she heard Nate moaning and groaning. Grabbing the lantern, she climbed down from the wagon to determine what had disturbed the injured patient.

"Damn that hurts," he said to no one in particular. "More medicine. I can't sleep."

Rachel set the lantern beside him, then padded barefoot to the wagon to retrieve Doc's black leather bag. She muttered in frustration when she saw the empty vial. She tried to rouse Doc to mix up more of his sedative but he didn't respond, just lay there like a slug and snored away.

"I should be the one with the medical degree," she grumbled as she sank down beside the flickering lantern to study the labels on the bottles of authentic medical compounds. She had learned from her Cheyenne grandmother to use curative herbs, and she had watched Doc mix painkillers for patients before. A little of this and that and she could duplicate the nostrum to relieve Nate's pain.

"More medicine," Nate groaned as he clamped hold of his injured ribs.

"I'm working on it," she replied, distracted.

A moment later, she held the vial up to the light. It looked to be the same amber-colored potion she remembered Doc dispensing to patients. She held it to Nate's puffy lips. He gulped quickly, then gagged.

"Water," he wheezed.

Rachel scrambled for the canteen.

In between muttered oaths, Nate gulped water. His breathing became irregular and his chest heaved. Rachel studied his reaction with growing alarm. Then to her dismay, he collapsed and lay motionless on the pallet.

"Dear God!" Rachel squawked as she bounded to her feet to rouse Doc. "I've poisoned him!"

Rachel darted to the tree and dropped down on both knees to shake Doc awake so he could undo the damage she had unintentionally done to Nate. The poor man had gotten the hell beaten out of him because of her and then she had poisoned him by mixing the wrong amounts of ingredients together.

"Doc!" She shook him again—harder this time.

All she received in response was a wobbly moan. Doc didn't open his eyes. He lay there, poisoned by rotgut nostrums—while Nate lay on the other side of camp, poisoned. Period.

"I accidentally killed Adolph Turner in self-defense and now I've killed Nate Montgomery. I'm only twenty-three and I have two deaths on my conscience already," she grumbled in dismay. "My life has gone straight to hell!"

Frantic, she bolted up and dashed to Nate. She encouraged him to sip more water, hoping to dilute the strong formula she had concocted erroneously to ease his pain. But he didn't respond. Nate lay there, looking dead.

Rachel laid her head on his chest to check for a heartbeat. She half collapsed in relief when she felt the weak thud against her cheek. She wasn't sure how long she remained hunkered over him, monitoring his pulse. Maybe ten minutes, though it felt like an hour.

Suddenly his arm encircled her to hold her close to his chest. Her first reaction was to shove the heels of her hands against him to break his hold on her, just as she had done when Adolph clamped hold of her. But she refused to crack another of Nate's ribs, especially after she had overmedicated him.

"Hello, darlin'," he purred seductively.

Rachel blinked, then stared into his shadowed face. What?

She tensed when his hand drifted down her spine to follow the curve of her derriere. Never had she allowed a man familiar privileges, even while she had supported herself as a singer and barmaid in a saloon in Leadville, Colorado. Her impulse was to slap his face, but she granted him leniency because it was her fault those henchmen had beaten him up. He didn't need to suffer more than he had.

"I'm dying for a taste of you, sweetheart," he whispered.

"You're dying all right. I accidentally poisoned you… And keep your hands to yourself."

Her curt command didn't faze him in the least. He kept caressing her leisurely, and she hated that she liked his gentle touch, which was so unlike the lusty attention of other men.

"Don't be so stingy with your kisses." He opened those vivid blue eyes briefly and she got lost in them. "You can spare a few for me and still have plenty left."

When he cupped his hand around the back of her head and drew her face to his, she tried to resist without hurting him. In the end, she gave up and kissed him.

It wasn't an altogether unpleasant experience.

It was nothing like the forceful kiss Adolph Turner planted on her. This kiss was pure seduction and it persuaded her to yield, while his straying hand brushed the tip of her breast, then glided down her belly.

Unbelievable! Her dazed mind scolded her for permitting his familiarity. The truth was that she was enjoying the embrace of a man she didn't know. Probably because she felt guilty for poisoning him and wanted to grant him his dying wish. If he wanted a kiss, then it behooved her to give him the best she had to offer before he flew off to the pearly gates.

Or straight into hell. Whichever.

Rachel put herself into kissing him, and she didn't object when his roaming fingers glided beneath the scooped neckline of her nightgown to circle her taut nipples. Pleasure seeped through her as he dragged his lips lightly over hers. Warm tingles that had no business assailing her shimmered through her blood and spread out in all directions at once.

"Feel what you do to me, temptress…"

Rachel forgot to breathe when he placed his hand over hers, guiding it to the bulge in his breeches. That set off forbidden memories of seeing him naked and she began to wonder what he'd look like when he was aroused, as he was now.

"You taste like heaven." He kissed her deeply, thoroughly, and rubbed his erection against her hand.

Sweet mercy! What was in that sedative she had concocted that made Nate respond so dramatically? Evidently, she had mixed a love potion rather than a painkiller. It was her fault he'd been hurt, and her fault that he was rubbing his hands all over her and kissing her as if she was the other half of his lost soul.

Then Nate collapsed suddenly. His head rolled sideways and his hands fell away from her. She snatched her fingers away from him as if she had been burned.

Now he was dead. She was sure of it. He hadn't moved a muscle and she couldn't tell if he was still breathing. She couldn't see the rise and fall of his chest. She hesitated to lay her cheek against his chest again, for fear he might rouse and she would find herself succumbing to what she presumed to be pure lust.

What else could it be? She didn't know this man well enough to like or dislike him. All she knew was that she was unwillingly attracted to him.

Finally, she worked up the nerve to place her fingertips on his neck. He had a pulse—barely. Thank God.

Rachel cuddled up beside Nate on the pallet, in case he needed assistance during the night. The poor man only *thought* he had encountered trouble when those three mean-spirited henchmen attacked him. Now he would be lucky if he survived a dose of Rachel's poisoned love potion.

She fell asleep hoping and praying Nate would survive. *In spite of* her bungled effort to relieve his pain.

Chapter Three

Nate came awake, then groaned miserably. Yesterday evening he swore he couldn't have felt worse. He was wrong. Every ache and pain had intensified. Not to mention the throbbing vibration in his skull. He was stiff and sore and he felt as if he had slept under a rock. And what the devil was that awful taste in his mouth? Doc's painkiller?

He frowned contemplatively—which made his face hurt. He tried to recall the last thing he remembered. He had awakened after dark, suffering severe pain. He remembered hearing the crackle of the campfire. He'd been starving and hurting until hell wouldn't have it—

"Nate?"

He pried open one eye to see a blurry face hovering over him. Something about the woman's voice triggered an arousing memory. For the life of him, he couldn't imagine why.

"Nate, can you hear me?"

Even though it hurt to think, he tried to remember what the doctor had called the woman traveling with him. He drew a blank.

"You're still alive," she reassured him as she draped a cool, wet cloth over his face.

"That's a relief. I was hoping dead didn't feel this bad." He sighed gratefully when the cool cloth soothed the puffy heat in his face.

"After last night I wasn't sure you were going to make it. You kept collapsing into a near-catatonic state. I kept trying to revive you."

"Last night is still fuzzy and confusing," he admitted. "All I know for sure is that I'm starving."

"I can remedy that problem. What about your pain?"

"It's still there—in spades." He tried to lever into an upright position but it made him dizzy and light-headed so he eased down on the pallet.

The smell of biscuits wafted toward him and he sighed in hungry anticipation. When she held the fluffy biscuit to his lips, he took a bite and chewed carefully—in case his tender jaw protested. When he'd swallowed, she offered him a drink of water.

"Tasty," he praised before she offered him a second bite.

"Thank you… I was wondering if I could ask you a few questions about the three men who attacked you."

He was curious about the sudden change in the tone of her voice but he didn't ask. "Sure. Fire away."

"Did the men mention what they were doing in the area?"

"That's a strange question. Why do you ask?"

"Just wondering what they were up to. Did they dress like cowboys from a Texas trail herd? Or drifters? I'm curious why they pounced on you, if you were simply minding your own business…as you claim."

Nate munched on the biscuit, amazed that he kept

noticing alternating inflections in her voice. He supposed being half-blind prompted his other senses to work overtime to compensate for his inability to see straight.

"I never saw the men before," he replied honestly. Then he fudged a bit, refusing to divulge information about his real reason for traveling through Kansas. The less anyone knew about why he was in the area, the easier it was to make discreet inquiries. "I'm on my way to Dodge City to take a new job. I simply stopped for the night."

"Why are you an *ex*-lawman rather than a practicing lawman? Were you fired, dismissed or voted out of office?"

She offered him another biscuit, dipped in gravy, to prevent him from taking offense to her straightforward interrogation. Usually *he* was grilling eyewitnesses and criminals for information, not the other way around.

Nate pulled the wet cloth from his face and tried to take a good look at her. He could tell she had dark hair and dark eyes—four of them. Her olive complexion made Lenora Havern, the socialite his father had earmarked for him, appear chalky and sickly in comparison.

"You sure ask a lot of questions…" He let his voice trail off, hoping she would fill in the blank that was her name. He couldn't remember who she was, and she didn't take the hint and prompt him.

"I'm curious by nature." She replaced the wet cloth on his face. "I've heard of several lawmen who have gone bad and turned to crime. I was just wondering if you were one of them."

"Anyone in particular that comes to mind?" he asked between bites.

"Henry Waggoner for one. Terrance Garfield for another. I could go on and on. So why don't you wear a badge these days?"

"I had to leave so I could tend to my ailing father." It was a half-truth—and it was his father's life-threatening illness that turned out to be a manipulative, outright lie.

"Very commendable."

He tried to smile but it was too painful. "I'm a commendable kind of man."

She laughed. He really liked the sound of her laughter. "You're a man, Mr. Montgomery. That's one strike against you. Time will tell how commendable you are."

"I'd give most anything to take a bath in the creek," he remarked. "Do you suppose your doctor friend could help me?"

"I'm afraid Doc is a bit under the weather," she said regretfully. "But I'll help you as much as I can."

"I'm, um, sorry about our awkward first encounter, Miss…or Mrs…?"

"I'll assist you to the creek so you can bathe, provided you don't bring up that incident again."

"Agreed." Nate propped himself on his elbow, then slowly came to his knees.

As promised, she steadied him when he wobbled on his feet. He could feel her shoulder lodging against the uninjured side of his rib cage to support him. He caught a whiff of the tantalizing scent of her and another jumbled memory skittered across his mind, then scattered before he could make sense of it.

"I forgot your name," he said as he draped his arm over her shoulders.

"Rachel."

"Rachel what?" He squinted at his bare feet to make sure he didn't trip over an obstacle and cause himself even more agony than he was experiencing already.

"Just Rachel, and you ask too many questions, too, Mr. Ex-Lawman," she countered saucily.

"I assure you that it's a difficult habit to break."

He shifted his attention from his feet, hoping to get a better look at his secretive nursemaid. He nearly stumbled when his vision cleared momentarily and he got his first good look at Rachel Whoever-she-was. She was about five feet four inches tall, incredibly curvaceous and wholesome looking compared to frail-looking, helpless Lenora.

Nate surveyed her bewitching features and the shiny mane of curly raven hair that tumbled around her shoulders. The trim-fitting blouse and riding breeches accentuated her appealing curves and swells to their best advantage. She had an expressive mouth and inviting lips—

A fleeting memory flashed across his mind. Something about a shadowy tryst. His hands roaming over her lush, shapely body. Her hand brushing against his aroused flesh—

She halted in midstep. "Something wrong, Nate?"

He stared at her again, but his vision clouded over, taking the puzzling memory with it. "No. I just need a breather. I'm sorry to say those three men beat the living hell out of me and I've lost my stamina."

"Wouldn't surprise me if those men beat up other people for a living, since they seem to be so good at it."

Again, there was a slight inflection in her voice that made him curious. However, she urged him forward and he had to concentrate on keeping his balance.

"Careful now," she insisted. "This is where the path descends downhill. Falling on your face would add insult to all your injuries."

* * *

Rachel guided Nate down the creek bank and silently cursed herself for making the comment about Adolph's henchmen being professional brutes. She had to remember to guard her tongue while she was talking to this former lawman. A man with a lawman's mentality was the very last kind she wanted to associate with now. If her name was plastered on a Wanted poster in Dodge City—where he was headed to take a job—he would know exactly where to find her.

Nate huffed, puffed and cradled his arm against his tender ribs. "Damn, walking down here is zapping my energy. I don't even want to think about walking uphill."

"Before long you'll be soaking away your aches and pains," she encouraged.

She steeled herself against admiring his physique while she helped him remove his shirt. Despite her best intentions, her feminine gaze skimmed over the dark furring of hair on his masculine chest that trailed into the band of his breeches. She stared appreciatively at the sinewy muscles on his arms that flexed, then relaxed.

She stepped back before she impulsively reached out to trail her hand over the scar on his shoulder. "You'll have to help yourself with your breeches." Especially since she knew there was nothing but *him* beneath the garment.

He grinned rakishly. Or so she assumed. It was difficult to tell since his face and eyes were still swollen. "Saw enough of me already, did you?"

She narrowed her gaze at him. "You promised not to mention that. I might leave you here permanently, Mr. Montgomery, if you refuse to behave yourself."

"Are you married to Doc Grant?" he asked out of the blue.

"Are *you* married?" she fired back. She was embarrassed enough about last night's passionate tryst. She was going to feel even worse if he had a wife or fiancée.

"No."

That was a gigantic relief. "Is it because of your nosy disposition and cranky temperament?" she teased playfully.

He smiled good-naturedly—or at least he tried. Only one side of mouth turned up. "Yeah, that's it…and I'm still waiting for you to answer my question."

"No, I'm Doc's part-time assistant nurse, a performer in the medicine show and sometimes his walking conscience that he tries to ignore."

"Because of the drinking," he guessed correctly.

"Yes. There are times when his demons catch up with him and he turns to the tonics he refuses to dispense to his patients," she confided, though she wasn't sure why. It must be because she was standing here admiring the muscled expanse of his chest instead of choosing her words carefully.

No doubt about it, Nate Montgomery could put a Greek god to shame, and looking at him while he was half-naked was very distracting. The thought of how he looked completely nude leaped to mind and she cursed herself soundly.

"What demons torment you into wandering around Kansas like a gypsy, Rachel?"

"Careful," she admonished. "The lawman is coming out in you again."

"I'm just curious."

"That was the cat's dying words, Mr. Montgomery."

He chuckled softly. "And I become *Mr. Montgomery* when I get too personal, is that it? Sorry. Old habits die hard. You're my guardian angel so it's only natural that I would be interested in finding out more about you."

He knew too much about her already, things no other man knew and that unsettled her. She had experienced forbidden pleasure with him. At least he didn't recall that he'd had his hands all over her—and vice versa—after he consumed the sedative-turned-love-potion she had stuffed down his throat the previous night.

She fished a bar of soap from her pocket, then gave him the other set of stolen men's clothing she had brought for him. As an afterthought she handed him the pistol she had confiscated from Adolph and had kept for her protection.

Nate arched a curious black brow as he tested the weight of the weapon she placed in his hand. "A pistol-packing female? Why am I not surprised?"

"Because it is a rough-and-tumble world and a woman has to defend herself." She knew it for a fact because she'd done it for years. "Unarmed is unprepared, I always say. If you need help, just fire off a shot to signal me."

She turned to leave but she halted when he said, "Rachel, one last thing before you go."

"What's the 'one last thing'?" she asked.

"I keep thinking there is something about you that I should remember, but with this pounding headache—"

"Go soak your aching head," she cut in quickly. "I'll come to fetch you after I get Doc on his feet and cram food down his gullet." *And do me a favor and please don't remember the love potion incident,* she mused as she strode to camp.

Rachel stopped short and sighed in exasperation when she saw Doc on his hands and knees beneath the shade tree where he had collapsed the previous night.

"How did I wind up caring for two men when I know how much trouble they are?" she asked herself.

She strode forward, crossed her arms over her chest and gave Doc a disapproving stare.

"Don't start," he said hoarsely.

"I was going to comment on what a lovely morning it is."

He glared at her with bloodshot eyes. "No, you weren't." He thrust up an arm, silently requesting that she assist him to his feet. "You covered me up and retrieved my pillow from the wagon last night."

"Don't I always?" She took his arm so he could climb to his feet. When he swayed, she hooked her arm around his waist. "Breakfast is ready and waiting."

"Not hungry."

"Too bad. You're eating. Like it or not."

"Coffee?"

"Piping hot."

"You're too good to me."

"I know."

Doc scrubbed his hand over his face, blinked a couple of times, then raked his fingers through blond hair that was sticking out in all directions. "Where's Nate?"

"I assisted him to the creek so he could bathe." She eyed him grimly. "I also had to mix a potion for him after you conked out because he awoke in severe pain."

"Good for you," said Doc as he shuffled up to the campfire.

"Not good for Nate," she replied. "I thought I killed him. Whatever I added incorrectly, when mixing the ingredients, made him act strangely, then collapse like the newly dead."

When Doc stared expectantly at her, she shrugged and

refused to elaborate. While he sipped coffee and munched on biscuits, Rachel hiked off to the creek to wash the utensils. She made certain she was nowhere near Nate's bathing site—for fear she'd get another eyeful of him. Once had been too much.

"Is that you, Rachel?" Nate called out.

"Yes. I'm rinsing the cooking utensils. Is everything going okay with you?"

"Soaking in the creek is working wonders. Except that I keep remembering something."

Uh-oh. Rachel huffed out her breath. "Whatever it is, it isn't important."

"Yes, it is."

She nearly leaped out of her skin and tumbled headfirst into the creek when his voice came from so close behind her. Blast it! He moved as silently as an Indian warrior. She ought to know. She had perfected the skill herself and had put it to good use on a number of occasions.

"Sorry. Didn't mean to startle you."

Rachel glanced over her shoulder to note that soaking in the creek had reduced the swelling in Nate's puffy face. His azure-colored eyes were partially open and his auburn hair was damp. The rest of him strained against the ill-fitting clothes, calling attention to his abundance of brawn and muscle. Rachel gave herself a mental slap for picturing him naked—for the umpteenth time.

"I want to talk to you about what happened last night." He moved closer, careful where he stepped since he was barefoot.

"I'd rather not. Besides, you promised—"

"—That was before I remembered what I did," he interrupted.

Nate found himself staring at Rachel's rounded rump,

which was displayed enticingly in the formfitting riding breeches. A round rump that he recalled having his hands all over. Not to mention full breasts that he had fondled, and those Cupid's-bow lips that he had kissed like a man starving for a taste of her. He couldn't imagine what had gotten into him last night but the memory had exploded across his mind the instant his headache eased off. First, he had unintentionally exposed himself to this woman, then he had caressed her familiarly.

That's gratitude for you, he chastised himself caustically. She'd saved his life and he'd treated her disrespectfully. It was a wonder she was speaking to him!

"I have to return to camp. Doc is awake and I need to pack up while he comes to the creek to bathe and sober up."

Nate clutched her arm as she walked by. Although he still couldn't see clearly, he noticed that she recoiled at his abrupt touch. He wondered if she had suffered through unpleasant experiences with men before. Probably. Given how naturally alluring she was, Rachel attracted men without trying and they probably pestered her constantly.

"I apologize," he said for starters.

"Apology accepted."

She tried to worm loose but he kept a firm grip on her arm. "I must have been heavily sedated. I never would have tried to force myself on you. I wasn't myself last night."

Her dark head snapped up and her obsidian eyes glistened in the sunlight. "No? Why is that? Because I'm not your type? Except when no one else is around in the middle of nowhere? Not respectable enough to warrant your polite respect? Don't think I haven't heard that before. Men are such asses—"

"Whoa!" He grinned when she tried to pull away again

and he held on tightly. "Calm down, hellcat. And do not try to put words in my mouth. I can speak for myself. All I meant was that I behaved badly. You saved my life and I repaid you by taking advantage of your compassion." He smiled again, hoping to tease her back into good humor. "Unless you found me so appealing that you couldn't resist my charm."

"Don't be absurd." She thrust out her chin, but she stared at the air over his left shoulder so she wouldn't have to look him in the eye. "I would have slapped you silly but you suffered from too many injuries already." She swatted the hand he had wrapped around her elbow. "Now, let me go before I have to hurt you."

"Just one more thing."

"You always seem to have 'just one more thing,' Montgomery. What is it this time?"

Nate didn't know why he angled his head toward hers. Maybe it was because he'd wanted to retest his response to her after he remembered how familiar they had been with each other last night. Maybe it was because those lush, inviting lips made him hungry. Whatever the case, he touched his lips to hers experimentally. She stood like a statue, refusing to react.

"That's not the way I remember our kiss," he whispered as he brushed his mouth languidly over hers.

"You must have been hallucinating."

.She made him smile. Lenora Havern couldn't have made him smile if her very life depended on it. However, this mysterious but prickly female amused him, aroused him, and intrigued him—to the extreme.

"You kissed me back last night. I remember." His lips drifted over her high cheekbones, the curve of her jaw.

"I felt sorry for you, was all."

"You should feel sorry for me now. I'm only slightly better this morning than I was last night," he teased, then kissed her as gently as he knew how because he liked the taste of her, liked the feel of her shapely body brushing up against his, liked the scent of this enigmatic woman.

He smiled when she finally began to respond to him. He hadn't imagined that she had leaned into him, had opened her lips so he could drink deeply from the sweet nectar of her kiss last night. Now *this* he definitely remembered—vividly.

Bad as he'd felt, after being beaten to a pulp, Rachel's kisses had revived him. *Now* she was curing him with kisses. The only place he ached severely was the place where he was most a man—the place he had moved her hand to touch him intimately last night so she'd know she had set him on fire.

The thought prompted him to loop his good arm around her waist and guide her curvaceous body against him. She felt incredibly good in his arms, on his lips, and he couldn't make himself stop kissing her.

The rustle of bushes captured his attention and he stepped back abruptly. He reached for the pistol Rachel had loaned him and tucked her protectively behind him. When Doc stepped into view, Nate relaxed.

"I'll pack up the supplies so we can hit the road," Rachel volunteered as she retrieved her six-shooter from his hand, then scooped up the cooking utensils.

She left without a backward glance.

Doc halted beside Nate and glared pointedly at him. "If you hurt that girl you will answer to me."

Nate stared at the physician who was four inches shorter, forty pounds lighter and fifteen years older—give or take. "I wasn't planning to."

"Good, because I can mix potions that can make you lose all interest in women, or concoct a sedative that will knock you off your feet. So don't cross me or use Rachel for your selfish interests. Got it?"

"Yes, sir."

Doc nodded, satisfied. "Besides, you owe her your life."

"I'm aware of that."

"Then become her bodyguard when we reach our next destination," he insisted. "Men always stand six-deep around her during, and after, her performances. Ludy Anderson, our banjo player, is usually around to keep an eye on Rachel but he isn't much use while he's performing for the bystanders."

Nate frowned curiously. "Where is Ludy now?"

"He likes to ride into town ahead of us to scout out a good place to set up shop and to entertain himself," Doc explained, then raised his eyebrows.

In other words, this Ludy person was a bit of a ladies' man who enjoyed spreading around his traveling-salesman charm.

Doc studied him consideringly through bloodshot eyes. "Do you have hidden talents you can use to perform for the folks who show up expecting to be entertained before I treat their ailments with legitimate medications?"

"I can shoot a pistol." Nate wiggled the fingers of his right hand but they were still stiff and sluggish. "Usually."

"Maybe you can earn your keep since you've been left penniless."

"Fair enough. I'll do what I can to help out." He smiled hopefully. "Could you extend an advance on my wages so I can buy suitable clothing and a firearm?"

Doc dug into his pocket, then handed Nate several large bank notes.

"I appreciate your generosity, Doc. I'll pay you back as soon as I have a chance to wire my brother to send money and replacement clothing. Until then, I'll make myself useful, even if I'm not feeling up to snuff… One more thing. Where is Rachel from?"

Doc shrugged nonchalantly. "She didn't say."

"And you didn't bother to ask," Nate presumed.

Doc cocked his blond head and smiled slightly. "I didn't ask where you were from or where you were going. I guess I'm suffering from a shameful lack of curiosity, aren't I?"

Nate studied Doc Grant for a long moment as he ambled toward the creek. He had spent years posing questions and solving mysteries while in law enforcement. It was only natural to dig beneath the surface to uncover all the facts.

Yet he was being a hypocrite because he refused to volunteer the information that he was headed to Dodge City to find out why Edgar Havern and his silent partner—who was also Edgar's father-in-law—had noticed a sharp reduction in the profits of their investment in the freight company the past eight months. Nate had agreed to assist Lenora's father—despite his own father's irritation. It was the very least he could do after he'd rejected the arranged marriage and beat a hasty retreat from Kansas City.

Nate intended to hire on at the freight company so he could discreetly observe the business practices. Once he had resolved Edgar Havern's problems, he planned to return to his federal duties in law enforcement. It was what he was good at, after all. He was *not* good at playing nice at elite social functions and allowing his father to dictate his life.

One thing Nate knew for sure was that the women in

his brother's and father's social circle couldn't compare to the sassy, independent-minded female named Rachel who was harboring secrets of her own and tempting him without the slightest effort on her part. In fact, if Nate were the sensitive type, Rachel's standoffish attitude toward him might hurt his feelings. Especially since women had been fawning over him recently because his family had scads of money they were all too eager to help him spend.

Nate grinned wryly, wondering if the feisty Rachel Whoever-she-was would be nicer to him if he paid her. Probably not. She didn't hold men in high esteem. Yet he recalled that for a few breathless moments, when she gave into the mutual attraction—one she refused to acknowledge—he thought she liked him just fine.

He chuckled as he walked barefoot back to camp. If he knew what was good for him, he wouldn't bring up the erotic details of their encounter. She'd bite his head off.

Chapter Four

$\infty\!\!\infty\!\!\infty\!\!\infty$

Muttering at the memory of her reckless abandon with Nate a few minutes earlier, Rachel crammed the utensils and cooking supplies into the knapsack. Then she toted them to the wagon and stashed them away. How could she have given in to forbidden pleasure with Nate the second time?

Once was bad enough, but twice? Apparently, her self-control wasn't as invincible as she thought it was.

How could she have forgotten how much trouble men caused? They had abandoned her, betrayed her and attempted to use her for their lusty purposes while she moved from one occupation to the next to support herself. Knowing that, why had she become instantly attracted to an ex-lawman who was so bruised and swollen that she didn't know if he were handsome or not?

Isn't that what lust was about? she asked herself. Pure physical attraction at its worst? For sure, all she knew about Nate was that he could kiss her deaf, blind and stupid, and leave her wishing for another glimpse of his incredibly masculine body.

"You are insane," she castigated herself as she stashed the knapsack in the covered wagon.

"Oh? Why's that?"

Nate's deep baritone voice rolled over her. His silent approach startled her to such extremes that she nearly cartwheeled off her perch on the back of the wagon.

"Stop doing that," she snapped, uprighting herself.

"Doing what?" He manufactured a stare of complete innocence, but she saw right through it.

"Stop sneaking up on me, that's what." She bounded to the ground, then strode off to hitch the horses.

"Doc specifically requested that I keep an eye on you."

She halted, glanced back at his ill-fitting clothes and bootless feet, then smirked. "How can you keep an eye on me when both of your eyes are all but swollen shut and you can barely see where you're going? Anyway, I can take care of myself, thank you so very much."

"I'm trying to be nice to you," he called after her.

She grabbed the ropes, then led the horses to the wagon. "I'm not worth the effort because I don't plan to be nice back."

"Why?"

"Go away. You're bothering me."

"I bother you? Interesting."

Yes, he did, damn it. More than any man she had ever encountered. But Nate Montgomery would only be around until he was well enough to strike off on his own. He was headed to the very last place on earth that Rachel wanted to go after the Adolph Turner fiasco. In addition, there were a dozen sensible reasons why becoming attached to Nate was a bad idea.

Refusing to rise to his baiting, Rachel clamped her lips shut, then hitched up the horses. Then she checked to ensure the reins and harnesses were in proper working order. All the while, she ignored Nate as if he wasn't there. Nonetheless, she could feel his intense gaze boring into her and she wondered if he was remembering their passionate embrace beside the creek. She certainly was.

The thought burned her cheeks and scorched her blood. Willfully she stifled the memory of his all-too-familiar touch, then strode down the path to the creek.

"Doc! We are ready to roll. Are you coming?"

Looking somewhat refreshed and revived, Doc Grant ambled up the path. "Thanks for taking care of things."

"That's what you're paying me to do. The nagging is free of charge."

"I told you. Do not start with me." Doc hitched his thumb toward Nate who was struggling to pull himself onto the wagon seat. "Take out your bad disposition on him."

"I already did."

Rachel climbed into the back of the wagon and left the men to themselves. She snuggled down on a pallet, determined to catch up on lost sleep after waking up at regular intervals the previous night to make sure Nate remained among the living, no thanks to her.

The first order of business when Nate climbed gingerly from the wagon in the small town of Crossville was to outfit himself in clothing and boots that fit properly. Thanks to Doc's generosity, Nate felt a little better about himself.

By the time he ambled from the dry-goods store, Doc and Rachel had set up shop. The medicine-show production was nothing like the usual ones Nate had seen before. The dimple-cheeked, frizzy-haired banjo player named

Ludy Anderson, who had ridden into town the previous evening, showed up with a wide smile on his face and began his musical act.

There was no question in Nate's mind about how Ludy had whiled away his hours the previous evening—and perhaps this morning, too. He had the look of a well-satisfied male.

Nate appraised the musician, who flashed another winsome grin while he played his banjo. Several women cast him flirtatious glances and Ludy soaked up the feminine attention. He winked rakishly at them as he played a fast-tempo tune, drawing the interest and attention of passersby on the street.

To Nate's stunned amazement, Rachel appeared from a nearby alley, dressed in the full regalia of an Indian princess. Her dark hair lay in braids that cascaded over her breasts. Her fringed and beaded buckskin dress and moccasins appeared to have been custom-made to fit her. She captivated the audience with her beauty and fascinated them when she spoke of ancient Cheyenne legends.

Nate hadn't acquired an appreciation for Indian tribes because of his stint in the army. He had seen the worst that Indians and whites could do to one another in ongoing battles over possession of land and the outrage of broken treaties.

However, Rachel's mystical presentation made him realize the Cheyenne tribe had a strong spiritual connection to the sacred sites and hunting grounds they fought to protect from white invasion. It also made Nate wonder how Rachel knew so much about the Cheyenne culture. Where she had picked up the ability to speak their native tongue and convey the Indian version of creation.

When Rachel finished her spellbinding presentation,

she bowed humbly while the crowd applauded. Then, with knapsack in hand, she strode toward the alley beside the dry-goods store. Nate followed her to block the path, making certain no one invaded her privacy.

Ludy Anderson struck up several lighthearted tunes to entertain the crowd while she was gone.

To Nate's relief no one followed Rachel. Since he looked and felt like hammered hell, he doubted he could intimidate anyone who decided to hassle her. If he had to back up his terse commands he'd likely end up in a world of hurt again.

His male pride was already smarting after his confrontation with the ruffians.

A few minutes later Doc appeared beside the wagon to address the crowd. Rachel joined him, dressed in a modest gown that was covered by a white apron. Doc didn't give the anticipated sales pitch about the never-fail cure-alls and nostrums stored in his wagon. Instead, he told onlookers the same thing he'd told Nate the previous night. He assured the audience that the so-called patented medicines sold by charlatan doctors were worthless.

"Don't be fooled by these fifty-proof elixirs," Doc declared as he held up a bottle that was labeled Wizard Oil. "Nothing replaces a certified doctor. The next time a medicine show pulls into town, enjoy the entertainment, take it for what it is and save your hard-earned money."

Nate smiled to himself, pretty sure Doc's honesty would drive shysters out of business eventually. He did seem to be on a one-man crusade to change misconceptions about patented medicines.

Then Doc asked if anyone in the crowd suffered sprains, broken bones, stomach ailments and such. While several more patients lined up for examinations by Doc and his lovely assistant, Ludy strolled up beside Nate.

"Don't know why Doc doesn't put down roots and reopen his private practice," Ludy remarked as he set aside his banjo.

Because Doc, like Rachel, was running from something, Nate speculated.

An hour later Rachel walked off to change clothes again, while Doc gave another spiel about proper treatment of ailments and the evils of wonder tonics.

Ludy inclined his frizzy brown head toward the alley where Rachel appeared in a stunning bright yellow gown. It was as if the sun had appeared from behind a bank of gloomy clouds. Conversation fizzled out as she took her place in front of the medicine-show logo on the side of the wagon—the backdrop that served as a makeshift stage.

Mesmerized, Nate stared at the Indian princess turned dignified lady. She had piled her dark hair atop her head, displaying her swanlike neck and the elegant line of her jaw. The neckline of the silk gown displayed the fullness of her breasts. The tapered waistline emphasized her enticing figure to its best advantage.

Nate did a double take when she smiled serenely. Was this the same spirited female he'd met on the creek bank the previous night? He was beginning to think Rachel was a chameleon who could portray several roles, as if she had been born to each and every one of them. Apparently, she was a woman of diversified talents.

"I don't know where Doc found this gem of a woman, but wait until you hear this," Ludy said as he strummed a cord on his banjo, then sauntered up beside Rachel.

When she began to sing a hauntingly tender ballad Nate stood there, stunned to the bone. Her voice was amazing and the transformation from feisty tomboy to Indian princess to physician's assistant to alluring songstress was astonishing.

Nate swore his mouth had dropped open wide enough for a pigeon to roost. He wasn't the only one mesmerized by her clear voice. It made him even more curious about her secretive past. If Rachel hadn't traveled with a musical troupe or appeared in theater, she should have. She had talent galore.

People poured from the doors of shops and saloons to listen to her sing and to admire her stunning beauty. The crowd tripled in size by the time she began her second song.

"I heard a little girl with a voice that big sing once," said a grizzled older man who stood off to Nate's left.

"Where and when was that?" he was compelled to ask.

"Colorado mining town nearly a decade ago," the man recalled. "Wonder if these two are related."

Nate wondered if it was the same woman grown up.

When she concluded her last song, a roar of applause filled Main Street. This time, when she walked away to change clothes, a passel of young men trailed behind her, tossing out propositions that she ignored. Nate hurried to catch up, despite the excessive strain on his bruised muscles and ribs.

"Go listen to what Doc has to say and leave the lady alone," Nate commanded as he stationed himself in front of the alley.

A young, cocky buck with straight brown hair, a long nose and protruding chin smirked as he looked Nate up and down. "You think you're gonna stop us from seeing the lady?"

"Yep," he confirmed with more confidence than he felt.

"In your banged-up condition?" Another strutting cock of the walk with a square face and oversize ears scoffed disrespectfully.

Nate had faced down hardened outlaws, but never when he looked like a human punching bag. He'd known a confrontation would be difficult, given his appearance and the fact that he hadn't had time to replace his six-shooters. But working as Rachel's bodyguard paid for his clothing, room and board while he traveled with the medicine show. He bided his time until he could contact his brother to send money and clothing to the freight office in Dodge City. Besides, Nate felt oddly protective of Rachel, who had likely saved his life. He would have confronted this drooling crowd of men for free.

"Need this?" Rachel appeared behind him, still wearing her sunshine-yellow gown. She discreetly stashed her pistol in the back waistband of his breeches.

"Yeah, thanks. I don't seem to be a believable threat."

"You scare me, if that helps," she teased playfully.

Nate was ashamed to admit that he showed off like a teenager while Rachel watched. He grabbed the weapon and shot the hats off the two young men who harassed him. Then, for dramatic effect, he blew on the smoking barrel of the pistol.

"Any more questions?"

Goggle-eyed, the men staggered back. They cast Nate cautious glances while they retrieved their damaged hats from the dirt. The crowd dispersed immediately and Rachel peered up at him with a wry smile twitching her lips.

"It appears that you *are* handy to have around," she said. "Who would have thought?"

"And you sing like an angel and look like one, too," he retorted as he returned her pistol. "Where did you practice voice lessons and study the Cheyenne culture before you joined Doc's unique medicine show?"

She smiled impishly as she pivoted on her heels. "I'll be back in two shakes. Guard the alley, sharpshooter."

"Whatever you say, angel face." He watched her walk away and he wondered if he'd ever get a straight answer out of Rachel Whoever-she-was.

Nate wasn't surprised to see the city marshal striding purposefully down the boardwalk five minutes after he'd fired off two shots to discourage the lusty hounds trailing at Rachel's heels.

The round-bellied marshal drew himself up in front of Nate. "I don't approve of gunplay in my town."

"I don't approve of young bucks throwing themselves on the lady I am paid to protect from unwanted attention," Nate countered in the same authoritative tone.

"That's not the story the two plowboys gave me."

Nate appraised the marshal, who looked to be a decade older. His thick red brows reminded him of fuzzy caterpillars. Same went for the mustache on his upper lip. "The plowboys lied."

The marshal smirked. "And why should I believe you? From the looks of you, you enjoy a good fight. Did you win or lose the last one?"

"Surprise attack. Lopsided odds. I lost."

Nate glanced over his shoulder when Rachel, dressed in a simple calico gown, emerged from the shadows of the alley. She took one look at the badge on the marshal's chest, nodded stiffly, then strode over to rejoin Doc. Clearly, she preferred to keep her distance from law officials. But then, he already sensed that Rachel had something to hide.

"There's the evidence." Nate directed the marshal's attention to Rachel. "Too temptingly pretty for her own good."

The marshal's appreciative gaze followed her progress across the street. "Yep, that explains it."

Nate gestured toward the marshal's office. "I'd like to file complaints against the three men who jumped me last night. They stole my horse, my saddlebags, my badge and a roll of cash. I'd also like to look at your Wanted posters to see if anyone fits their descriptions."

The marshal regarded him pensively, then offered his hand in greeting. "Daniel Stocker," he introduced himself.

"Nathan Montgomery, U.S. Marshal. I've been on a six-month leave of absence." He was glad he hadn't divulged that information to Rachel. Leery as she was, she would have steered clear of him completely, he predicted.

Marshal Stocker gave him another quick once-over. "On leave because you were injured in the line of duty?"

"No, tending an ailing father." Nate made a supreme effort to keep the seething irritation from lacing his voice.

Every time he recalled his father's deception, it annoyed the hell out of him.

"I hope your father is better now," Marshal Stocker said.

"Miraculous recovery."

Casting Rachel a sideways glance to make sure she was still safe, Nate walked down the boardwalk with Dan Stocker. Nothing he'd like better than to find out the names of the men who had attacked him, round them up and haul them to jail. He smiled at the gratifying thought. Those brutes would be his first order of business after he checked out the goings-on in Edgar Havern's investments in the Dodge City Freight Company.

While several of the locals approached the wagon to praise Rachel's singing and acting ability, she kept a watchful eye on Nate's departure. The fact that he was chumming with the city marshal shouldn't have surprised her. Birds of a feather, after all. She also predicted that he was going to check Wanted posters so he could identify his attackers. Still, it made her anxious, wondering if a sketch of *her* face was printed on a poster.

She didn't want to be forced to leave town in a flaming rush. Traveling with Doc and performing in the medicine show was the perfect occupation. She never remained in the same place for too long.

"You look tense, hon. Has someone been bothering you?" Doc Grant asked as he circled the wagon to examine his next patient.

Rachel pasted on a nonchalant smile. "I'm just a bit on edge because Nate had to confront those pesky men while I changed clothes."

Doc nodded in understanding. "You can lie low this afternoon if you'd like. I'll treat the last few patients myself, then we'll be on our way this evening."

Casting another apprehensive glance at the marshal's office, Rachel walked off. She decided to look over the bolts of fabric at the local boutique and dry-goods shop. The owner of the boutique had allowed her to change her costumes in the back storeroom, then exit into the alley. Making a purchase was her way of showing her appreciation to the shopkeeper.

Thanks to Jennifer Grantham's instructions, Rachel had become an experienced seamstress, and it was an easy task to design her costumes and clothing. Of course, she had learned to sew her own garments years earlier as part of her Cheyenne training, but the practical styles were drastically different from Jen's fashionable designs.

The thought of Jen provoked Rachel's rueful smile.

She had lost contact with a good friend because of Adolph Turner. Even now, he was tormenting her life. Not knowing if he had survived, and wondering if his henchmen would show up to capture her, frustrated her to no end.

Adolph Turner swore foully when his three henchmen showed up in his office—empty-handed again. It was the fourth time in three weeks that they had reconnoitered the area and had turned up not one productive lead or sighting.

"Where the hell could she be? How is it possible that one pint-size female can disappear into the night and three experienced ex-hunters can't track her down?" He scowled.

Max Rother shrugged his thin-bladed shoulder. "Don't know, boss. We've tracked all over three counties and haven't seen anything of her."

Adolph absently rubbed the shoulder he had dislocated the night Rachel St. Raimes had plowed into him and sent him sprawling backward. Plus, he'd had to have stitches in the back of his head, thanks to clanking his skull on the sharp edge of the shelf. Then there was the blow from the point of the heavy anvil that had gouged him in the breastbone. It had hurt to breathe for two weeks. He'd been in bad shape, thanks to that scrappy hellcat.

"Maybe you oughta file charges against her," Warren Lamont suggested. "A few Wanted posters floating around might turn up some information."

Adolph shook his head adamantly. "In the first place, too much time has passed since the incident, and I explained my injuries as a careless accident caused by stumbling around in the dark storeroom."

An angry snarl puckered his lips. "But most importantly, *I* want to personally get my hands on that firebrand.

She is *mine* to deal with." He shook a lean finger in his henchmen's faces. "When you find her, *I* want her first. Do you understand me? Don't cross me…or else."

"Yeah, boss, we get it," Bob Hanes replied. "We'll bring her to you straight away."

Adolph frowned speculatively. "Are you certain you checked every boutique in every town in the area you've searched? She hasn't taken up her profession again?"

"We're sure," Warren Lamont confirmed.

Adolph flapped his arm dismissively. "Before you head out to scout around tomorrow, I want you to collect from the sodbuster west of town. He's delinquent on making his payment for the goods we ordered and delivered to him. Make sure he knows better than to hold out on me again."

When all three men trooped from the office, Adolph plopped into his chair behind his desk. "Where the devil has Rachel gotten off to?" he asked himself bewilderedly.

He supposed it was possible that she'd been set upon and perished. The thought ruined his mood because he had spent three weeks planning his revenge.

He huffed out his breath, then frowned pensively. Enough time had passed for him to approach Jennifer Grantham with a casual inquiry about her employee at the boutique. If Adolph sensed that Jen was concealing information, he would send his men to pay her a visit after she closed up shop. Threatening to harm her young daughter should encourage Mrs. Grantham to talk.

However, he preferred that his hired gunmen track down Rachel St. Raimes and drag her to Dodge City so Adolph could deal privately with her. The less anyone knew about the confrontation in the storeroom the better for him.

Especially after the circumstances surrounding the

death of his former mistress. No one tried to blackmail Adolph Turner and lived to brag about it!

Adolph had grown up in the East and had battled his way out of destitution. Years ago, he had vowed to do whatever was necessary to gain wealth and influence. No one was ever going to look down on him again, as if he counted for nothing. No one was going to strip him of his possessions, either. Nothing was going to stand in the way of the good life he had designed specifically for himself.

He only had to answer to those two uppity businessmen in Kansas City occasionally, he reminded himself. It wasn't as if the citified dandy or his silent partner would lower himself to interrupt his life of leisure and tramp out West to check on one of dozens of wide-ranging investments.

Adolph scowled, remembering the feisty woman who had resisted his attempts to charm her. Rachel could have benefited from his wealth, for as long as she amused him. However, that hellion refused his offers to set her up in a suite at the hotel so she could be at his beck and call.

When Adolph located Rachel, she would serve his purpose—*without* the fringe benefits of expensive trinkets and a furnished hotel suite. She could have had it all, but she had rejected him. When he finished taking out his revenge on her, she would *have* nothing, *be* nothing.

The thought brightened his mood considerably.

Max Rother counted out the money he had received when he sold the U.S. marshal's horse and pistols to a besotted Texas cowboy on South Side. If he had found the badge in the saddlebag *before* they rode away, he would have made sure the lawman was dead. He hoped like hell the oversight didn't come back to bite him in the ass.

"You should've let me keep the horse," Warren Lamont

complained as he pocketed his share of the money. "It was a helluva lot better than the nag I'm riding."

Bob Hanes rolled his eyes at his younger cohort, then scoffed. "You're dumb as a rock, boy. If somebody recognized that horse, you'd be arrested for horse thieving. You think Adolph Turner would defend you and save your scrawny neck?"

"Hell, no, he wouldn't." Max snorted. "The minute you cause Turner problems you're gone." He took a step closer to the man who was sixteen years his junior and got right in his unshaven face. "You are *never* to mention the U.S. marshal we beat up to anyone, especially Turner. The extra money we make robbing and plundering is our private business. Understand?"

Warren bobbed his head and his stringy brown hair flopped around his face.

Bob shoved the rolled-up clothing and boots into Warren's midsection. "Sell this stuff to one of the cowboys who's headed back to Texas. Don't take nothing but money for the items we stole from the marshal."

"Then bring us our third of the profit," Bob insisted. "It's share and share alike."

"Right. But when we find the St. Raimes woman, don't think I'll keep quiet if you make me wait my turn until last, just because I'm the youngest," Warren grumbled.

Bob crowded Warren's space, forcing him to back up a step. "We'll draw straws when the time comes, kid. But I'm telling you that no one will lay a hand on that chit before Turner takes his turn with her. I watched him kill the man you replaced because he took a turn with Turner's mistress of the moment. Turner may dress like a dandy but that bastard is crazy and he's as ruthless as they come."

Warren's Adam's apple bobbed noticeably when he

swallowed. He clutched the clothes and boots they'd stripped off the unconscious marshal the previous day, then strode off.

"And hurry it up," Max called after him.

Warren headed for the nearest boardinghouse on South Side to sell the clothing to the highest bidder.

"That kid will never see thirty," Max predicted as he spit a wad of tobacco in the dirt. "He doesn't have the brains God gave a goose."

"I'll drink to that." Bob spun on his boot heels and swaggered toward his favorite saloon to quench his thirst.

Chapter Five

Rachel kept to herself during their jaunt from Crossville to their next destination at Riverview. Nate hadn't mentioned seeing her sketch on a Wanted poster at Marshal Stocker's office. All he'd said was that he hadn't found any information about the men who had attacked him. But Marshal Stocker had agreed to ask the circuit judge to write out bench warrants for their arrests.

When they made camp for the evening, Ludy helped her unload their gear while he taught her the lyrics and melody to a new song to add to the show.

"Don't know why you don't settle into a big city where you can perform regularly in the theater," Ludy commented as he arranged logs on the campfire. "The accommodations have to be better than this."

"I like wide-open spaces," she insisted as she watched Nate and Doc stroll toward the creek for a refreshing bath.

Nate was ambulating faster this evening, she noted. The swelling in his face had decreased noticeably. She wondered how much longer he would remain with the wagon. She knew he was anxious to reach Dodge City so he could begin his job.

Rachel frowned pensively as she unloaded the food supplies. She hadn't thought to ask if Nate had a particular line of employment in mind. Was he hoping to become a deputy to the city marshal…?

"Rachel. Yoo-hoo," Ludy prompted.

She smiled apologetically. "My mind is a million miles away. What did you say?"

"I said…why not head to Saint Louis or Kansas City? You could live in the lap of luxury instead of roughing it out here like a homeless vagabond."

I am a homeless vagabond. "Maybe I will eventually." She shrugged lackadaisically. "Right now I enjoy the spirit of adventure and touring the Kansas plains." *I also have to lie low until I know for certain if I've become a fugitive of justice.*

"Not me." Ludy stirred the kindling, and sparks popped and crackled as the logs caught fire. "I'd settle into the theater without a backward glance. But I'm a mediocre talent who entertains pioneers when they need a pleasurable diversion." He waggled his eyebrows playfully. "Of course, I do enjoy the added benefit of meeting scads of women. Maybe one day I'll find one who suits me perfectly and we'll settle down to raise our own four-piece band."

Rachel chuckled as she added dried beef to the pot of water. "You can start your own theater while you're at it."

"I just might do that, so don't be surprised if I invite you to be my star performer."

Ludy frowned curiously when Rachel motioned for him to follow her to the back of the wagon. She grabbed several bottles of elixirs. "Keep an eye on supper while I drain these bottles, then replace them with water."

Ludy clucked his tongue. "Doc is going to pitch a fit when he finds out you're destroying his stock of alcohol."

"It's for his own good," she defended.

"Try telling him that. And *please* do it while I'm not around."

"I've already told him that drinking his inventory of elixirs—the very same ones he refuses to sell to his patients—is burning holes in his stomach," she grumbled. "He won't listen, so now I've moved to my last resort."

"Cure him or kill him. Good thinking." Ludy winked and grinned before he lurched around to tend the fire while Rachel scurried off with an armload of glass bottles full of patented medicine that had become Doc's spare supply of alcohol.

Eventually, Doc would come upon the bottles she had replaced with water. She knew he would rant and rave at her. She also knew she couldn't restrain him from buying bottles of whiskey at saloons in the nameless towns they visited. Yet she vowed to do what she could to deter Doc's self-destructive tendencies. If he'd just tell her what tormented him she would find a way to help him.

Besides, it would help distract her from this ridiculous fascination with Nate, who would never be a part of her future.

The next evening Nate sighed audibly as he sank into the creek. He completely submerged, enjoying the feel of the cool water soaking his puffy skin and bruises. Bathing had become his favorite pastime lately.

By now, most of the swelling in his face was gone. His ribs were still tender. But thankfully, every step and every breath weren't new experiences in agony. Honestly, he had suffered gunshot wounds that hurt less. And that was saying something.

His thoughts trailed off when thunder rumbled overhead. The wind picked up and rustled through the overhanging trees, signaling the approach of a storm. Nate had endured inclement weather plenty of times during his forays of tracking criminals. He wondered if storms worried Rachel. Then again, he doubted that she frightened easily. That was one of the things he liked about her. Clinging, sniveling women didn't interest him. Rachel's courage, free spirit and self-reliance captivated him thoroughly.

Which was the main reason he planned to leave the medicine show after the two upcoming performances in Possum Grove and Evening Shade. This dead-end attraction to Rachel exasperated him. She took great pains to keep her distance from him, after the intimate encounter at first meeting. In fact, the only time she wanted him around was to guard the alleys when she hiked off to change costumes for her performances.

Maybe he should follow Ludy, who had ridden off an hour earlier to spend the night in Possum Grove, he mused as he lathered himself up with soap. Ludy had struck off to scratch an itch. For damn sure Nate's itches were acting up, compliments of his frustrated fascination for Rachel, who treated him as if he had contracted the plague and should be cautiously avoided.

After paddling around in midstream to exercise his strained muscles, Nate came ashore to dress. He grabbed the new pistol he had purchased before leaving Crossville. Then he walked toward camp. He wasn't surprised to see Doc propped up against a tree, guzzling a drink from a bottle of nostrum labeled Female Remedy. Specifically Adapted for Female Constitution. Whatever that meant.

"I'm so sorry, Margie," Doc mumbled pitifully as he stared skyward. "I should've been there."

"Come on, Doc." Nate grabbed him by the scruff of his jacket and hauled him on to his wobbly legs.

"Leave me alone." Doc nearly threw himself to the ground in his effort to wrest loose of Nate's grasp.

Nate held him fast. "The storm is going to hit in about five minutes." To confirm his prediction a blast of cold wind swept through the campsite and lightning streaked across the gloomy sky. "You'll get struck and explode because of your high alcohol content."

"Doesn't matter," said Doc. "I'm in hell."

"No, you aren't. I've been there. This isn't it."

When Doc tried to take another sip, Nate snatched the bottle from his hand.

"Hey!"

"Get in the wagon," Nate commanded sternly. He glanced this way and that. "Where's Rachel?"

"Dunno. Haven't seen her."

"Couldn't see her if you tried," he said under his breath as he hustled Doc to the back of the wagon.

"Maybe she's wandering around on foot in men's clothes. Same as she was when I found her," Doc slurred out.

Nate frowned curiously at that tidbit of information. "When was this?"

"Three or four weeks ago. Don't recall for sure."

Nate boosted Doc into the wagon. He tumbled against the pallet he had rolled up to save space. With an audible sigh, and a last call to the mysterious woman named Margie, Doc sagged into inebriated oblivion.

Nate glanced around, then bellowed, "Rachel!"

The howling wind drowned him out.

He pulled himself onto the seat to guide the horses and wagon down the grassy knoll that offered better protection from the wind. Leaving Doc to sleep off his most recent bout with his fifty-proof elixirs, Nate strode off to locate Rachel. Why he bothered he didn't know. She had told him countless times that she could take care of herself. For the most part, she could—and he admired that about her.

A high-pitched shriek carried in the wind and put Nate on instant alert. He jogged toward the sound, greatly relieved that jarring his ribs wasn't as painful as it had been the past few days. Another yelp caught his attention and he veered west to skirt the bushes along the clear-water stream. When he heard an inhuman snort and squeal, he lurched around to scan the underbrush.

There was a wild pig hereabouts but he had yet to see it.

"Rachel! Where are you?" he called out loudly.

"Be careful!" she called back. "The boar charged at me twice. Those tusks will rip skin from bone!"

The underbrush off to his right rustled and another grunting snort erupted. The last thing Nate needed was to go head-to-head with a vicious wild boar when he couldn't move with his usual agility. He took off toward the sound of Rachel's voice, then stumbled to a halt when he saw her standing waist-deep in the stream.

The sight of her silky flesh glistening with water droplets and her bare breasts exposed to his masculine gaze paralyzed him. She yelped in embarrassment, covered herself, then sank neck-deep. But the water was so clear that he could still see her all too well. He swore the titillating image of her lush body would be branded forever on his brain.

A man never forgot some things.

This was one of them.

"Watch out behind you!" Rachel yelled at him.

The thud of hooves and the angry snort put him into motion. Nate dashed into the water to avoid being attacked, but the boar charged after him. Before the vicious beast came too close, Nate grabbed his pistol. When the hoary brute lowered his tusks and charged forward, Nate was forced to shoot it. The boar's stocky legs buckled and its head submerged in water. It lay there, unmoving in knee-deep water.

"I thought I was going to have to do the same thing," Rachel said from behind him. "I tried to come ashore to get my pistol but he came after me. He didn't back off until I was in the water. Crazy as he was acting, I was afraid he had rabies."

Nate wanted to look over his shoulder, but he forced himself to scan the area to locate Rachel's clothing and pistol. When thunder boomed overhead, he reminded himself that being in the water when lightning struck could get a man killed quicker than a cantankerous-boar attack.

"We need to take cover." He swerved around the dead boar to retrieve her clothing. Already raindrops splattered the water's surface, sending out ripples in all directions.

"Promise me that you won't turn around," Rachel demanded as he strode toward her discarded garments.

"Why not? Turnabout is fair play. You've seen me naked."

"Not on purpose. Besides, you've seen enough of me already," she mumbled.

No, he hadn't. He was afraid that the tempting glimpse he'd had earlier was going to drive him crazy. He wouldn't be satisfied until he'd seen—and touched—every luscious inch of her shapely body.

Nate doubled at the waist to pick up her discarded clothes and weapon. Then he held them at arm's length so she could walk up—*naked*—behind him to cover her shapely *nude* body and deprive him of the very thing he wanted to see most.

She dressed hurriedly in her breeches and white blouse. "Where's Doc?"

"I stuffed him in the back of the wagon and moved it downhill to provide more protection.... Who is Margie?" he asked, staring straight ahead, although the man in him was shouting at him to take a peek.

"I don't know. He mentions her name when he's drinking heavily. I've asked him before but he's close-mouthed."

"Sort of like you."

"There, all dressed," she declared, ignoring his remark.

Nate half turned to see the white blouse clinging enticingly to her wet skin. Rain splattered around them and her blouse became more transparent by the second. Desire hit him—hard—below the belt.

This is what visual torment feels like, he mused as he grabbed her hand and barreled through the underbrush to return to camp.

The sky opened up and they became drenched in less than a minute. Nate ducked reflexively when a lightning bolt struck a tree on the other side of the stream. A flash of light burst in front of his eyes and the loud boom shook the earth.

Dragging Rachel along behind him, Nate raced as fast as his injuries allowed to reach the wagon. The fierce wind whipped around them as they crawled beneath the wagon to wait out the storm.

"So much for a cleansing bath," Rachel grumbled as she surveyed her mud-splattered clothing.

"And so much for a hot meal." Nate inclined his wet head toward the smoke rising from the doused fire.

"That leaves canned beans and peaches. I'll fetch them."

Rachel crawled toward the back of the wagon, then pulled herself to her feet to rummage through the supplies. Sure enough, Doc had passed out. He'd sprawled among the bottles and satchels stacked in the wagon bed.

"Doc is oblivious to the storm," she reported as she propped herself on her elbows beneath the wagon. "I swear, if he doesn't stop drinking those cure-alls, he is going to kill the only good friend I have left."

"You've got *me*," Nate reminded her.

She didn't change expression as she opened a can of beans, then handed it to him.

Nate leaned over to thank her with a kiss. "The beans aren't going to appease the hunger gnawing at me," he murmured.

When he raised his head, she frowned disapprovingly.

"Nectar of the gods," he insisted as he accepted the can of food.

"I'd call beans the staple of life, not the nectar of the gods," she disagreed.

He stared steadily at her. "I was talking about you." Then he leaned forward and kissed her again.

"This is a bad idea, Nate," she murmured, shying away.

"It feels good to me. Not kissing you is impossible…"

Rachel's resistance melted into a puddle when his sensuous lips skimmed ever so gently over her mouth. Damn it, this man tempted her but he possessed the power to hurt her—if she allowed him to get too close, if she allowed herself to care too much. Before long, she wouldn't want him to leave—and she *knew* he was leaving soon. He was headed to the very last place on earth she wanted to go, too.

Her breath sighed out of her as his arm glided around her waist to draw her sensitized body familiarly against his. She hadn't realized that she'd draped her arm over his shoulder until her fingers speared into his thick auburn hair.

"You've been driving me crazy for the better part of a week," he said as he spread a row of moist kisses down her throat.

She didn't tell him that she couldn't get him off her mind. She didn't dare arm him with that knowledge. Men always left, no matter how much women cared for them. Nate was no different. He was only interested in a moment of pleasurable diversion.

Even knowing that, suddenly Rachel didn't care about what tomorrow held, as long as she could be with Nate tonight. He made her want things that she had never wanted before from a man.

The reckless thought made her arch wantonly toward him. When his hand cupped her breasts she didn't protest, only enjoyed the sensations he aroused in her. He unbuttoned her blouse to brush his thumb over her beaded nipples and another jolt of pleasure sizzled through her. He looked into her eyes, holding her gaze while the back of his hand drifted from one aching crest to the other. She wondered if he could read the helpless surrender in her expression. He must have, she decided, because he smiled at her before he angled his head down to draw her nipple into his mouth and suckle her.

Rachel gasped as burning pleasure seared her body and scorched the very core of her being. She shivered with forbidden delight when he nipped playfully at her with his teeth. His hand was on the move again, drifting back and forth across her belly before it dipped beneath the waistband of her breeches.

She forgot to breathe when he touched her intimately. Desire and need, unlike anything she had ever experienced, cascaded over her, washing away every cautious inhibition she relied on when it came to the wiles of men. When Nate traced her damp flesh with his fingertips, then withdrew his hand to brush the evidence of her desire for him over her nipple, she moaned at the intimacy between them. Then, when he bent his head to taste the feminine essence he'd brushed over her breast, she trembled in maddening torment.

As if he hadn't set her on fire enough already, he trailed his hand downward again to unfasten her breeches, granting himself free access to her body. He cupped her mound, rubbed his thumb against the sensitive nub between her legs and left her groaning in desperate need.

Rain poured off the wagon and rivulets of water trickled across the grass, but Rachel barely noticed because Nate's erotic seduction was burning her alive. When he glided his finger inside her, she arched toward him in shameless abandon. Then he twisted away to skim his lips over her belly, while stroking her repeatedly, maddeningly.

"Nate—?" she whispered breathlessly as his warm lips drifted over her inner thigh, circling ever closer to where she burned the hottest, where she ached the most for him.

"I won't hurt you. I promise," he murmured against her sensitive flesh.

Yes, you will. You can promise me the moon, but you'll leave me behind and I'll be tormented by the memory of forbidden pleasure as long as I live, she thought.

Then suddenly she couldn't think at all, didn't care if there was a tomorrow or the day after. There was only tonight and the incredible sensations he summoned from her.

He flicked at her with his tongue and stroked her gently

with his hands. Pleasure intensified with each erotic glide of his fingertip. Each intimate kiss made her want to scream his name and urge him to take away the wild ache that threatened to consume her. Sweet mercy! Rachel swore she couldn't tolerate another second of the exotic torture. She was burning alive and Nate kept fanning the flame with his intimate kisses and caresses.

She gasped in astonishment when her body practically came apart at the seams. Unfamiliar spasms of indescribable pleasure ricocheted through her. Rachel clutched frantically at him, pulling him above her, feeling him hard and eager beneath the fabric of his breeches that separated them.

"I want you like hell blazing," he growled against the curve of her neck. "But if you don't want me, too, tell me now. In another minute I'm not sure I'll be able to stop—"

A lightning bolt crackled above them and thunder boomed like a cannon. The horses, still hitched to the wagon, lunged forward, leaving them exposed to the downpour.

Rachel fumbled to fasten herself into her clothes as Nate rolled to his feet to reassure the jittery horses. She wondered if the roar of thunder was a sign from the Cheyenne gods, warning her to come to her senses before she passed the point of no return and lived to regret her recklessness—as her grandmother and mother had.

Despite the soaking rain, her body was still on fire. Rachel bounded to her feet to help Nate unfasten the harnesses, then tether the horses. When their arms collided while they worked hurriedly, Rachel glanced into his intense blue eyes, which reflected the flash of lightning that streaked across the sky.

"Rachel—"

She pressed her forefinger to his full lips to shush him,

then shook her head. She didn't want to hear what he had to say. She was too vulnerable to him, too aroused by unprecedented feelings and sensations. No matter what he said, it would be wrong. She just wanted the moment to pass, even if the memory of the astonishing intimacy between them would remain with her until the end of time.

When Nate crawled beneath the wagon to wait out the storm, Rachel walked over to a tree and sank down. Knees drawn up to her chest, her arms encircling her legs, she closed her eyes and begged for sleep to take her away from the lingering sensations that hummed through her body. Nate had aroused her. He had pleasured her in ways she had never experienced, yet she was oddly dissatisfied, as if she had been deprived.

She wanted more, needed all he could offer. But if she shared her body with him completely she was afraid that she would want to keep him with her forever. Rachel was realistic enough to know that she had to keep moving while Nate settled in Dodge City.

"This is what ill-fated attraction feels like," she muttered under her breath.

Forbidden. That described Nate Montgomery perfectly. There was one man on earth she wanted—and she couldn't have him. The grim realization seemed to fit with the never-ending struggles that were her life.

"It rained," Doc said the next morning when he thrust his tousled blond head from the back of the wagon to look around. "When did that happen?"

Rachel expelled a tired sigh. She hadn't had much sleep and it made her cranky. Doc, on the other hand, had fallen into a stupor and slept through the storm.

Rising, she worked the kinks from her neck and back—

the result of sleeping propped up against a tree trunk. She plucked at her wet clothing, then glanced around discreetly to locate Nate but he was nowhere to be seen.

After last night's steamy tryst, she wasn't sure how she would react when their eyes met. Nate knew her body better than she did. If he made one teasing remark… Well, she wasn't sure what she'd say or do since she was feeling awkward and embarrassed.

"Morning," Nate said as he appeared from the bushes. He smiled at Rachel and his azure-blue eyes swept possessively over her, making her blush furiously. However, he didn't say a word about her reckless abandon or behavior as if she were his midnight conquest. His respectful consideration made her want to hug the stuffing out of him.

Doc climbed down from the wagon, scrubbed his hands over his face, then squinted at his surroundings. "Since the firewood is wet, we'll grab some hardtack and head to our next destination. We might even stay at the hotel in Possum Grove."

While Nate ambled over to fetch the horses, Rachel grabbed dry clothing from the covered wagon. When she returned from changing clothes in the bushes, Nate approached her. She tensed, wondering if this was when he planned to taunt her about the passion that had blown up between them like last night's storm. Again, his intense gaze roamed over her, knowing exactly what was beneath her breeches and blouse. Yet, he didn't voice a humiliating comment.

"I went down to the creek earlier," he said. "I removed the wild pig carcass from the water. If you want to bathe I'll make sure Doc gives you time before we leave."

"Thank you, but I'm fine," she said as nonchalantly as

she knew how. "That was considerate of you not to con-
taminate the water supply for the next travelers."

He turned away, paused, then glanced over his shoulder
at her. "One more thing, Rachel."

There was always one more thing with Nate. "What's
that?"

"I wanted you so badly last night that I didn't get much
sleep. I'm not expecting my condition to improve during
the day. If I become out of sorts that'll be why. Just thought
you needed to know that keeping my hands off you is
taking all the noble self-restraint I have left."

When he walked off, Rachel battled a yearning so
intense that it frightened her. And very little frightened her
these days…except for her ill-fated feelings for this blue-
eyed, incredibly handsome ex-lawman.

Chapter Six

⁓⁓

Adolph Turner swaggered into Grantham Boutique. He smiled pleasantly when the two women, who were talking to Jennifer Grantham, glanced at him. Mrs. Grantham inclined her blond head ever so slightly to acknowledge his presence.

The attractive widow had made a name for herself in town and she was doing a thriving business. Adolph had considered courting her, but he hadn't wanted a pesky child underfoot. His mother had told him hundreds of times what a nuisance *he* was and he wasn't about to put up with someone else's brat.

While the two older women studied the bolts of fabrics on display, Jennifer Grantham approached him. "May I help you with something, sir?"

Adolph shrugged elegantly, though it caused a twinge in his mending shoulder. "I'm looking for a gift for a lady friend. Perhaps a bracelet or necklace."

"Any particular color?" Mrs. Grantham gestured toward the glass case beside the cash register at the back of the shop.

"No, just something that catches my eye." He followed

her, watching the sway of her hips beneath the expertly tailored blue gown.

While she placed several items on the counter, Adolph studied her discreetly. She wore a carefully schooled expression that gave away none of her personal feelings for him. It was difficult to determine if Rachel St. Raimes had confided in Jennifer Grantham about the fiasco in the storeroom and had influenced the shop owner's opinion of him.

"These are nice." Adolph pointed out two necklaces. One for his new mistress and the other to clamp around Rachel's neck while she was wearing nothing else when he finally had her in captivity.

And damn those three morons he'd sent to track her down! They still hadn't overtaken that elusive hellion.

Mrs. Grantham named the prices of the items and Adolph retrieved his wallet to pay without blinking an eye.

He laid the bank notes on the counter, then glanced around the shop. "What has become of the woman who works for you?" he asked with what he hoped was mild interest. "Is she ailing?"

"No," was all the petite blonde shopkeeper said while she made change.

Adolph mentally cursed Jennifer Grantham's unwillingness to offer him information. "Now that I think of it, I don't remember seeing her around town the past month."

"She left town and I haven't heard from her," Mrs. Grantham said finally. "I'm looking for a replacement that is as efficient and skilled as she was."

Although Adolph pretended to stare at the change Jennifer Grantham counted out to him, he was studying her expression beneath his lowered lashes. Damn it, he was pretty certain that the shopkeeper was telling the truth.

She didn't look as if she was purposely withholding information.

She simply didn't like him, he decided.

Obviously, those whispered rumors about the circumstances surrounding his dead mistress weren't winning him friends. Not that he gave a damn. Money purchased all the acquaintances and harlots a man needed until he tired of their company.

Except for Rachel. He had unfinished business with that scrappy female who had made him look the bungling fool when he tried to coerce her into bed with him.

It's only a matter of time, Adolph assured himself confidently as he picked up the jewelry and exited the shop. He vowed to hear Rachel *begging* him to take her. The appealing thought aroused him and he sauntered off to let his new mistress appease his lust for the elusive woman who got away.

Nate surveyed the quaint community known as Possum Grove. It sat on the bank of a clear-water creek in a copse of tall cottonwood trees. Apparently, the local beautification club members had taken it upon themselves to provide the flower gardens and rosebushes that surrounded the park swings and teeter-totters set up for children.

Judging from the businesses that lined the street facing the creek-side park, the community. catered mostly to farmers, ranchers and trail drovers on their way to Dodge City to deliver their cattle herds to the main railhead for shipment to slaughterhouses in the East. There were feed stores, two blacksmith shops, a general store, a bakery, a boutique, three restaurants and four saloons that advertised the additional entertainment of billiard rooms and gaming halls—and who knew what else—on the second story.

Two hotels bookended Main Street. They appeared well maintained, though they didn't begin to compare to the elegant establishments in Kansas City where Brody Montgomery held his annual social ball—and tried to arrange a betrothal for his youngest son.

"Something wrong?" Rachel questioned while she sat on the wagon seat beside him.

"No, just thinking unpleasant thoughts that sprang up uninvited from my past." He guided the horses and wagon along the shaded street. "I usually prefer to keep the past dead and buried."

"I can't think of a better place for it myself," she inserted.

"Unfortunately, some vivid memories have a nasty way of sneaking up on you when you let your guard down."

"Indeed they do," she agreed.

Nate clamped down on his tongue when questions about *her* secretive past leaped to mind. Rachel intrigued him and he wanted to know everything about her. What circumstances had made her the woman she had become? Had a man from her mysterious past made her wary, cautious and mistrusting? Where was her family?

Was she interested in him or had he simply managed to seduce her into yielding to him at a weak moment last night when the passion he aroused in her tempted her past the point of resistance?

The scintillating memory of coming so incredibly close to burying himself in Rachel's moist heat bombarded him. The hungry need that had gone appeased throbbed heavily through his body. Hell! Wanting her and wanting to know all about her was coloring all his thoughts. Why couldn't he get Rachel off his mind? He usually had more mental control than that.

Nate sighed inwardly and told himself that his fascination for this exotic-looking female was going nowhere fast. He had an investigation to conduct in Dodge City and Rachel was determined to continue her gypsy lifestyle as an entertainer and assistant in Doc's medicine show. The longer Nate traveled with them, hanging in limbo, the more emotionally involved he became with Rachel. That wasn't good and he knew it.

"I'm going to remain with the show while you perform in Possum Grove and then travel with you to Evening Shade," he announced. "Then I'm headed to Dodge City to take another job."

He halted the wagon on the side street next to a two-story brick hotel. It looked to be the nicer of the two, he decided.

He watched Rachel closely. He noted a flicker in her obsidian eyes, but he couldn't tell if the announcement pleased or disappointed her.

After a moment, she smiled nonchalantly. "Why delay? You should be on your way now. Your new life and a new profession await you. Doc and I can manage just fine. Besides, Ludy is around here somewhere."

Nate didn't correct her assumption that he had given up law enforcement. She'd run like hell in the opposite direction if she knew he was still a U.S. marshal, he predicted.

When he reached over to steady her when she climbed down, she avoided his touch. In other words, she didn't need his help. Didn't need *him* in her life.

Not mattering to Rachel aggravated him. If he had any sense he would march down the street to one of the saloons and find an accommodating female to ease his needs. No doubt, Ludy Anderson was seeing to his personal pleasures in one of the rooms above a saloon. *He* damn sure wasn't depriving *him*self.

Too bad that Nate's interests centered on a certain secretive, dark-eyed beauty who had the voice of an angel but who had already written him off as a past acquaintance.

"I'm going to stop by the marshal's office," he said in a clipped voice, unable to smother his frustration.

"I'll rent our rooms for the night." Rachel didn't glance in his direction. "I'll see to it that Doc beds down for extra rest to compensate for ingesting too much of his own fifty-proof nostrums again last night."

"We're short on a few basic supplies. I'll pick them up at the dry-goods store on my way back to the hotel," Nate volunteered.

"Thank you. Charge them to Doc and I'll come by to pay for them this afternoon."

Nate turned away when Rachel scurried around to the back of the wagon to rouse Doc, who was lounging on a pallet. Making a beeline for the marshal's office, Nate strode inside to appraise the young marshal who lounged behind the desk. The officer had rocked back on the hind legs of his chair and rested his boot heels on the corner of the scarred desk. His hands were linked behind his curly brown head and a shiny new badge decorated his shirt. The officer was in his mid-twenties, Nate guessed. The kid-marshal's expression implied that he thought he was tough and owned the world.

He had a helluva lot to learn.

"I'm here to file a formal complaint against the men who robbed me and stole my horse." Nate placed his hands on the desk and got down in the kid's face. "I gave descriptions of the men to Marshal Stocker in Crossville and I requested that the circuit judge sign bench warrants. When will the judge pass through Possum Grove?"

The kid's hazel eyes widened when Nate employed the domineering tone his father was famous for. "Ah, sure, mister. I'll, uh, get some paper."

Nate shook his head and swallowed an amused grin. "No, you'll get the standard written forms from the file cabinet and fill them out because that's customary procedure."

"How come you know so much about my business?" the kid asked challengingly.

Nate walked over to the cabinet to rifle through the forms. "Because I was a city marshal before I became a U.S. marshal." He thrust the forms at the wide-eyed kid. "Three men. One of them was about your age and your size."

The young marshal started scribbling hurriedly.

"How long have you been on the job?" Nate asked curiously.

"Four days. I'm filling in for my grandpa. His horse threw him and he's recuperating. I'm Phillip Dexter."

Nate rolled his eyes heavenward, asking for divine patience, then gave descriptions of his assailants. He told himself that it wasn't the greenhorn marshal who agitated him.

It was wanting Rachel like hell blazing that preyed so heavily on his disposition. Knowing that he was leaving soon, and Rachel didn't seem to care, put him in a surly mood—and kept him there.

Rachel shepherded Doc up the stairs and into his hotel room. "The attendants will be along soon to bring water for your bath," she informed him.

Doc nodded his disheveled head, then dug into his pocket to hand her a roll of banknotes. "Pay for the rooms and give yourself a bonus for putting up with me. Give Nate his fair share, too."

She had noticed immediately after she'd joined Doc Grant on his circuit that a lack of funds was not an issue. He paid her generously, even though she'd had a small supply of money in her purse—plus the banknotes she had taken from Adolph's wallet to pay for her dress—when she left Dodge posthaste.

"Nate offered to pick up a few supplies to restock the wagon so I'll pay for it later." She guided Doc to the bed and he sprawled upon it.

"Buy yourself some new clothes while you're in town," he suggested. "Women always like a new gown or stylish hat. My—" He clamped his lips shut, then shooed her on her way with a flick of his wrist. "We'll open the show late this afternoon. Until then, you're free to do whatever you want."

Tucking away the money Doc had entrusted to her, Rachel descended the steps to fetch their luggage. She shrank back and plastered herself against the side of the wagon when she saw Adolph's henchmen exit the local boutique four doors down the street.

Immediate panic set in and her heart pounded like a tom-tom while she watched Max Rother, Bob Hanes and Warren Lamont swagger down the boardwalk to veer into one of the saloons.

Curse it! Those bullies still hadn't given up their search. She would never be able to stop looking over her shoulder, waiting for her past to catch up with her.

The moment the men disappeared from sight Rachel sagged against the wagon and expelled a gusty sigh of relief. She grabbed the luggage, ducked her head and scampered back to the hotel as fast as her legs would carry her.

From the second story-window of her room, which overlooked the street, she waited for the men to reappear. However, ten minutes passed and she saw nothing of them. She presumed they were drinking their fill or had latched on to harlots who agreed to accompany them upstairs to trip the light fantastic.

Rachel knew that particular routine because she had witnessed it numerous times while she had worked in a tavern in Leadville, Colorado. Hubert Solomon, owner of the Golden Goose, had told his "girls" that they were hired to engage miners and prospectors in conversation, flirt and dance with them for a quarter of a dollar—that was paid directly to Hubert—and encourage them to buy drinks. He had paid Rachel additional wages to sing and dance for his customers.

Thankfully, Hubert had made it clear that he didn't expect his "girls" to entertain men in the upstairs rooms. However, several of the barmaids were eager to engage in amorous pursuits if the price was right. Rachel wasn't one of them. She never accompanied men upstairs.

Dealing with inebriated patrons who refused to take no for an answer had taught her how to defend herself quickly and efficiently. It turned out to be good practice for her fiasco with Adolph Turner. The pushy, overbearing bastard, she fumed.

Mentally preoccupied, Rachel knocked on Doc's door, then barged inside without awaiting permission. She heard a squawk erupt from behind the dressing screen. Water sloshed on the floor as Doc poked his disheveled head around the edge of the colorful screen to glare at her.

"I'm bathing!" he huffed. "Try knocking next time."

"Sorry…I don't like this town much," she blurted out. "Let's rest in our rooms for a few hours, then continue on our way to Evening Shade."

"We've already paid for the rooms," Doc reminded her. "Furthermore, there are likely citizens here who are in need of medical attention. I intend for them to receive it. I might save a life. That matters, girl. It's the ones you lose that haunt you forever. Believe me."

"Save one life and lose my own," she mumbled to herself.

Doc frowned curiously. "Pardon?"

"Nothing, Doc. I'll have someone fetch us some food from the restaurant. We'll catch up on lost sleep before we set up for today's show."

Rachel closed the door behind her, then groaned when a troubling thought bombarded her. Nate! He might happen on to the three men who had attacked him. If she tried to help him apprehend them, she would expose her identity and give away her whereabouts. Adolph—if he was still alive and kicking—would be hot on her trail.

On the other hand, if Nate *didn't* stumble on to Adolph's goons, and she kept silent about their presence in town, then he wouldn't run the risk of another brutal attack when he tried to arrest them. Unfortunately, he wouldn't receive restitution for the loss of his horse, his personal belongings and his money, either.

However, she was dying to know if Adolph had survived. "Maybe *dying* isn't the best word," she mumbled as she paced the hallway, debating with herself about what action to take—if any.

"See what happens when you keep secrets?" she grumbled as she descended the stairs to ask one of the hotel attendants to fetch food for their lunch. Keeping secrets compounded on top of one another. They became entangled and they complicated a person's life to the extreme.

Rachel was deeply concerned about Nate running headlong into the brutes. If she informed him of the men's presence in town, her life would be in jeopardy, too.

She stopped breathing when she saw Nate exit the marshal's office, then veer toward the same saloon the men had entered twenty minutes earlier. She waited, expecting to hear shouts or gunfire. Nothing happened. She sagged in relief when Nate reappeared a minute later, carrying a bottle of whiskey—and it better not be for Doc because he didn't need to stock up. Rachel was doing her best to fill Doc's embossed bottles of patented remedies with water.

Apparently, Adolph's henchmen had latched on to willing prostitutes and had traipsed upstairs to ease their lusty needs. Nate and the three men had missed a confrontation by a few minutes. Her luck had held—for now.

Whirling around, Rachel bounded upstairs to pace the floorboards in her room. She had to keep Nate off the street while the bullying threesome was running around loose. In addition, she couldn't perform with the medicine show until she knew for certain that the men had left town. If they recognized her… She grimaced at the gruesome scenarios that leaped to mind.

Hell and damnation! Why did those three men have to show up in this particular town of all days? Why not tomorrow when she was on her way to Evening Shade?

Rachel told herself that she was going to have to do something drastic to protect Nate from potential danger and to save herself. Those ruffians wouldn't leave an eyewitness alive to point an accusing finger at them for assault and thievery.

It wasn't that she didn't think Nate was competent, but look what had happened to him when he faced three-to-one odds with those brutes last time they clashed.

Tensely, she watched Nate stride into the general store to restock supplies for the wagon. She waited apprehensively for the three men to exit the saloon. Thirty minutes later the men still hadn't returned to the street when Nate strode toward the hotel with the supplies. She breathed a gigantic sigh of relief, assured that Nate was safe for the moment. Of course, she would have to distract him until those ruthless bastards rode off to another town to search for her.

No matter what, he was *not* leaving his room, she told herself resolutely. Not until Adolph's thugs rode away!

Nate stopped at the front desk of the hotel to order water for a bath. While the attendants trooped upstairs to fill the tub, he strode off to send a telegram to his brother, Ethan, asking him to ship clothing, money and his spare badge to Nate in Dodge City. He also insisted that Ethan *not* mention the telegram or request to their father. Nate didn't want his father showing up to check on him. Or rather to order him to return home and settle down with a wife of Brody's choosing again.

Then he entered his room to shave with the razor he had picked up at the dry-goods store. He decided to remove the beard and mustache he'd worn the past six months in Kansas City.

I'm starting fresh, Nate reminded himself. Besides, summer temperatures were soaring and a clean-shaven face was much cooler. He was anything if not practical. Something his father and older brother had difficulty understanding.

Nate was halfway through shaving when someone knocked at the door. One of the young boys hauling water opened the door and Nate saw Rachel standing in the hall, holding a tray of food. She gaped at him when she noticed the beard on the left side of his face was gone.

He inclined his head toward the end table. "Thanks for lunch. Set it down over there, please."

She waited until the second attendant exited, carrying an empty bucket, before she walked inside. Something about the way she fidgeted around the room and darted uneasy glances at him made him frown curiously.

"Is there a problem?"

She smiled a little too brightly. "No. Of course not."

Nate didn't believe her, but he couldn't imagine what might have happened the past hour since he'd seen her. "Is Doc okay?"

"He's dining." She paced the confines of his room. "He decided to start the show late this afternoon so we can rest." She stared pointedly at the whiskey bottle on the end table. "That better not be for Doc."

"It isn't."

It was the substitute for what Nate really wanted—Rachel, naked and yielding in his arms. If she knew what he was thinking, she'd leave his room—at a dead run—right this very minute.

She must have read his mind because she whirled toward the door and disappeared from sight.

Nate finished shaving, then stared at his reflection in the mirror. He looked more like his old self—the lawman he'd been before he'd rushed to Kansas City to be sucked into his father's scheme to marry him off to a wealthy social-ite.

The poor woman wouldn't have survived a day traveling with the medicine show. Rachel, on the other hand, seemed capable of adapting to almost anything.

"Stop making comparisons," he scowled as he plunked down on the edge of the bed to eat lunch.

Nate had told his father and older brother the previous month that he wasn't interested in settling down—and certainly not with Lenora Havern. Furthermore, Rachel Whoever-she-was didn't need him to make her life complete.

And he didn't need her, either.

It was the *wanting* her that tormented him to no end.

Nate intended to fulfill his duties as a U.S. marshal, just as he always had. He liked the challenge of solving mysteries and problems. He liked being on the move.

"So there you have it," he told himself between bites of fried potatoes and steak. "This is the life you designed for yourself." Even if his father objected strenuously to Nate working in law enforcement when he didn't have to work a day in his life.

"So don't be like Dad who thinks he should have a say in how you live your life. You don't get to decide what Rachel wants for herself."

Still… He wanted to insist that she accompany him to Dodge City. He wanted her to want him, too, because he enjoyed being with her. She intrigued him. The thought of leaving her behind disturbed him.

Nate shook his head in amazement. How could a woman he'd known for a week make such a vivid impact? Why was he compelled to invite her to travel to Dodge City while he conducted the investigation?

He supposed it was the combination of her striking appearance, her indomitable spirit, the mystical sound of her voice and the enticing feel of her lush body meshed to his that had him rethinking his decision to leave her behind.

He barked a laugh. "Must've been the aftereffects of that brain-numbing potion she gave you that first night you met her." The thought made him frown pensively. Not that he believed it for even a moment…and yet…

Nate scoffed at the ridiculous thought, then munched on the potatoes that had an under taste. There was something vaguely familiar about the flavor. Where had he noticed it before?

After finishing his meal, he poured himself a tall drink and downed it quickly. Then he shed his clothes and stepped into his bath. Strange sensations streamed through him as he lathered himself with soap. The frustrations that had tormented him since the previous evening faded away, leaving him amazingly relaxed. Exotic memories of kissing and caressing Rachel skittered across his mind.

Suddenly, wanting her exploded with killing force.

He wondered how she would react if he marched down the hall to her room, naked as the day they had met, and took up where they had left off last night. The impulsive thought hammered at him as he grabbed the towel. When he stood up to dry off, the room tilted sideways and a fuzzy haze clouded his vision. Yet nothing curbed the ever-present need that gnawed at him. Instead, the ache intensified.

"Another drink," he mumbled as he wrapped the towel around his waist and padded over to the end table.

He pivoted around when the door swung open. He reflexively reached for the pistol that usually hung in a holster on his hips but he grabbed nothing but towel. His gaze widened when Rachel stepped inside the room, then closed and locked the door.

He appraised the low-cut green satin gown that he'd never seen her wear before. The diving neckline exposed the tempting swells of her breasts. She dazzled him as she walked toward him, her dark eyes riveted on his barely clad body. Need coursed heavily, hungrily, through him.

"This is not a good time for you to be here," he warned.

She halted less than an arm's length away. "No? Why not?"

"Because I want you too much," he told her flat-out. "I also think I'm going to miss you like crazy when I leave."

Damn it, the drink he'd ingested all too quickly must've loosened his tongue. *Think before you blurt out comments like that one,* he criticized himself.

"I'm going to miss you, too, Nate." She stepped closer to glide her arms around his neck. Then she studied his face for a long moment—while the feel of her luscious body brushing provocatively against his drove him another step closer to crazy. "I like you clean shaven. You are incredibly handsome. But I'm sure dozens of women have told you that before."

"None that mattered," he mumbled before he yielded to overwhelming temptation and kissed her as if she were the dying wish granted a condemned prisoner.

Lord, he loved the taste of her. He reveled in the feel of her body molded familiarly against his. "Just one more thing, though," he whispered against her cheek.

She chortled softly and the appealing sound went through him, touching every fiber of his being. "With you, there is always one more thing. What is it this time?"

"Your dress is stunning," he complimented.

"Thank you. I made it myself."

He grinned roguishly as he reared back to appraise her again. "But as much as I like your dress, I'd rather you were wearing nothing but me."

His straightforward remark made her breath stall out. But Nate didn't retract the comment. What he wanted was right there between them. He waited anxiously, expecting her to turn around and hightail it from his room. When she didn't retreat, he stared into those dark, hypnotic eyes through the cloudy mist that teased his vision. Before his eyes blurred completely he reached down to unfasten the delicate buttons on the bodice of her green satin gown.

"Last chance, angel face," he said hoarsely. "If you don't leave now I—"

She pressed her forefinger to his lips, then stepped back to remove the dress. Nate swore he was drooling all over himself as he drank in the titillating sight of Rachel standing before him in a lacy chemise that extended a few inches past her hips. His appreciative gaze roamed over her full breasts and trim waist, then settled on the silky flesh of her thighs.

Desire hit him like a rock slide. He managed a smile when he noticed her attention had shifted to the towel he had fastened around his hips. His arousal couldn't have been more evident.

He held his breath when she unfastened the knot in the towel and let it drop to the floor. When she traced his hard length with her fingertips, he stopped breathing altogether.

"I don't want *you* to wear anything but *me*," she said as she guided him to the edge of the bed, then knelt between his legs.

Chapter Seven

The instant her lips skimmed over his throbbing shaft Nate swore he was going to pass out. Pleasure sizzled and burned through him and he braced himself on his hands before he collapsed beneath the onslaught of blazing sensations.

"Rachel, don't—"

"I want to know you as well as you know me," she insisted as she brushed her lips back and forth across his aching flesh. "I want to know what pleasures you, what drives you wild with need."

"*You* do," he rasped.

Another tidal wave of fiery sensations buffeted him. He clenched his fists in the bedspread to steady himself when she took him into her mouth and suckled him. Then she nipped playfully at him with her teeth, causing his overworked heart to slam into his rib cage so hard he swore he'd cracked another rib—and didn't care if they all shattered.

"Damn," he said on a hissed breath, and fought like hell for control.

"That bad?" She looked up at him while she continued to hold his pulsing shaft in her hand.

"That *good*. But I swear you're killing me." His comment made her smile impishly so he added, "I can't think of a better way to die—"

His breath fizzled out completely when she stroked him repeatedly, tenderly. Another round of indescribable sensations blazed through him. His vision kept fading in and out, leaving him swearing that he was floating in a dreamlike trance. If he'd had the slightest reservations or inhibitions before now, they had fled in the holocaust of fire that scorched him inside and out.

Rachel was giving him such tantalizing pleasure that he surrendered without the slightest objection to her intimate kisses and caresses. When she urged him to sprawl on the bed, he obliged willingly. He watched, entranced, as she removed her chemise and tossed it aside. Seeing her in the darkness the previous night had aroused him, but it didn't compare to marveling at every exquisite inch of her body in the light of day. She was feminine perfection and he wanted her like hell burning.

"Lord, you're incredibly beautiful," he whispered roughly. "Come here."

"Not yet." She pulled the pins from her hair, then let the rich raven strands tumble over her shoulders, concealing the tips of her breasts. "I'm not finished becoming acquainted with you, Nate."

He sighed in utter defeat when she set her hands upon him again. He craved her touch with mindless obsession. He savored the riveting tingles of pleasure she called from him. His breath came out raggedly when her silky hair drifted over his chest and belly in an erotic caress that sent his mind into another dizzying spin. His body shuddered when her hand drifted over his abdomen to sketch the muscles of his inner thighs.

Unholy torment engulfed him when her feathery caresses skittered ever closer to his arousal, then drifted away. He was shameless—and desperate—to feel her fingertips and lips on him again. He had never granted any other woman access to his body, but Rachel could do whatever she wanted to him, for as long as she wanted, however many times she wanted. He was at the mercy of her tender touch and his ravenous need for her.

When she traced his hard length with her tongue, then flicked at him, he heard a wobbly groan that must have been his. Then her hands began to move over him and the burning ache intensified. Flames licked at his body and the room went completely out of focus.

This better not be a fantasy, he thought as mind-boggling pleasure vibrated through every nerve and muscle. He was a *little* dizzy and a *lot* out of breath. This helpless condition became worse when she cupped him and suckled him until he arched toward her in frantic abandon. He quivered with so much unappeased need that he groaned again.

Urgently, he reached for her, but she pressed him back to the bed and she continued to work her passionate magic on him. He wasn't sure how much more pleasure he could endure before he exploded. Already he swore the top of his head was about to blow off. His body was completely sensitized and need pummeled him, making it nearly impossible to draw breath.

"Enough," he panted as he buried his fingers in the long silky strands of her dark hair and drew her head up to his. "I want you, Rachel. I swear I've never wanted anything more."

Despite the shimmering haze floating around him, he noticed she was smiling down at him. "I want you, too, Nate."

That's all he needed to hear. He hooked his arm around her waist and rolled over so that she was beneath him. He wished his vision would clear up so he could see every detail of her face, every thick strand of hair that fanned out on his pillow. Yet feeling her soft flesh beneath his hand was enough to satisfy him for the moment.

Hearing her quick intake of breath when his fingertips skimmed the taut peaks of her breasts pleased him immensely. He was rewarded with the sound of her quiet moan when he skimmed his open mouth over her concave belly to spread a row of kisses up and down the satiny flesh of her inner thighs.

When he lifted her hips to his lips to taste her warm essence she cried out his name. And when he suckled her, and then probed her heated flesh with his tongue, he felt the fluttering tremors of passion assail her. He vowed to offer her the same intense pleasure she had given him before he buried himself deeply inside her. Rachel had driven him as close to desperate urgency as he had ever been but he swore he'd hold himself at bay—even if it killed him, and there was a very real possibility that it would—until she was consumed by the maddening sensations that dragged him to the crumbling brink of self-control.

"Nate—?"

"I'm here," he whispered against her skin.

"But not close enough. You're driving me cra—"

Her voice broke on a shuddering sigh when he traced her softest flesh with his thumb, then glided his finger into her shimmering heat. He stroked her slowly, deliberately, and felt her come apart in his arms.

He'd never spent so much time pleasing a woman, but he dedicated himself to drawing Rachel to the edge of mindless oblivion and making the last of her inhibitions flit off in the wind. When he took her, he wanted her clutching frantically at him as they tumbled into breathless ecstasy together.

To that dedicated end he pleasured her, aroused her over and over again. He smiled triumphantly when she grabbed him by the hair on his head and pulled him above her.

"Make the empty ache go away," she demanded shakily.

He settled exactly upon her and whispered, "Whatever you wish, Rachel. Whatever you wish…"

Rachel couldn't name a time in her life that she'd felt so wildly frantic and out of control. The pleasure Nate had given her with his skillful kisses and caresses defied description. It was even more intense than the sensations she had experienced with him the previous night. He seemed to know how and where to touch her and make her shiver with so many astonishing feelings that they converged to overwhelm her. Her body was so attuned to his kisses and caresses that she responded intensely, wildly, wholeheartedly.

When he moved intimately toward her, she clasped her hands on his hips and urged him ever closer. Even the unexpected pressure of his masculine penetration didn't prevent her from urging him deeper and arching shamelessly toward him—anything to satisfy the burning ache inside her.

When he stopped suddenly and looked down at her, as if he was seeing her for the very first time, her body begged for more, begged for something that he withheld from her and she needed desperately. She couldn't imagine what that something was because the passion he had summoned from her already was enough to stop her heart and make her swear she had died twice the last few minutes.

She was still arching toward him when he mumbled something she couldn't interpret—and she was too impatient to ask him to repeat. Then he began to move inside her, satisfying her with each gliding stroke. The wild, sweet crescendo built until indefinable pleasure burst over her like fireworks streaming down from the sky. He drove into her, harder, faster, and she gave all that she was to him, desperate to satisfy the insatiable need clamoring for release inside her.

Her eyes flew wide open and she stared at Nate in baffled astonishment when the most phenomenal sensation she had ever experienced claimed her mind and body. Pleasure expanded, vibrated, through every part of her being until it consumed her completely. She swore she was spiraling weightlessly through time and space, soaring directly into the sun. She held on for dear life when even more incredible sensations bombarded her.

When Nate clutched at her, then shuddered above her, she understood the meaning of wild, splendorous ecstasy. Nothing seemed as important as holding on to him, feeling his heartbeat hammering against her breasts, while her accelerated pulse beat in perfect rhythm with his. The tumultuous pleasure of passion poured over her, through her, draining her energy and strength. She was locked in Nate's sinewy arms but she didn't feel restrained or imprisoned. She felt as free as an eagle soaring with the wind beneath its wings.

For that timeless moment, all was right with her world, and she never wanted to forget how amazing it felt to be here, like this, with him.

Nate nuzzled his chin against her neck and she felt his smile of satisfaction—the same silly smile she suspected was curving her lips.

"You are absolutely incredible," he mumbled drowsily. "But you should've told me it was your first time, sweetheart. I would've been gentler with you."

She pressed an affectionate kiss to his forehead. "I'm not complaining."

"Good. Didn't want to disappoint you."

"Never that," she confided softly.

She felt him sag heavily against her and she decided she had better scoot away before the potion she'd mixed into his fried potatoes took full effect.

"You're leaving so soon?" he said groggily. "Stay…"

That was the last thing he said before his eyelids slammed shut, his head lolled against the pillow and he fell into a deep, motionless sleep.

Rachel smiled in amusement as she traced his sensuous lips with her forefinger. So much tender emotion welled up inside her when she stared at him that it nearly squeezed her heart in two. She could easily fall in love with Nate— if she hadn't already. And what a disaster that would be! He was strikingly handsome—especially without the beard and mustache. Plus, he was undeniably virile, intelligent and quite charming when he wanted to be. But also he was an ex-lawman and most likely she was wanted for murder.

Her mother and grandmother had fallen for the wrong men and they had ended up pining away in misery. Rachel had vowed long ago that history wouldn't repeat itself with her.

She knew Nate would leave her behind to begin his new life in a place that was off-limits to her. She also knew she would never see him again. She needed to devote her life to another purpose, just as her grandmother, Singing Bird, had devoted her life to healing the Cheyenne with her natural curatives.

Rachel frowned pensively, wondering if that's why she felt a natural affinity to Doc Grant. His crusade for tending the sick was similar to her grandmother's.

Too bad her mother hadn't found a worthwhile purpose when her father broke his pledge to uphold the law and turned to a life of crime. Her mother had begun to drink excessively—also like Doc Grant. She had lost the will to live, even for the sake of her young daughter, and she had died in a nameless Colorado town while Rachel sang for handouts to pay for their food and lodging.

Rachel had reaffirmed her vow never to care so deeply for a man that he stole her soul and her reason for existence when he walked away. She was a survivor. She might be dangerously close to losing her heart to Nate, but she refused to give up as her mother had.

Resolved, Rachel donned her chemise and gown, then returned to stand beside Nate's bed. A myriad of intense emotions tumbled helter-skelter through her. She felt guilty for giving him the same potion she had mixed the first night they met.

That first time had been an accident. This time wasn't.

This was proof positive that her concoction had made him extremely susceptible to her and it had aroused him past the point of resistance. He had been unaware that all she knew of men was what she overheard promiscuous barmaids whispering to each other. That is, until that moment when Nate realized she had been innocent of men.

Since the aftereffects of the love potion made Nate

drowsy, she expected him to sleep the afternoon away. Good. She wanted to avoid a possible confrontation with the three scalawags who were out for her blood.

Rachel was still at odds with herself about preventing Nate from discovering the whereabouts of Adolph's henchmen. However, three-to-one odds provoked her to protect him, as well as herself, from harm. He might be outraged by her deception but he couldn't argue with the fact those ruthless bastards got the best of him recently.

Yet she knew Nate and those ruffians would clash eventually in Dodge City. Also, Nate would discover the truth about her, she mused as she poured the remainder of his bottle of whiskey into the chamber pot. She suspected that her strong love potion and the liquor he'd ingested were a potent combination.

She bent over to press a light kiss to Nate's unresponsive lips, then draped the corner of the bedspread over his muscular body. She smiled, knowing there was no other man alive she wanted to introduce her to the pleasures of intimate passion. Even if he was a former lawman she couldn't care less.

After checking her reflection in the mirror to ensure that she looked presentable, she pinned her hair atop her head, then exited. She returned to her own room and stood guard at the window for a few minutes. She tensed reflexively when the scraggly-looking thugs staggered from the saloon, each carrying a half-empty bottle of whiskey. She cursed in frustration when the men veered into a restaurant for a late lunch.

"Darn it, are they ever going to leave town?" she grumbled in frustration.

Although Rachel was willing to give Nate another dose of love potion and experience the same incredible pleasures again, she didn't want to have to sedate him all day while those three goons lollygagged around town. Heavens, if they spent the night in Possum Grove she would have to keep Nate occupied in bed until morning. Wickedly appealing as that thought was—

"Stop it," she scolded herself. "You can't hold Nate— naked—in his hotel room and turn him into your love slave by giving him that potion continuously."

Pivoting away from the window, Rachel shed her gown and crawled into her bed. Her lack of sleep during last night's storm—and her passionate interlude with Nate—left her exhausted. Not to mention the mounting concern about the possibility of being apprehended by Adolph's henchmen.

Rachel dozed off almost immediately. The erotic memories of the passion she had discovered in Nate's arms were there to greet her, luring her into rapturous dreams.

Rachel awoke with a start. Her pleasant dream had transformed into a nightmare in which those three hounds from hell, sent by the devil himself, interrupted her tryst with Nate and dragged him away, leaving *her* to face Adolph the demon.

Scrubbing her hands over her face, she stared at the ceiling and reassured herself that it was only a bad dream. She rolled from bed to dab her eyes and cheeks with cool water. Then she stood guard at the window, uncertain how much time had passed while she slept.

Were those goons still eating their fill? Had they wandered back to the saloon to ingest more liquor? Although she didn't approve of imbibing large amounts of whiskey, she wished Adolph's men would drink themselves blind so they wouldn't recognize her or Nate.

"Damn it, where are they now?" Her anxious gaze darted back and forth between the restaurant and the four saloons. Well, there was only one way to find out what had become of those scoundrels, she reminded herself.

She whirled around to rummage through her satchel, locating the men's clothing she had altered to fit after Nate had purchased garments for himself in Crossville. The baggy breeches still concealed her feminine physique but she had hemmed them up so she wouldn't trip over them constantly. She had shortened the long cuffs on the oversize shirt and added a brown vest that she had stitched together from a scrap of fabric she'd picked up at the dry-goods store in Crossville.

Tucking her hair beneath the floppy hat, Rachel exited her room to take the narrow metal steps that served as a fire escape at the back of the hotel. She scampered down the alley, then inched up to a café window to survey the interior.

The three men weren't there.

Pulling her cap low on her forehead and ducking her chin to conceal her identity, she stepped onto the board-walk to amble past the first saloon. She glanced inside but she didn't see the men bellied up to the bar or sprawled negligently at a table. Then she walked to the second tavern to have a look-see but she saw nothing of the men.

Simmering with impatience, she headed to the third saloon—and glanced inadvertently toward the park near the stream bank. The men were watering their horses and sipping whiskey. Rachel leaned a shoulder against the supporting beam of the saloon and kept surveillance for several minutes. She entertained the thought of dashing downhill to shove the drunken men facedown in the water and letting them float away.

Of course, that would add more crimes to her list. Damn, if nothing else she wished she could walk up and ask them if Adolph had survived their fracas in the storeroom. At least she would know for certain what she was up against. The *not* knowing frustrated her to no end.

When the men led away their horses, then mounted up, Rachel thanked the Powers That Be—both Indian and white. She had bought herself crucial time.

"Whew! Talk about dodging the bullet," she said to herself as she scurried across the street to pay for the supplies Nate had purchased earlier in the day.

Now that the ruffians had ridden away, she could breathe easy. Also, she could perform in the medicine show without the fear of being recognized and captured.

Rachel climbed the fire escape, then checked the hall to ensure no one saw her duck into her room. She had avoided disaster—even if Nate wouldn't see it that way if he found out she had purposely detained him.

Nate awoke with a dull headache and a feeling of lethargy. He blinked, befuddled, when he realized he was lying spread-eagle in bed—nude. "What the hell—?"

He raked his fingers through his hair and frowned thoughtfully when he noticed the empty bottle on the end table. How much whiskey had he consumed? He didn't remember guzzling the entire bottle.

A feeling of amazing satisfaction thrummed through him and he tried to figure out whether he was recalling a hazy dream or reality.

Then it hit him like a doubled fist between the eyes.

"Oh, damn. I did it again." He scowled.

This time he had taken advantage of Rachel completely. That was no dream. It must have been the result of a whiskey-induced lust attack. She probably hated him with a vengeance.

Not that he blamed her.

Nate levered himself upright on the bed, then glanced around. He remembered Rachel walking into his room, wearing a bewitching gown that he'd wanted to rip off her—with his teeth. He tried to recall what had happened next but the sequence of events became fuzzy and disjointed. Thoughts and sensations buzzed around him and he frowned in absolute concentration. One thing he definitely remembered was the tantalizing feel of her hands and lips on his sensitized body. Had he asked her to pleasure him or had she volunteered?

He massaged his throbbing forehead, then squinted at the late-afternoon sunlight that streamed through the window. Erotic images darted across his mind, then spun in dizzying circles. He remembered Rachel making a feast of him before he made a feast of her. Then he had taken her in a wild rush of obsessive passion.

The problem was that she'd been a virgin and he hadn't realized it until it was too late. He hadn't cared because the pleasure he'd discovered with her had overshadowed his conscience and any sense of decency he had going for him. He'd acted selfishly and shamelessly and he didn't blame Rachel if she refused to speak to him again.

"Damnation," he muttered as he flopped back on the bed.

He stared at the ceiling—as if it held all the answers to the tormenting questions swirling in his brain. It didn't. He didn't understand why he'd been so reckless and inconsiderate of Rachel. He wasn't sure why his vision seemed impaired, either. Must've been too much whiskey, he decided.

And what was that odd taste on his tongue? It must have been the fried potatoes, he decided. He'd thought they'd had an unusual flavor. Obviously, the seasoning didn't agree with him. That, added to too much whiskey, must have made him behave recklessly and irresponsibly.

Now he'd have to apologize to Rachel all over again because he couldn't remember if he had said or done anything else to offend her.

Other than stealing her innocence, he amended with a wince.

Hell's bells! He didn't really want to apologize for something that he'd do again—and again—if she gave him the chance. She hadn't trusted men before. *Now* he'd given her every reason not to.

Scowling, Nate heaved himself on to his feet and wobbled to the tub to thrust his head into the cool water. If he didn't clear his fuzzy senses quickly, he would be stumbling around all evening. For all he knew the medicine-show performance might be under way and he was staggering around in his room while Rachel changed costumes without him there to protect her privacy.

Not that he'd respected her privacy or modesty this afternoon, he thought with a grimace.

Would she be too proud and ashamed to discuss what had happened between them? he wondered. Probably. She had been awkward with him this morning after their interrupted tryst during last night's storm.

Nate shook the water from his hair, then grabbed a towel. He grumbled sourly when his thoughts cleared up enough for him to realize there might be serious consequences to today's intimate liaison. Rachel hadn't been with a man before. If she conceived a child…

His thoughts stalled, knowing this unexpected turn of

events would probably have Brody Montgomery jumping for joy. His father might not like the fact that he hadn't been the one to handpick the mother of his grandchild from Kansas City's socially elite, but perpetuating the family name was his father's ultimate objective.

He wondered how Rachel would react if she conceived his child. Not happy, he predicted.

"Well, damn," he mumbled as he cast aside the towel, then donned his clothes.

He strode down the hall to knock on Rachel's door. When she didn't answer, he tried Doc's door. Doc didn't answer, either. Assuming the two were setting up for a performance, Nate hurried downstairs to locate the medicine wagon.

Chapter Eight

A few minutes later Nate noticed that Ludy Anderson had pulled the wagon into the creek-side park and set up beneath a shade tree. Curious bystanders wandered downhill to listen to Ludy strum his banjo and sing a few lively tunes. His voice didn't compare to Rachel's, but he sang a helluva lot better than Nate, so who was he to judge?

A short time later Rachel appeared. As always, she captivated the crowd with her Cheyenne costume and the Indian version of creation. Curiosity ate Nate alive while he watched her performance. He wanted to know when and where she had learned to speak fluent Cheyenne. Her dark hair and dark eyes indicated Indian ancestry. How much? he wondered. He also wondered why she refused to divulge her last name. If she became the mother of his child, he was entitled to know such things.

Mother of his child? Nate wasn't sure what he thought about that. Nevertheless, he wasn't a man who turned his back on his responsibilities. Not that the mysterious Rachel would have him as a husband. She might change her mind, however, if she discovered the Montgomery name came with a sizeable fortune he had inherited from his maternal grandparents.

Money had a way of changing a woman's mind, he assured himself cynically. Several females had crawled all over him in years past in attempt to charm him, deceive him or lure him into marriage. Since that hadn't worked, his father had decided to manipulate him into settling down in Kansas City.

Nate shook himself from his wandering thoughts when Rachel completed her performance and the crowd applauded enthusiastically. As Rachel approached him, wearing the bead-and-buckskin squaw dress that fit her curvaceous figure like a glove, he watched her astutely.

As anticipated, she was reluctant to meet his gaze. No doubt, she felt uneasy about their passionate encounter. Damn, he hoped like hell that he hadn't made the experience unpleasant for her. He hated that he couldn't remember all the intimate details.

She spoke not one word as she walked uphill to change clothes in the storeroom of the general store. When two men scurried after her, Nate blocked their path and thrust out his arm to forestall them.

"Why don't you enjoy the rest of the show," Nate suggested pleasantly. "The young lady will return shortly to give another performance."

The two men, dressed in cowboy boots, jeans and tattered shirts, looked him up and down and smirked disdainfully.

"What are you supposed to be? Her bodyguard?" the tall, lanky cowpuncher asked sarcastically.

"That's right. Doc Grant has a special place in his heart for the young lady. He pays me extremely well to make sure no one bothers her."

The stocky cowboy grinned and waggled his bushy brows suggestively. "Wasn't planning to harm her, just gonna show her a real good time."

Nate suspected Rachel had had enough of men for the day. He'd taken advantage of her already and these two men would likely upset her with their bungling attempts to seduce her.

"Go away," he said curtly, discarding all tact.

When they didn't back off, Nate practically stood on top of them and bared his teeth while his hand hovered threateningly over his pistol.

"Okay," the skinny, long-faced cowboy replied, then added defiantly, "but we'll be back."

"And I'll still be here," Nate assured him.

Ten minutes later Rachel appeared in a stunning green satin gown… Nate jerked to attention when he remembered this was the dress Rachel had been wearing when he'd unfastened those dainty buttons on the bodice—and hadn't stopped touching her until he was buried deeply inside her.

"I'm sorry," he blurted out when she approached.

She halted and blinked at him. "Sorry for what?"

"I'm terribly sorry about this afternoon," he hurried on. "For some reason I can't recall everything that happened but I do remember this dress. You said you made it yourself…then I unbuttoned it off of you."

Her face turned the color of steamed beets and she tried to brush past him, but he grabbed her arm and held her fast.

"Let me go," she demanded sharply. "People are staring."

"That's because you look stunning," he insisted. "I want you to know that if I hurt you…if I forced you—"

"You didn't," she cut in quickly. "It was my fault and I

apologize to *you*. Now let me go. I have to give a performance and I can't do it properly if you get me rattled."

"I rattle you?" He tilted his head to study her pinched expression. "In what way?"

"Every way imaginable." She clamped her mouth shut, then blew out her breath. "Just let me go. We can talk about this later…or not at all. Not at all would be best."

He released her arm and she surged downhill, moving as quickly as the stylish gown permitted.

Nate frowned—which only made his head hurt worse. What did she mean that what had happened was her fault? *He* had made his intentions toward her quite clear that morning, he recalled.

He shook his head, trying to sort out the jumbled thoughts. Maybe he was having a relapse from that brain-scrambling blow to his skull earlier in the week.

He stared pensively at Rachel's departing back as she made her way to the medicine wagon. "We *are* going to discuss the incident—at length. Like it or not," he vowed, though she was out of earshot.

Rachel barely remembered giving her musical performance that afternoon. Guilt, embarrassment and concern hounded her constantly. Plus, she wasn't sure what Nate wanted to discuss about their passionate interlude. Did he remember the taste of the potion? Did he think it was his responsibility to propose to her when he realized that he was her first time? Probably.

He seemed to be an honorable man. However, Rachel refused to become his obligation. Despite common sense, she cared about him. Because she did, she refused to settle for being his obligation when she wanted to be the object of his deep, everlasting affection.

Not that it mattered what she wanted, she reminded herself sensibly. Nate was headed one direction and she was going another.

"Rachel?"

She flinched at the sound of Ludy's voice floating from the darkness that had settled over the park.

"You okay? You don't seem yourself today," he observed.

She flashed him a saucy grin. "No? Then who am I?"

He grinned back. "That's the burning question. Doc, Nate and I don't know who you are, today or any other day. Why don't you tell us?"

"Clever of you to try to pry information from me," she remarked as she turned away. "Sorry but it won't work. My past is a closed chapter…and not a very interesting one at that."

"Seriously, Rachel, you've looked tense all day. Is there something wrong that I can fix?" he asked earnestly.

Rachel pivoted to face him, then reached out to poke playfully at the dimples in his cheeks. Before she had become involved with Nate, she had kept her distance from all men—Ludy included. Now that she had come to trust Nate, she felt more confident with physical contact with other men. Ludy might be a ladies' man who flirted outrageously with other women, but he was respectful to her and he was her friend.

"You are a sweet man, Ludy, but there is nothing to fix."

Ludy grasped her hand, gave it an affectionate squeeze and held it in his own. "If you need something, Rachel, all you have to do is ask me. You know that, don't you?"

His sincere offer prompted her to press a sisterly kiss to his cheek. "Thank you. I am honored to call you my friend."

As she walked away to change clothes her eyes welled up with tears. Well, honestly, she thought as she brushed the moisture from her cheeks. It wasn't like her to become sentimental mush at the drop of a hat or at the utterances of her newfound friend.

Yet, there was no denying that her emotions were in a tailspin after juggling the apprehensive events of the day to avoid disaster. She'd gone into a panic when she sighted Adolph's dangerous henchmen and quivered with concern over Nate's welfare. She'd fretted about the possibility of being discovered and captured. Then she'd become hopelessly consumed by the intimacy of passion.

The intensity of emotion and conflicting turmoil she'd endured all the livelong day exhausted her. Not to mention the additional mental strain of performing for the public while she felt at such odds with herself. What she needed was to venture off alone to sort out her troubled thoughts.

That was what Singing Bird always recommended when the emotional burdens of life closed in on you. There were times—like now—that Rachel wanted to seek the comforts she had known while living with her Cheyenne grandmother.

Come to think of it, this would be the perfect time to leave Kansas. She should have left a month ago, but she had stumbled on to Doc Grant, who needed her as much as she needed him to travel in anonymity.

Rachel jerked upright when someone grabbed her from behind and tried to clamp his hand over her mouth. The smell of sweat and liquor clogged her senses and she cursed herself for being so distracted that she hadn't paid close attention to her surroundings. Damn it, she knew better. She had been *trained* to know better.

"Now that your human guard dog wandered off we can have ourselves some fun… Ouch!"

The ruffian behind her yelped in pain when she bit a chunk out of his finger, then gouged his soft underbelly with her elbow. Rachel tried to lurch sideways and dart around a tree so she could make a beeline for the safety of the medicine wagon. Unfortunately, a second man lunged from the shadows to grab the nape of her gown. He jerked her backward so hard that she lost her balance and landed on the ground with a thud that knocked the wind out of her, making it impossible to scream for help.

"Where do ya think yer going so fast, honey?" the second foul-smelling rascal jeered as he plopped down on her belly, forcing the air from her lungs again.

When she finally caught her breath, she tried to scream bloody murder but the first attacker crammed his smelly kerchief in her mouth and held it in place, even while she turned her head from side to side in an attempt to evade him.

Alarm spurted through her veins when the wiry-looking man on top of her held her wrists above her head with one hand, then shifted to jerk up her skirts with the other. Anger and outrage pulsated through her as she bucked and twisted, trying to unseat him.

Rachel was instantly reminded of dealing with drunken miners in Colorado and with Adolph in Dodge City. But this time she wasn't carrying a pistol or her weighted purse to counter attacks. Her mistake. She hoped she survived, never to repeat the careless error.

Damn men everywhere! she fumed. The lusty bastards treated women as if they were theirs for the wanting and the taking. Fury riveted her when her assailant clamped his beefy hand around her knee to force her legs apart. When he shifted, she upraised her leg and slammed the heel of her shoe against the back of his head. He yelped in surprise and teetered sideways.

When he released her hands unintentionally, she took immediate advantage by clawing at the other attacker who held the kerchief over her mouth.

"You little wildcat," he muttered while he tried to dodge her raking nails and still hold the kerchief in place.

Rachel curled upward and lashed out to scratch her assailant's bearded face. When he recoiled in pain, she spit out the gag and shrieked at the top of her lungs. Serenaded by both men's foul curses she rolled to her knees, then bounded to her feet. Unfortunately, she became tangled in her skirt and the men pounced, forcing her facedown in the grass.

She was still fighting for all she was worth when she heard two dull *thunks* behind her. Both men collapsed half-on, half-off of her. Before she realized what happened, Nate was kicking the men aside so he could pull her to her feet and hold her protectively against his chest.

"Damnation, I'm sorry, Rachel. Some bodyguard I turned out to be," he said with a self-deprecating scowl.

While she panted to catch her breath, she saw him stuff his pistol into his holster. She presumed he had knocked out both men with well-aimed blows to the backs of their heads. Impulsively she struck out with her foot to kick both unconscious men in the shoulders, hoping to relieve her frustration with them. But it wasn't enough. She kicked each one in the hip for good measure.

"Feeling better now?" he murmured as he rested his chin on the top of her tousled head.

"No—" Then Rachel did something she hadn't done since she was a bereaved child who had lost her mother. She bawled her head off.

She hated displaying weakness of any kind. Unfortunately, the day had been too much. Conflict and tension had finally taken their toll on her composure. She clung to Nate as if he were her lifeline. She buried her head against his sturdy shoulder and cried—then cried some more.

"I…h-hate…c-crying—" *sob* "—like a b-baby," she blubbered, humiliating herself further.

"You're entitled." He gathered her even closer, rubbing his hands up and down her back in a comforting gesture. "Let it all out, sweetheart."

"I b-bet you—" *sob* "—n-never b-bawled your—" *hiccup* "—head off," she mumbled as she dampened his shirt with salty tears.

"I've wanted to. Lots of times. Does that count?"

He bent to brush a gentle kiss over her cheek, then said, "Whatever you need, sweetheart, to make you feel better, I will see it done. I promise. Just name it, because your every wish is my command."

The generous offer was the crowning blow that made her wail hysterically. It was at that precise moment—when his embrace became her port in an emotional storm, when the sound of his baritone voice soothed her tormented soul, when his comforting words overwhelmed her—that she fell in love with him. Utterly and completely.

She knew it was a foolish mistake because she was probably wanted for murder. Or had a price on her head—at the very least. In addition, Nate was an ex-lawman who would be leaving in two days. She had to let him go without breathing a word about the depth of her feelings for him.

She should pack up and rejoin her grandmother's people. In fact, she shouldn't have left the Cheyenne's mountain camp in the first place. She'd thought she wanted to strike off on her own to make a place for herself in white society but that hadn't worked out. Her dreams kept crumbling around her like windblown sand castles.

"Come on. Let me escort you to your room so you can bathe and rest," he insisted as he guided her through the trees.

"Nate? What's going on?"

Doc Grant's concerned voice prompted Rachel to raise her head from Nate's shoulder, but he continued to hold her protectively against him.

"Two drunken drifters attacked Rachel," Nate said grimly.

"Oh, God. I should have paid more attention!" Doc howled.

"It was *my* duty and *my* fault. I was on the other side of the wagon, detaining the two men who chased after Rachel between her performances earlier this evening. So much for this laid-back little town and all its good citizens," he said, then snorted in disgust. "There are always a few rotten scoundrels lurking in the shadows to ruin a town's reputation."

"What happened?"

Nate glanced over his shoulder to see Ludy walking swiftly downhill.

"Rachel was attacked. Go fetch that young marshal and have him lock up these two men. Tell him I'll be at the office in the morning to file charges against them."

"No!" Rachel reared back, then shook her disheveled head adamantly. "Just let them go."

Nate frowned, bemused. "Why? They tried to—"

She cut off his objection with the slash of her arm. "I just want to leave this place bright and early in the morning without timely delays. I need to put the incident behind me."

When Nate opened his mouth to reason with her, she

peered up at him with watery eyes and a vulnerable expression that he rarely saw on her face. He felt his resolve falter.

His resolve split wide-open when she said, "You told me I could have whatever I needed," she reminded him. "You *promised,* remember? What I *need* is to quit this town and head for Evening Shade first thing in the morning."

He didn't like the idea of allowing two lusty bastards to walk away scot-free. His strong sense of fair play protested strenuously. Nevertheless, he'd promised to give Rachel whatever she wanted to ease her suffering. He couldn't imagine why she allowed those drunken drifters to go free, but she was insistent and he didn't argue with her for fear of upsetting her more than she was already.

"Ludy, would you help Doc close up for the night and secure the wagon?" Nate requested.

"Sure. Be glad to," Ludy agreed without hesitation.

Doc didn't move downhill toward the wagon, just continued to stand there. He stared intently at Rachel, then looked directly at Nate. "No matter how hard you try, sometimes it's impossible to save someone from harm, isn't it?"

Nate had the feeling Doc was referring to something besides Rachel's harrowing ordeal. He looked as if he were staring through a window of time, lost to an unpleasant memory that held him in its grips and refused to let go.

"Come on, Doc." Ludy latched on to his arm. "Let's get the wagon locked down. Rachel is in good hands."

Not good enough, Nate mused as he escorted Rachel uphill. He hadn't been there when she'd needed him and he felt guilty as hell about it. That, compounded with what had transpired between them in his hotel room this after-

The Reader Service — Here's how it works:

NO POSTAGE
NECESSARY
IF MAILED
IN THE
UNITED STATES

BUSINESS REPLY MAIL
FIRST-CLASS MAIL   PERMIT NO. 717   BUFFALO, NY

POSTAGE WILL BE PAID BY ADDRESSEE

THE READER SERVICE
PO BOX 1867
BUFFALO NY 14240-9952

GET FREE BOOKS & FREE GIFTS WHEN YOU PLAY THE...

Lucky 7

777

SLOT MACHINE GAME

*Just scratch off the gold box with a coin.
Then check below to see the gifts you get!*

YES! I have scratched off the gold box. Please send me the 2 free Harlequin® Historical books and 2 free gifts (gifts are worth about $10) for which I qualify. I understand I am under no obligation to purchase any books, as explained on the back of this card.

We want to make sure we offer you the best service suited to your needs. Please answer the following question:
About how many NEW paperback fiction books have you purchased in the past 3 months?

❑ 0-2	❑ 3-6	❑ 7 or more
E4MQ	E4M2	E4NE

246/349 HDL

FIRST NAME	LAST NAME

ADDRESS

APT.	CITY

STATE / PROV.	ZIP/POSTAL CODE

Visit us online at www.ReaderService.com

7	7	7	**Worth TWO FREE BOOKS plus 2 BONUS Mystery Gifts!**
🍒	🍒	🍒	**Worth TWO FREE BOOKS!**
🔔	🔔	🍒	**TRY AGAIN!**

DETACH AND MAIL CARD TODAY!

noon, was weighing down his conscience something fierce.

"I hate men," Rachel muttered resentfully as Nate shepherded her into the hotel lobby.

"Bastards one and all," he agreed to pacify her. "But I'm *your* bastard. Use me however you wish. If you don't want those two worthless heathens jailed, how about if I beat the hell out of *them* to make *you* feel better? I can tell you from recent personal experience that having the hell beat out of you makes a lasting impression."

"No." She muffled a sniff, then groaned when the lighted lobby revealed the ripped shoulder seam and grass stains on the full skirts of her elegant green gown.

Dismayed by the damage to her garment, she teared up and sobbed again. Nate didn't understand why. It was just a dress, even if she had made it herself, even if it held some sentimental attachment he didn't know about. For certain, it was uncharacteristic for this iron-willed woman to cry over something as inconsequential as a dress.

"I'll buy you another dress," he offered as he opened the door to her room.

Anything to make her stop crying. Whimpering women usually didn't get to him, but for some reason Rachel's tears hit him right where he lived. "You can have two new gowns if you want," he added generously.

She shook her head, and her silky raven hair tumbled over her shoulders in disarray. "You have enough expenses to cover after you lost everything you owned when you were attacked," she said raggedly.

He clamped down on his tongue when he nearly confided that he could easily afford to replace his wardrobe—and hers—without putting the slightest dent in his funds. He liked that Rachel didn't judge him by the money at his disposal and he preferred to keep silent about his family's wealth.

"I'll have the attendants fill your tub," he volunteered.

She wiped away the tears that dribbled down her cheeks with the back of her hand. "Thank you. A bath sounds wonderful."

"Anything else to make you feel better?"

"Ridding the world of men would be good for starters," she said vindictively.

His lips twitched as he reached out to brush a speck of grass and dirt from her chin. "I'll get right on it."

Nate closed the door behind him and gave Rachel her privacy. Damn it, if he was going to shoot all men everywhere he had to start with himself. He had no doubt that Rachel was still reeling over this afternoon's tryst, even if she'd tried valiantly to pretend she wasn't upset.

He had taken her innocence, probably in a heated rush, but he couldn't remember for certain. Which tormented him to no end.

If that wasn't enough to ruin her day, he hadn't been on hand to protect her when those scruffy bastards attacked her.

Rachel was right, he realized as he strode off to summon the attendants. Men were the bane of her existence. But he still couldn't figure out why she objected to having those two ruffians arrested. It made no sense, given her low opinion of the male population. She should have wanted them locked in the calaboose so she could toss the key in the creek.

Yet, she didn't want to press charges and she wanted to clear out of town, first thing in the morning. That's what they would do. Anything to prevent her from dissolving into tears again. Clearly, she was embarrassed to expose the slightest weakness to him or anyone else.

He wondered which part of her mysterious past compelled her to be so self-reliant that she refused to count on anyone but herself and to conceal every vulnerability.

"One of these days, you're going to tell me," Nate said resolutely to the vision floating above him. "I am going to sit you down and demand answers to all my questions. Then we are going to discuss today's tryst and its possible consequences."

One of these days. The words skittered through his mind and he realized there weren't too many days left before he rode to Dodge City to do the job he'd volunteered to do. He was running out of time with Rachel and the thought of leaving her behind didn't set well with him. Not well at all.

An hour later Rachel felt rested and revived—to some extent, at least. Soaking in the tub gave her the chance to relax for the first time all day. It did nothing, however, to soothe her guilty conscience. She kept thinking she should inform Nate that she had seen the three men who'd attacked him and she scolded herself harshly for refusing to arrest the drifters who attacked her. However, she was afraid the city marshal might mention that he had seen Nate's assailants.

Of course, if the marshal *had* seen them, he might drop by to inform Nate, anyway. In which case, she couldn't stop him for tracking them down.

Rachel expelled a sigh and rested her head against the back of the tub. She knew Nate would confront Adolph's goons soon enough in Dodge City. She had to tell him before he left the medicine show and headed north. He needed to be forewarned before he rode into Dodge City and found himself at the mercy of those heartless bullies again.

What if he learned about Adolph's attack and perhaps his death—well deserved though it would be. Nate might figure out that she was most likely the one who had killed Adolph. Or perhaps the one who seriously injured him before she stole several items from the storeroom, then dashed off into the night to confiscate the first available horse.

How would the former law-enforcement officer react to that information? She wasn't sure she wanted to know.

Rising, Rachel dried herself off, then padded across the room to dress in her nightgown. She plunked down on the bed, then drew up her knees to her chest. She felt angry and oddly restless. Yet she wasn't going out after dark, even disguised in mannish clothing. Not after tonight's unnerving encounter.

When the memory of being held down by those drunken drifters bombarded her, she gritted her teeth and cursed them half a dozen times. They had stolen her feeling of confidence that she could come, go and do as she pleased on a whim. This had been a hellish day and the unexpected attack had been the last straw.

She jerked upright when someone knocked on the door. "Who's there?" She reached for her pistol and mentally reminded herself to sew hidden pockets into her gowns so she wouldn't end up as vulnerable as she had tonight. She was also going to purchase a bigger knife—one that discouraged miscreants from pestering her, she decided.

"It's Nate. I brought you a supper tray."

"Not hungry."

"Of course you are," he contradicted. "Open the door

so I don't have to break it down. No matter what, I'm coming in. Guaran-damn-teed."

She huffed out her breath, whipped open the door, glared at him and said, "I didn't realize you were so pushy. And here I was just beginning to like you."

He smiled charmingly as he brushed past her. "It's the lawman coming out in me."

"Try to keep those lawman characteristics to a minimum in my presence, *please,*" she requested. "I told you, I'm not particularly fond of marshals and such."

"I remember. Let's talk about why you become defensive and you rebel against symbols of authority…" His voice trailed off when he became distracted by her nightgown.

Rachel followed his gaze, noting the fabric was too sheer to be worn in mixed company. However, considering how intimate they had become this afternoon, it was too late for modesty. She told herself to get past her embarrassment and resist the urge to cover herself with a robe. Nate had seen her completely naked already. There was nothing left to hide from him—except the possibility that she was a murderess and a thief. Couldn't forget that.

"Don't you have a robe?" he asked hoarsely as he dragged his gaze upward to stare at the air over her head.

"Yes. Would you like to wear it?"

Nate chuckled. "No, but you're distracting me to the extreme so put it on, *please.*"

She rummaged through her satchel to don the simple cotton garment she had made while working for Jennifer Grantham at the boutique. Then she sank down on the edge of the bed to nibble at the bread and cheese. "The supper tray was very thoughtful of you."

"I want to know who you are and what you're hiding," he said without preamble. "No more elusive games, Rachel."

Her skinned chin shot up and she stared at him defiantly. "Am I a criminal you were sent here to interrogate?"

"No."

"Am I a witness to a crime that you came to interview?"

"No."

"Then what makes you think you have the authority to pry into my personal life?"

He fisted his hands on his hips and a muscle clenched in his jaw. Clearly, he was struggling to keep his temper. "What happened between us this afternoon gives me the right," he countered.

When he stared at her with such intense sky-blue eyes that searched out the secrets in her soul, she focused her undivided attention on the tray rather than on him.

"You believe you have the right to have this sort of conversation with *all* the other women you've slept with?" she said caustically, and realized that she felt annoyed there had been other women in his life. She had no right to be jealous and possessive. But still...

"No, just the ones with whom I've discovered, *at the last possible moment,*" he said meaningfully, "that I am their first experiment with sex."

"How many of us are there?" Although she blushed profusely at the personal direction of their conversation, she wanted to know how many inexperienced women had fallen beneath his seductive spell.

While he stared her down, she tried not to fidget awkwardly. She wanted to appear nonchalant, but she doubted she'd be able to pull it off.

"Counting *you?*"

She nodded her head jerkily, then crammed a chunk of cheese in her mouth.

"You're the one and only."

That pleased her immensely but for the life of her she didn't know why. Maybe she wanted to be the first at *something* with Nate. After all, she'd made the ridiculous, stupendously foolish mistake of falling in love with him, no matter how hard she'd tried not to.

And she *had* tried extremely hard not to!

Apparently, she had been cursed with the same critical flaw that afflicted her grandmother and her mother. Rachel had lost her heart to a man who was all wrong for her. Not that any of them were right for her, she amended. Because of her mixed heritage and varied background, she was a misfit of the worst sort. Not the proper, genteel lady most men dreamed of marrying...

She suddenly remembered the insulting comment Adolph Turner had made the night he'd pounced on her. He'd said she wasn't a dignified lady so there was no reason to bother courting her respectfully. She deserved no more than to be propositioned to become his most recent mistress—after the last one did him the discourtesy of dying mysteriously and leaving him surrounded by a fog of suspicion.

"Rachel, if there is a possibility of a child—"

She flung up her hand to silence him. "Don't you *dare* tell me that you would do the honorable thing and fulfill your obligation by marrying me," she practically snarled at him.

"But I would, you know," he said softly and sincerely.

It didn't matter how softly and sincerely he uttered the vow. It was the last thing she wanted to hear from the only man who had ever touched her heart.

"You can leave now," she muttered as she chewed on a slice of bread.

"No," he said gruffly.

"Yes." She made a stabbing gesture toward the door, as if he were too dense to know where it was. "Get…out…"

"Not a chance in hell, angel face. You are *not* getting rid of me that easily."

Chapter Nine

Nate walked purposefully across the room. He halted to tower over her, but she refused to look up. She decided to pretend he wasn't there and see how that worked.

"I don't know what came over me this afternoon," he blurted out unexpectedly.

She knew. He'd been at the mercy of her potion. Her conscience kept reminding her that her actions weren't as noble as she wanted to pretend because it wasn't a purely unselfish act.

"I made it clear last night and this morning that I wanted you," he reminded her. "But I hadn't intended to force you into—"

She bolted up in front of him before he could finish the sentence. Feeling self-conscious, she spoke directly to the buttons of his shirt that covered the muscular wall of his chest. "I told you that what happened was *my* fault. *I* came to your room. *I* wanted to be with you. Therefore, I hereby declare that you aren't responsible for possible consequences. I don't know how to make it clearer than I have, Nate."

He curled his forefinger under her chin, forcing her to raise her gaze to his wry smile. "I get it now. You don't mind using me for experimental sexual purposes, but you don't consider me worthy husband and father material, is that right?"

She nearly drowned in those hypnotic eyes, surrounded by thick black lashes, and she practically melted beneath that sensuous smile. Damn, he was incredibly handsome without the heavy beard and mustache that concealed his striking features.

She shored up her faltering resolve and said, "I was trying not to hurt your feelings, but yes. If you aren't the Queen of Sheba's crowned prince with a kingdom and a fortune at your disposal, then I'm not interested."

A strange flicker passed through his eyes and his face closed up quickly. "So you plan to marry for money?"

She suspected that she had hurt his feelings, in her effort to make him back off. That played hell with her conscience, too. Nevertheless, she had to do whatever necessary to make him understand that she did not hold him responsible.

"I told you that I'm not planning to marry at all. Having a man around, who thinks he is entitled to tell me what to do, is an offensive prospect. I've been on my own too long to sacrifice my independence for love *or* money."

"So…if I strike it rich, you still won't be interested?" he prodded relentlessly.

He was studying her with fierce intensity, as if her response was vitally important to him. She couldn't fathom why. He was leaving soon and she wasn't going with him. So that was that. Period. End of their story.

"Definitely not interested," she reaffirmed. "Wealth might change your attitude and personality." She thought of

Adolph's lust for power and domination. Disgust shot through her like a speeding bullet. "I like you just the way you are."

"Do you?" He scrutinized her closely again and she fidgeted beneath his probing stare. *"How much?"*

What did it matter? This dead-end affair would be over in less than two days.

"Rachel?"

She dodged his gaze, afraid to admit how deeply she felt about him, tormented by the knowledge that this might be her last opportunity to be alone with him before he rode to Dodge City.

"Whatever you're hiding about your past, I can—"

She pushed up on tiptoe to press her lips to his. "You vowed to do whatever makes me feel better tonight," she reminded him again. "Being with you is what I want. No strings, no questions, no promises."

"You drive a hard bargain," he murmured against the curve of her throat.

"All I'm asking for is tonight." She moved provocatively against him, noting that he was already aroused.

"You can have whatever you want…me included. No argument there," he whispered roughly.

His mouth came down hard and insistent on hers. Rachel gave herself up to the heat that burst instantly through her body. She desperately wanted to replace her assailant's hurtful manhandling with Nate's skillful lovemaking. She wanted to feel his brawny body moving familiarly against hers. To taste him, to lose herself in his appealing scent, to have him as close as possible for as long as the passion between them lasted.

If tonight was the last time they were alone, she refused to waste another moment. She knew sizzling pleasure awaited her and she yearned to send the world and all of its problems away in the wind of ungovernable passion.

"A shame I didn't know what I've been missing these past few years," she teased playfully as she splayed her hands over his broad chest. "You, Mr. Montgomery, have been quite an education."

He chuckled in roguish amusement as she unbuttoned his shirt, then raked her nails over his hirsute flesh. "I aim to please, ma'am," he drawled. "Whatever you want, however you want it, all you have to do is ask."

She wanted to ask what it took to make a man like Nate fall in love with her. Instead she said, "Just make me forget what a lousy night I've had."

"I'll be more than happy to try," he whispered as his head came slowly, steadily toward hers.

This time his lips touched hers with such incredible tenderness that she melted against him, surrendering immediately to her heartfelt affection for him. When he scooped her into his arms, then laid her on the bed, her gaze never left his as he stretched out beside her. His hands drifted sensuously over her body and every ounce of tension that had pelted her during the day evaporated instantly.

His moist lips brushed the beaded tips of her breasts and her body radiated with the exquisite pleasure he offered her. His fingertips skimmed over her skin, sensitizing every inch of her flesh, making her tremble with erotic anticipation.

"Feeling better yet?" he murmured as he flicked his tongue against one taut nipple and then the other.

She felt so relaxed and aroused that it took a moment to register his question. "I can't remember anything before the moment you walked into my room."

That was the honest truth. He had appeared and he'd filled up all the lonely corners and crevices in her world.

His dynamic presence had obliterated her ordeal with the drunken drifters. The ardent sensations created by his skillful caresses left no part of her untouched.

"Good. Glad to hear it." His warm breath feathered over her belly, making her quiver with pleasure. "Now let's see if I can make you forget everything you ever knew."

When he slid his finger inside her heated core to drive her crazy with intimate caresses, she couldn't think past the frantic needs burgeoning inside her. He stroked her with maddening thoroughness, then withdrew, leaving her arching shamelessly toward him, begging for more of his erotic touch. He caressed her again and fiery sensations expanded until she swore she'd burst into flames.

His name tumbled from her lips, repeatedly, as the crescendo of white-hot need fed upon itself like an uncontrollable wildfire. When his lips grazed her secretive flesh and he flicked at her with his tongue, a coil of searing heat unfurled inside her, robbing her of breath, shattering her composure like fragile crystal.

"Please…" she gasped as aching need pulsated through her.

"I'm trying," he teased, then offered her another intimate kiss that drove her mad with wanting. "How am I doing so far?"

"You're incredibly good—" Her voice fizzled out completely when spasms of rapture rippled through her. She reached for him in frantic desperation, wanting him as she never wanted anything in life.

He came to her when she needed him most, filling her at the exact moment when she teetered dangerously close to the edge of mindless oblivion. He drove into her with the same kind of urgency she felt clamoring through her. She clung to him, desperate to appease the burning ache that consumed her. But to her surprise—and her impatience—he rolled sideways, then set her above him so that she was riding him.

Rachel stared down at him, feeling him pulsing deep inside her, watching a roguish smile spread across his handsome face. She felt him arch into her and heard him groan in pleasure. When he clamped his hands on her hips and moved her up and down on his hard shaft, need welled up inside her all over again. Her lashes fluttered shut when another tumultuous wave of ecstasy crested over her and indefinable sensations rippled through every fiber of her being.

"Open your eyes and look at me," he demanded hoarsely. "I want you to see what you do to me."

Despite the incredible intimacy that made her blush, she watched passion overtake him, saw his entrancing blue eyes drift over her body like a possessive caress. He cupped her breasts in his hands, then tugged gently at her nipples, summoning yet another spasm of hungry need from deep inside her.

While he arched into her, thrusting upward, over and over again, she fought to draw breath. Overwhelming pleasure riveted her. When he whispered her name, then pulled her down on top of him, she felt him shudder convulsively beneath her. She clutched at him urgently and savored the incredible moment she shared with him.

She wanted to pull him closer, though they were already as close as two people could possibly get. He had become the burning flame inside her, a living breathing part of her, the other half of her soul…and she never wanted to let him go.

Inexpressible pleasure and roiling emotion bombarded her from all directions at once. It was at that exact moment, while she was suspended in sublime ecstasy, that Rachel did forget everything she ever knew. She couldn't think past the intimacy of being one with Nate to remember what her life had been like before he taught her the meaning of passion and willing surrender. Her world began and ended within the sinewy circle of his arms and nothing satisfied her more than feeling his muscular body joined completely with hers.

For this night, this one magical night that transcended time and space, nothing else mattered to Rachel. Nothing could harm or frighten her because she had discovered a slice of heaven on earth.

That was her last thought before sleep overtook her and erotic dreams began where reality left off.

When Rachel slumped against him, fast asleep, Nate eased away. He smiled as he combed his fingers through the silky raven tresses that tumbled over her shoulders and spilled across the pillow. He didn't know if Rachel had forgotten everything she knew, but *he* certainly had.

He'd never known a woman like Rachel. She was tough and resilient. She was also a dozen kinds of passion waiting release. She was the symbol of indomitable spirit and independence, and he admired her strength and determination.

He seemed to have no self-control whatsoever when Rachel was in his arms. When she responded to him with pure instinct and reckless abandon, his ravenous need for her knew no restraint.

Nate walked over to cover up Rachel, then brushed a feathery kiss on her forehead. He still wasn't sure if he was relieved or insulted that Rachel insisted she wouldn't marry him under any circumstances. All he knew was that the prospect of some other man coming along to take his place—even temporarily—in the future didn't set well with him.

Lost in thought, Nate tiptoed over to douse the lantern. With the supper tray in hand, he exited the room. He pulled up short because Doc Grant stood in the hall, glowering at him in blatant disapproval. How did Doc know what had gone on behind the closed door? Nate asked himself.

He followed Doc's disparaging gaze to his torso—and noticed his shirt was buttoned improperly. Well, hell. That was a dead giveaway.

"Damn you, I told you not to toy with Rachel." Doc stabbed his index finger into Nate's chest for emphasis. "She's like the daughter I never had. I won't let you or any other man hurt her."

Nate had never seen Doc so puffed up with anger and indignation. Usually he was wallowing in his own misery and battling his demons. Now his hazel-eyed gaze filleted Nate and his lips curled with disdain. If Nate were easily intimidated, he might have backed away from the skewering glare. However, Nate had confronted heartless criminals who preferred to kill him rather than look at him, so Doc's murderous glower rolled off him like water off a duck's back.

When Doc growled a few epithets to his name, then tried to stalk past him to open the door to Rachel's room, Nate blocked his path. "She's asleep. She needs to stay that way. You can speak with her in the morning."

Doc flashed him another killing stare. "Maybe you need to schedule your departure for *right now*." He dug into his pocket, then thrust a roll of banknotes at him. "Purchase whatever else you need before you leave. Don't bother paying me what you owe. Your leaving will be payment enough."

Nate slapped the money back into Doc's hand but Doc countered by cramming it in Nate's shirt pocket. "I'm not leaving until after the performance at Evening Shade," Nate insisted. "And I will repay all the money you loaned me. Every last penny of it. Plus interest."

Doc shook his blond head briskly, then lurched around. "I misjudged you, Montgomery. I won't make that mistake again."

Nate watched Doc storm off, then he blew out his breath in frustration. Just what he needed, Rachel's adopted father crowing at him like an offended rooster.

When Doc reached the door to his room, he halted to glare daggers at Nate once more before he disappeared from sight. Nate made a mental note not to drink any potion Doc might offer him in the future. He suspected it would be laced with arsenic.

The next morning Rachel awoke with a smile on her face and an incredible sense of well-being. Nate's skillful brand of seduction left her swearing that she was floating on a puffy cloud in a universe far, far away from harsh reality. Whistling a tune, she dressed, then packed her belongings. She planned to eat a hearty breakfast at one of the restaurants, store her satchels in the back of the wagon, then leave town.

She crossed her fingers, hoping Adolph's men wouldn't be there to greet her when she arrived in Evening Shade. She didn't want to put her emotions through the meat grinder again so soon.

When she walked past Nate's room, she slowed her pace, wondering if he was awake. Then she strode away, reminding herself that she wasn't one of those clinging-vine types who needed constant reassurance and protection from a man.

If anything, Rachel was a realist. Spending every spare minute with Nate would only make his inevitable departure more painful.

Rachel was halfway down the staircase when a man with brown hair and a lean, tanned face halted in front of her. He looked to be only a year or two older, and had a shiny badge pinned to his shirt. She tensed, wondering if there was a Wanted poster with her sketch on it and the young marshal had come to arrest her.

To her relief the law officer didn't slap handcuffs on her wrists. Instead, he looked her up and down with masculine appreciation, then flashed a flirtatious smile.

"Morning, miss. I'm Marshal Phillip Dexter." He touched the brim of his hat politely. "You're with the medicine show, aren't you?"

"Yes, I am." She returned his smile, but since lawmen made her nervous, she was poised to break and run if he posed the slightest threat.

"Incredible voice," Phillip praised, then gave her the once-over again. "I thoroughly enjoyed your performance."

"Thank you."

"I'm looking for the U.S. marshal," he commented. "Have you seen him this morning?"

Rachel's hand clenched around the banister until her knuckles turned white. It took all of her acting ability to appear unconcerned when she learned there was a federal marshal in town. Had Adolph survived the fracas in the storeroom and sent a federal marshal to track her down, since his goons hadn't had success apprehending her?

Dear God, she was going to have to commandeer another horse and thunder away again, leaving Doc, Ludy and Nate without an explanation for her sudden disappearance.

"I didn't know there was a federal marshal in town," she said, willing her voice to remain steady.

"Sure there is." He looked at her as if she ought to know. "It's Montgomery."

Rachel kept a stranglehold on the banister because her knees wobbled to such extremes that she feared she was going to pitch forward and tumble down the steps. *Nate was a federal marshal?* Holy hell! That was infinitely worse than being a city marshal or county sheriff!

For God's sake, the president of the U.S.A., no less, had appointed him! Plus, Nate had misled her purposely. *Ex*-lawman, my eye! she thought furiously. If Adolph had sent him, what was Nate waiting for? For her to incriminate herself so he could arrest her?

She opened her mouth but no words came out. Her tongue was stuck to the roof of her mouth. Not that it mattered because her heart was pounding so hard that she couldn't draw enough breath to voice a sentence.

Finally, she pulled herself together enough to speak, but it took several moments. "Oh…right. You mean Nate. Of course, what was I thinking?" She smacked herself on the forehead, then managed a false smile. "He's been traveling with us and I've come to consider him part of our troupe."

"Montgomery came by my office yesterday to file a report," Phillip explained—and let his gaze wander at will over Rachel's trim-fitting calico gown. "He was looking for three men. I came by to tell him that I asked around town last night while I was making my rounds. I heard several reports of sightings from local businessmen. Unfortunately, I haven't seen anything of them this morning."

When the young marshal started past her, she clutched his arm. "I'll tell Nate the news," she insisted.

"I'm not sure that would be a good idea," Phillip said hesitantly. "Montgomery is sort of a stickler for rules and regulations. Maybe I better tell him myself."

Learning that Nate was a by-the-book law officer caused her alarm and anger to escalate with each passing second. The voice in her head kept shouting, *Get out of town while the getting is still good!*

"I'll deliver your message to Nate the moment I return upstairs." She directed Phillip's attention to the satchels she had dropped accidentally when he announced that Nate was a U.S. marshal. "Would you mind carrying my satchels to the wagon for me?" She batted her eyes at him a few times—and silently cursed herself for resorting to deceptive measures to divert Phillip's attention.

"Sure, I'll be glad to." He scooped up her luggage, then reversed direction.

Although Rachel walked alongside him, posing questions about his life in Possum Grove, she was silently seething. Nathan Montgomery had outright lied to her. There was nothing *former* about his profession. If he was a U.S. Marshal and he was taking a new "job" in Dodge City, it was entirely possible that he was, at this very moment, investigating Adolph Turner's murder. Either that or he had interviewed the *supposed* victim of assault and robbery during her absence in Dodge. Then again, Nate might not have the details of the case yet and he was on his way to Dodge—soon to discover that *she* was the fugitive he was to track down.

Oh, God! she thought, on the verge of panic. What if he already knew what she'd done and this was a setup?

Her mind whirled like a windmill, wondering whether Nate was trying to force a confession out of her by probing into her past with his cat-and-mouse game. And what if

Adolph had twisted the truth until it was almost unrecognizable? He'd certainly done it before in the case of his departed mistress. He could be hell-bent on having her captured and tried for robbery, horse thieving—and only God knew what else he'd dream up to add to her list of crimes.

Sure enough, dead or alive, Adolph was driving her crazy with dread and fear.

Calm down! Rachel shouted silently at herself. She was allowing her imagination and anxiety to get the better of her. Surely Nate didn't know who she was. But from now on, she'd watch him astutely, just in case he knew more than he was telling and waiting for her to incriminate herself.

The feeling of well-being that had greeted Rachel this morning fizzled out. She felt confused, betrayed, outraged and apprehensive. It was worse than the tormenting emotions that had hounded her the previous day, for her heartfelt affection for Nate had shattered in the wake of the shocking information Phillip Dexter had delivered.

The urge to flee nearly overwhelmed her again. There was no question that she would have to abandon the medicine show very shortly. When Nate reached Dodge City and discovered her involvement in Adolph's death— or injury—he would know exactly where to find her. He would place her under arrest—for *something*.

If Adolph had his way—which the bastard did all too often—she would rot in jail…or hang.

Neither option appealed to Rachel.

Having Nate apprehend her would be too humiliating. She loved that deceptive rascal, damn him! She still couldn't figure out why he'd told her that he was an *ex*-lawman. For certain, he had downplayed his profession after she had confided that she knew too many corrupt officers and lacked faith in any of them. And to think he had the nerve to fire questions at her about her past when he hadn't been honest about his *present* occupation!

Angry frustration ate her alive as she listened to Marshal Dexter try to charm her while he tucked her satchels in the medicine wagon. He wasted his breath, because she was finished with men forever and was too busy conjuring up tortuous ways to dispose of Nate.

What was another murder to her credit now? she asked herself bitterly.

You could only hang once, right?

When the marshal continued to follow her around like a puppy, Rachel buzzed around the wagon, checking to ensure it was in proper working order. Then she hitched up the horses. Still, Phillip didn't wander off to do whatever marshals did when they weren't making arrests or rounding up posses for manhunts. Or *woman*hunts, as her case happened to be.

The thought of having men with guns on horseback chasing after her made her twitchy.

Phillip tagged along when she announced that she was going to eat breakfast at one of the restaurants before leaving town. Although she had lost her appetite, she cleaned up every morsel on her plate while Phillip regaled her with his entire life story. She had plenty of secrets to keep, but evidently he didn't have even one.

On the way back to the hotel Rachel silently cursed Nate for deceiving her. Then she reminded herself that *she* had detained him in his room to avoid Adolph's ruffians. In addition, she had doctored Nate's food with a love potion and had diverted his attention by seducing him before he had conked out to sleep for several hours.

You are a hypocrite, she chided herself.

Nevertheless, she still felt betrayed. The man she loved turned out to be the worst thing that had ever happened to her.

Chapter Ten

Nate had received the silent treatment from Doc, starting the moment the older man stamped downstairs to stash his gear in the wagon so they could travel to Evening Shade. Judging by the red streaks in Doc's eyes and the expression on his face—that made him appear as sour as curdled milk—he'd drunk himself to sleep in the privacy of his room.

No doubt, seeing Nate walk from Rachel's room, looking ruffled and half-put-together was the perfect excuse for Doc to drink. As if he needed another one besides battling private demons that escaped at dark most every night.

Doc's hostility Nate understood. It was the cold-shoulder treatment he'd received from Rachel all day that he didn't understand. She had detained him in her room the previous night—not that he had complained about the erotically satisfying passion they had shared. He thought they were getting along extremely well.

Suddenly, she treated him like the enemy—after they had been as close as two people could get. He was at a loss to explain why.

"Something going on that I should know about?" Ludy asked as he shifted on the wagon seat beside Nate.

He lifted his shoulder in a noncommittal shrug, then popped the reins to send the horses into a faster clip.

Ludy hitched his thumb toward the wagon bed where Doc slept. And beyond to where Rachel, dressed in men's clothing, rode Ludy's horse. "What did you do to annoy those two? And it better not be what I think it is," he added darkly.

Nate sighed when Ludy puffed up, much the same way Doc had last night. Doc's and Ludy's protective instincts toward Rachel couldn't have been more obvious.

"What do you think it is?" Nate questioned.

Ludy's green eyes narrowed accusingly and his usual good humor disappeared in nothing flat. "You *know* what I think."

"You can think what you want, friend, but it is none of your business."

The frizzy-haired banjo player straightened on the seat, then gave Nate the evil eye. "If it pertains to Rachel I'm making it my business. I was looking after her before you showed up."

"When? In between jaunts to bordellos to make your rounds in every nameless little town in Kansas?"

"That's none of *your* business, *friend*," Ludy snapped defensively. "That's entirely different. We are discussing Rachel, who was exceptionally leery of men until you came along."

Nate blew out his breath in exasperation. He'd never had to explain himself to a woman's substitute father or brother. Not even to a woman's blood kin. Yet, here he was trying to soothe Ludy's ruffled feathers.

"I don't have to tell you that she is very special and unique," Nate commented.

Ludy scoffed. "That goes without saying. I figure Rachel's refusal to confide her past indicates she's had problems and now you've come along to complicate her life further. And here you are an ex-lawman." He stared pointedly at Nate. "I expected more from the likes of you."

So did Nate. His code of conduct had taken a direct hit when confronted with his obsessive desire for that onyx-eyed siren who had the voice of an angel and a body built for sin. Who could resist that devilishly sweet combination?

Nate figured he was headed to hell and there was a bonfire with his name on it awaiting him.

Ludy crossed his arms over his chest, twisted on the seat to face Nate directly and said, "So what are you planning to do about what you did?"

"I do not want to have this conversation," Nate muttered.

"Too bad. We're having it, anyway," Ludy insisted. "Rachel is the only woman friend I have and I intend to see that she is treated fairly."

Nate gave a caustic snort. "Judging by all your stops in the towns we've frequented, I'd say you have a lot of woman friends, so don't be so self-righteous."

"You know what I mean. Rachel isn't a passing fancy…so what are you planning to do about it?" Ludy prodded.

Nate glanced over his shoulder to ensure Rachel wasn't within earshot. She'd kill him if she knew she was the hot topic of conversation. She'd acted as if she'd wanted to kill him all morning and he had no idea what had set her off.

"I offered marriage and she turned me down flat," he confided reluctantly.

Ludy blinked like a startled owl. "What? Why?"

"She said she didn't want a man hovering around, thinking she needed his constant protection and trying to tell her what to do."

Ludy smiled reluctantly. "Sounds like something she'd say."

"I'm leaving tomorrow to take a new job in Dodge City so I'm hoping I can count on you to keep me updated on how things are going with Rachel and Doc. If you need me, I'll be here as soon as I can."

"Good to know. But I'm still not happy with you."

"Neither am I. My resistance isn't as invincible as I used to think," Nate said in a begrudging tone.

Ludy chuckled wryly. "That's a difficult thing for a man to admit, I reckon. At the tender age of seventeen, I discovered that I have a hopeless attraction to all shapes, sizes and dispositions of women. I haven't been the same since."

Nate thought Ludy was going to let him off the hook, but the banjo player added, "I did, however, show enough restraint not to tamper with Rachel. Especially with Doc, the scarecrow of vengeance, flapping his wings around the medicine show."

There was no doubt that Nate had made a resentful enemy in Doc Grant. Yet, it was Rachel's refusal to acknowledge his existence this morning that bothered him most.

Speaking of the devil… Nate cast Rachel a wary glance when she trotted the horse up beside the wagon seat. She didn't glance at him, didn't smile or frown. In fact, her bewitching face lacked all expression.

"Let's stop at the creek to eat the picnic lunch Ludy was thoughtful enough to purchase for us."

Having said that, she trotted ahead of the wagon.

Fifteen minutes later, Nate halted the wagon beneath a sprawling shade tree, then strode off to fetch water for the horses. When Rachel walked past him on her way to the creek, Nate set aside the buckets and blocked her path.

"Mind telling me why you have nothing to say after last night's—"

She made a slashing gesture with her hand to silence him. "I have told you repeatedly that I do not have to answer to you, Mr. Montgomery."

"So now we are back to formality, are we?" he said irritably. "I helped you make it through a bad night and you're finished with me?"

She glowered at him with her dark eyes flashing. "Precisely. Consider yourself used and discarded. It happens to women all the time. Now you know what it feels like."

When she started past him, he latched on to her arm. She hatchet chopped his wrist with the side of her hand. Despite the sharp pain, he didn't release her.

"You may be a gifted actress and performer, but you aren't fooling me one bit, angel face. I was there last night, if you recall—"

"More's the pity in that," she snapped disparagingly.

He ignored the insult. "You liked me well enough then."

She avoided his pointed stare by glancing at the tree limbs above his head. "It's a new day, Montgomery, and you're leaving very soon. I have nothing else to say to you but good riddance and goodbye."

When she jerked her arm from his grasp abruptly, Nate let her go. She was bristling with hostility, but as usual, prying information from Rachel required a crowbar. He didn't have one handy.

Huffing out his breath, Nate picked up the buckets and

returned to the wagon. Doc had climbed down to scrub his hands over his head and face. His blond hair was jutting out in all directions.

The instant Doc saw Nate he scowled and wheeled around. "You're still here. I told you to leave."

"I told you that I'm staying until after the Evening Shade performance." Nate set the buckets in front of the team of thirsty horses.

Doc glanced around to note that Ludy and Rachel had vacated the area. "Fine, then. I've changed my mind about what I expect from you. I'm holding you responsible for what happened."

"I already hold myself responsible," Nate declared as he walked up to Doc.

"Good. You and Rachel are getting married in Evening Shade."

Nate barked a laugh. "You'll have to drag her, kicking and screaming, to the altar. I offered last night and she rejected me."

Doc's bloodshot eyes shot open wide. "Why?"

"Not good enough for her?" Nate suggested helpfully. "No honor or integrity? Do you have anything else to add to the possible list? You seemed to have several complaints about my character and personality flaws last night."

Doc grumbled sourly. "I was just plain mad at you last night. This morning I'm thinking about how the future might play out for Rachel."

"Then you'll have to talk sense into her. She's barely speaking to me."

"Just why is that?" Doc asked suspiciously.

"I honestly don't know. Last night she was the one who—"

He clamped his mouth shut, cursing himself for even

hinting that Rachel had held him to his solemn promise to do whatever necessary to make her forget the drifters' physical attack. "I don't understand women. Rachel especially," he admitted. "She has me completely baffled."

That got a smile from Doc, who removed his wrinkled jacket and draped it over the back of the wagon. The midday sun beamed down on him, calling more attention to his peaked face. "That's the beauty of women. The *never knowing* and always wanting to make them happy."

Apparently, a fond memory had flooded over Doc because his smile widened and his eyes glistened in a way Nate hadn't noticed before. All too soon, however, Doc's smile turned upside down. The mysterious demon was back to torment him, Nate was sorry to say.

Doc turned away, then strode off. "I'll talk to Rachel."

Nate grimaced. If she thought he had bragged to Doc, she would likely skin him alive. "That might offend her. Or at least make her uncomfortable. I should talk to her."

"When?"

"Tonight."

"All right. We'll camp near Evening Shade and wait until tomorrow afternoon to open the show."

Nate breathed a sigh, hoping he'd dodged the bullet by preventing Doc from approaching Rachel—and very likely embarrassing her. She was such a private person that he had no doubt that she'd be offended by Ludy's or Doc's prying questions and unwanted advice.

She'd certainly let him have it with both barrels blazing when he'd tried to question her about her past and discuss the consequences of their trysts.

"Rachel, I want to talk to you." Ludy walked up beside her on the creek bank, spoiling the peaceful tranquility of the setting. "I wasn't going to interfere, but this thing with you and Nate is—"

She cut him off at the pass. "Nate and I are old business. I needed comfort and distraction last night and he was it."

And curse him to hell and back for boasting about his conquest. No doubt, this was his way of getting back at her because she had wanted nothing more to do with him. No doubt, his male pride was smarting something fierce.

"I shouldn't have to explain such things to you. After all, you've given new meaning to the word *distraction* in every town we visit," she remarked.

Ludy reared back as if she'd slapped him. Rachel felt guilty for lashing out at him.

"Sorry. I have no right to take my anger and frustration out on you when it's Nate I'd like to roast over a campfire."

Ludy frowned, bufuddled. "But he said he was prepared to do the right thing by you."

There was that infuriating turn of phrase again. It made Rachel gnash her teeth in irritation. "I might be a lot of things—" like a thief, murderess and fugitive "—but I will never be a man's *right thing* to do!"

Ludy held up his hands in supplication and smiled cajolingly, showing his dimples. "Easy, buttercup. I usually know what to say to appease women, but I'm at a complete loss with you. Are you telling me that you are opposed to getting hitched to Nate?"

"That is exactly what I'm telling you. Now go away—"

"There you are. I want to talk to you, Rachel."

She rolled her eyes heavenward, asking for divine patience when Doc's voice wafted toward her. "He tattled to Doc, too?" She glared at Ludy, who had the good sense to back away. "What is this? A two-sided assault? Did Nate put you and Doc up to this?"

Ludy shook his head vigorously while he retreated uphill. "No. Honest. I took it upon myself to talk to you."

"Nate asked me not too broach the subject, but I decided I want to talk about this right now," Doc declared as he halted in front of Rachel. "Now what is this nonsense about refusing to accept Nate's proposal? Of course you are going to accept!"

Her fingers curled, wishing she could put a chokehold on Nate's thick neck and squeeze until his eyes popped out. Damn him! Next thing she knew he'd be posting notices of their affair in every town on the circuit!

"I've decided to become a hidebound spinster. So yes, wedding proposals from anyone aren't in my future," she retorted hotly. "Furthermore, you can tell Blabbermouth that I'm never speaking to him again. Ever."

"He didn't boast," Doc insisted. "I came to check on you last night and I saw him exit your room. I am certainly old enough to know what's what, young lady," he added pointedly.

"Oh." She glanced the other way, unsure what else to say.

"You should give serious thought to accepting his proposal," Doc advised. "Nate looks to be a strong, healthy man who can support you in case—"

Rachel flung up her hand to forestall him. "There are extenuating circumstances that make any proposal impossible."

Doc blink, startled. "You're engaged? You're a runaway bride?"

No, she was running from the law—and Nate was it. He was the worst kind of law and order, in her book. A U.S. marshal, for heaven sake! His jurisdiction was wide ranging and he had influence, and he had friends in the very highest of places. One word from him and her head would roll. Even if, by some remote chance, he believed her story and stood up for her, she suspected his reasons for siding with her would draw speculative smirks that insinuated she had slept with him to ensure his assistance.

Damn it, she really needed to pack up and head to Colorado. She'd leave tonight, she decided suddenly. Having Ludy and Doc know that she had become intimate with Nate, who had lied to her about his federal appointment in law enforcement—the cad—was too humiliating and awkward. She'd have to confiscate Ludy's saddle horse to make her fast getaway, but she would leave him all the monetary compensation she could spare.

Doc jostled her from her mental arrangements by snapping his fingers in front of her face. "I could use a good soaking. Give me some privacy, please."

Rachel spun around and walked off. She didn't want to leave Doc behind for fear he would use her disappearance as another excuse to consume the fifty-proof patented remedies. Of course, very soon he would encounter the water she had replaced in the amber-colored bottles. That would really set him off, she predicted with a wince. Maybe it would be better if she wasn't around for that inevitable explosion—

She squawked in surprise when Nate suddenly appeared in front of her.

"I know what you're thinking," he said.

She glared at him. "You have no idea."

"You think I told Ludy and Doc about what happened last night," he hurried on. "I didn't. I also think you should marry me so we can resolve this uncomfortable predicament and appease your two, highly affronted protectors."

"Fine," she said, startling him—and herself.

It suddenly dawned on her that this was the perfect way to pacify everyone. She could agree to anything…because she was leaving tonight. If accepting the proposal that Nate really didn't want to offer—because he didn't love her and only felt obligation—would shut him up and satisfy the other two men, then she would agree to marry him.

Besides, Nate wouldn't want to hold her to the arrangement when he reached Dodge City and realized she was a fugitive—if he didn't know it already.

She gave that a second, *rational* thought and decided he didn't know it yet. Unfortunately, he would very soon.

His dark brows shot up his forehead and his jaw sagged to his chest. "You will marry me?" he chirped, incredulous.

His startled expression was a dagger through her heart. He hadn't expected her to agree, because he was only soothing his nagging conscience and Ludy's and Doc's indignation on her behalf. She was no more than a physical diversion to him. After all, *she* had seduced *him* twice. She was pretty sure ingesting the strong potions that appeared to have long-lasting effects accounted for his interest in her.

"Sure," she said belatedly. "I've thought it over and I've changed my mind. After tomorrow's performance in Evening Shade we'll tie the knot." *I'd rather tie a knot around your neck and put one on your head because you lied to me, Mr. U.S. Marshal!*

Leave it to Nate to appraise her carefully after his initial surprise wore off.

"Okay, what's the catch?" he asked warily.

She shrugged lackadaisically. "No catch. I'm madly in love with you and I don't want to live without you. You're the light of my life and all that."

He cocked his head to study her from a different angle for a long, thoughtful moment. Then he said, "While you're being so incredibly agreeable, tell me your last name and where you lived before you joined Doc's traveling medicine show."

"Rachel Waggoner," she replied, using her father's last name, hoping to shock him.

Sure enough, it did. He blinked in astonishment. "Henry Waggoner is your father?"

"None other. Which is why I have such a low opinion of corrupt lawmen who turn to crime and abandon their young daughters and wives burdened with their shame."

"And your mother?" he questioned. "Where is she?"

"She died of a broken heart, with the help of whiskey," she confided, certain her questionable background would prompt him to retract his offer of marriage. It didn't, surprisingly.

"Which explains why you have become Doc's guardian angel," he mused aloud.

She lifted her shoulders nonchalantly. "I tried to rescue Doc, but as you can see, I haven't been very successful yet."

"Where were you living and working before you joined the medicine show?"

Damn, he sounded exactly like a marshal firing questions, didn't he? "Colorado. I stayed with my Cheyenne grandmother after my mother died."

"Where you learned about the culture and learned to speak the language," he guessed correctly.

"I'm one-quarter Cheyenne." She wondered if her mixed ancestry might offend him. But he didn't so much as blink. Just peered intently at her, as he had an unnerving habit of doing when he was trying to sort out facts.

"My grandfather was a French trapper, who used marriage to my grandmother as a useful tool to become accepted by her tribe and have access to its hunting grounds. Of course, when he'd gathered enough furs to make himself wealthy, he returned to white society to get himself a proper wife," she added, unable to quell the bitterness in her voice, refusing to mention the name St. Raimes.

"You also sang for audiences in a mining town," he prompted. "When was that?"

It was her turn to blink in surprise. "How do you know that?"

"A bystander in Crossville mentioned that you reminded him of a little girl with an incredibly big voice. He heard you sing at a theater years ago. I figured it must have been you. You're musical gift is without equal."

The compliment pleased her enormously, but she was still mad at him because he hadn't been completely honest with her about his occupation. Therefore, she refused to feel guilty for feeding him half-truths and making crucial omissions about her past.

"I've also worked in several saloons the past few years."

She cast him a challenging stare, but if he found that offensive, he didn't let it show on his ruggedly handsome face. But then, he was a lawman who had likely heard it all and he probably could wear a deadpan expression with the best of them.

"That is where I practiced deflecting unwanted advances from drunken men. However, last night was not a good indication of my skills of self-defense." She stared meaningfully at him. "I was extremely distracted all day."

His sensuous lips twitched, but he kept silent on the subject and posed another question. "Where did you learn to sew expertly?"

She hadn't anticipated the question but she replied smoothly, "From my grandmother. She taught me a great deal about other things, such as making healing potions and surviving in the wilderness.

"Now that I've answered your questions, you can answer a few of mine," she insisted. Let him squirm, she thought to herself. She knew his present occupation and she knew he would lie about it.

"Where do you call home?"

"I was born in Kansas City." He gestured for her to accompany him back to the wagon and their waiting picnic lunch. "I joined the Army of the West and it fulfilled my sense of adventure. Turned out I was skilled with weapons so I decided to accept a position as city marshal in a dusty little town called Dover Flats. My main duty was corralling rowdy cowhands and drovers that stopped by while driving cattle to Abilene. After the city of Abilene quarantined longhorns because of the ticks that caused Texas Fever and infected local herds, the town became a quiet farming and ranching community. It was too far from the railroad tracks to draw gamblers and outlaws looking for easy money and drunken targets."

"So you ran for sheriff in the county?" she pressed.

He nodded his dark head. "That provided the opportunity to move from town to town and track renegades. The nomadic lifestyle suited me."

"But you gave it up to visit your ailing father?" She watched him carefully, wondering if she'd catch him in the lie.

He chuckled. "I couldn't fulfill my duties when I was called home. It turned out that my father used the ruse, in hopes of planting me in my hometown permanently. *He* decided I needed to settle down and *he* handpicked a young woman for me to marry."

"So you are a runaway groom?"

"I didn't bolt and run, if that's what you're asking," he corrected. "I politely refused to be shanghaied into marriage."

"Then you came west to coerce me into marrying you." She frowned when a disturbing thought struck her. "Are you proposing to me to make sure your father can't marry you off to someone of his choosing? If I am to be the consolation prize—"

Nate flung up both arms. "Whoa! You are nothing of the kind."

"Then what kind am I?" she huffed, offended.

"The grand prize. Now don't get bent out of shape more than you already are," he insisted. "I came here as a favor to Edgar Havern, my *ex*-future father-in-law, and *his* father-in-law because they are having a problem with an investment in Dodge City. That was the consolation for rejecting Lenora."

He knew he was revealing more than he should because the information was confidential. But he'd finally gotten Rachel to confide the details of her past so he had to return the favor. Otherwise, the feisty little termagant would cancel the wedding plans.

The fact that she had agreed to marriage surprised him. And hell, he still wasn't sure if he was pleased or disappointed that she had. All he knew was that he had the instinctive feeling she was still keeping secrets and she didn't trust him enough to confide in him.

Then again, he couldn't be completely honest with her, either. Her corrupt father had turned her against lawmen and he didn't relish telling her that there was nothing *former* about his occupation.

"Are you still in law enforcement?" Her dark eyes riveted on him.

"I'm doing private investigation during my leave of absence," he hedged.

She studied him for a few moments. He suspected she was processing the facts and trying to decide if she believed him. Damn, she was cautious. She would make an exceptional law officer because she didn't take anyone at his word and she reserved judgment until she had gathered all the information.

"So basically you are still in law enforcement?" she asked again.

"More or less."

"Which is it? *More* or *less?*" she demanded.

That was all he intended to say about that so he ignored the pointed question and said, "I'm sorry your father soured you against lawmen, but not everyone is corrupt."

"I wonder what percentages of lawmen are honest," she said, then strode off to set out the lunch basket.

"One more thing—"

She waved him off. "We are finished talking. There are no more *things* I wish to discuss with you."

Nate watched her go, wondering how honest she had been with him. He doubted he'd heard the whole truth and nothing but.

When Ludy and Doc arrived on the scene, he had no opportunity to grill her with the other questions swirling around his head.

To his shock and amazement, she set the basket on an outspread blanket and said to Doc and Ludy, "Nate and I are getting married, so you can stop badgering me."

"Really?" Ludy grinned broadly. "Congratulations. When?"

"Tomorrow. The sooner the better." This from Doc.

"We are thinking about waiting until after the performance in Evening Shade," she elaborated.

"That works." Doc munched on his meal. "I'm giving you away. I never had the—" He stopped talking abruptly.

Nate noticed the familiar flicker of pain cross Doc's face. He wondered what it would take to exorcise those demons that followed Doc like his own shadow.

"This calls for a celebration—"

"No, it doesn't. Not here and not now." Before Doc could take a drink of his Swamp Root Liver Tonic, Rachel snatched the bottle from his hand. "We have a long ride ahead of us. We will celebrate tonight and not a minute before."

Doc's head snapped up and he flashed a challenging stare. "Who is running this show, young lady?"

She tilted her chin to a defiant angle. "For now, I am."

Nate swallowed a grin when Rachel dared any man present to dispute her. It wasn't going to be him, that was for sure. He was glad to be on speaking terms with her again. With any luck, he could poke and prod until she told him why she had been upset with him today.

The future groom had a right to know such things… didn't he?

Chapter Eleven

Rachel made certain she wasn't alone with Nate the rest of the day. She refused to answer his questions. Instead, she spent her time mapping out her unannounced departure for this evening. She didn't want the men to suspect her intentions so she discreetly removed her satchels from the wagon and stashed them near the place where Nate had tethered the horses.

"You put together a fine supper this evening," Doc praised as he added another helping of stew to his plate. "We used to—"

He fell silent, then reached for a bottle of Skunk Cabbage Worm Destroyer Tonic. Rachel held her breath, hoping it wasn't one of the bottles she had replaced with water. She didn't want to be on hand when he discovered what she'd done—for his own good, of course. But try telling him that, she mused as she watched him tip the bottle to his lips. She breathed a sigh of relief when he drank without commenting.

After the meal, the men washed and put away the utensils. Things were working out perfectly for her evening departure.

"I'm going down to the creek to bathe," she announced, sticking to her planned nightly routine.

"Pay attention to your surroundings," Nate cautioned. "Do you have your pistol with you?"

She patted the pocket of her boyish breeches.

"If you want me to stand guard—"

"I'll be fine, thank you," she interrupted Nate.

While the men were occupied, Rachel sidestepped down the steep embankment that overlooked a creek choked with trees, bushes and tangled vines. Even from the cliff where Doc had decided to make camp, it would be difficult to tell exactly where she was—and that was good.

Hurriedly Rachel stripped from her clothes and waded into the water. She glanced around cautiously. The very last thing she wanted was to encounter Adolph's henchman. They would be upon her before she could alert Nate.

So far so good, she thought to herself as she sank into the water. She sighed appreciatively when the cool, invigorating water swirled around her. All the while, she scanned the area for unwanted guests—both the two-legged and four-legged varieties. Fortunately, all she saw was a few frogs, turtles and one snake that slithered into its hole on the muddy creek bank.

Rachel bided her time until dark, then walked ashore.

"Rachel? Is everything all right down there?" Nate called from atop the stony cliff.

"The water feels so refreshing that I plan to stay a little longer," she called back, thankful she hadn't sneaked away before he checked on her.

She didn't need the U.S. marshal hot on her trail. She didn't want Nate to realize she was gone until she had a decent head start. He had confided earlier that day that tracking down fugitives was one of his favorite parts of his job. She predicted he was exceptionally good at it, too.

Grabbing her clothing, she returned to the shallow water, then walked upstream so Nate couldn't detect her tracks easily. When she was a good distance away from her bathing site, she came ashore to dress. She had taken the precaution of studying the lay of the land before dark so she wouldn't get off course in the dense trees and bushes that clogged the valley. She knew the horses were tethered on the northern bend of the creek and she located them easily.

Breathing a sigh of relief, she saddled Ludy's horse. She reached for the bridle, then felt a pang of regret coiling inside her. She was going to miss Nate. It still amazed her that she'd fallen head over heels so quickly for that big, handsome rascal. She would never see him again, never enjoy the pleasure of his touch and the passion they ignited…

"Forget him," she muttered at herself. "This is no time to become sentimental. You can be sentimental all you want while you're traipsing around the mountains with Singing Bird. She will understand what you're feeling."

Nate strode away from the edge of the rocky cliff to gather up the blanket and basket supper. Ludy was propped against a tree on the south side of the campfire, playing a forlorn tune on his harmonica.

"I figured you'd head for Evening Shade," Nate commented as he strode past.

Ludy stopped playing and glanced up at Nate. "Can't tonight."

"Why not?"

"Have to make sure you keep a respectable distance from the bride-to-be." He stared directly at Nate, then grinned, displaying his dimples. "I'm the self-appointed chaperone."

"Good of you to make the noble sacrifice," Nate remarked, then glanced this way and that. "Where's Doc?"

Ludy hitched his thumb toward the back of the wagon. "He's drowning in his cups, I suspect. He's come up with all sorts of excuses to celebrate and to mourn—and whatever else he chooses to call these bouts. I've tried not to hang around camp for too many of them since I joined the medicine show. Besides, Rachel handles Doc better than I do."

Ludy flicked his wrist to shoo Nate on his way. "If I were you, I'd be spending my time contemplating how my life will change after the wedding. I'm sure it's going to be an adjustment for you. Would be for me."

When Ludy took up on the harmonica again, Nate ambled back to the edge of the cliff. He didn't like that Rachel was still lounging at the creek after dark. Then he reminded himself that Rachel didn't appreciate a man hovering over her as if she were helpless. Still, his future wife had needed him the previous night when the drifters jumped her so he felt justified. Besides, he was a lawman and he was in the business of protecting people.

Future wife… His thoughts circled back to the shotgun-wedding plans that Doc and Ludy insisted on. Of course, he wasn't the one who protested hotly, he reminded himself—and felt a mite offended. It was Rachel who didn't want to marry him. She obviously had thought far enough ahead to foresee problems. Such as, where would they live? Did she plan to continue traveling with Doc? And when would he work up the nerve to tell her that he was a

U.S. marshal when she had a strong dislike for lawmen already?

He decided he'd tell her *after* her name was on the dotted line of their marriage license.

"Rachel? Is everything still going okay down there?" He pricked his ears and waited but she didn't respond. "Rachel?"

Nothing, not even a peep.

"Well, hell!"

Instant alarm pulsated through him as he sidestepped down the steep slope. He grabbed hold of one cottonwood sapling and then another to keep his balance as he hurried downhill. He headed for the place where she had gone to bathe, but in the darkness he wasn't sure he'd found the right spot.

"Rachel?" Frantic, Nate lurched around, but he wasn't sure which direction to run first.

He held position—difficult though it was to stand and do nothing. Over the sound of chirping crickets and croaking frogs, he thought he heard the thud of horse hooves on the opposite side of the creek.

He surged through the water, holding his pistol over his head as he sank chest-deep in the stream. The thrashing of underbrush indicated a horse was about twenty yards ahead of him, moving at a steady pace. Nate came ashore, shoved his pistol in its holster and took off, running parallel to the horse and rider.

The instant he spotted a break in the tree line he shot sideways and launched himself at the horse and rider.

The startled horse bolted, then reared up when Nate slammed into it broadside. Snarling, Nate grabbed the rider, jerked him off the horse and shoved him to the ground.

"Where is she—?" His voice dried up when he realized he'd yanked his bride-to-be off the horse and held her to the ground. The very same bride-to-be who was *supposed* to be bathing at the creek and had agreed to a wedding before she had swiped Ludy's horse. "You sneaky little hellion!" he snapped furiously. "Where the hell do you think you're going?"

"I c-can't b-breathe," she panted while he was sprawled atop her, pressing her to the ground.

"Doesn't matter," he muttered. "I'm planning on strangling you for this devious prank, anyway."

Nate wasn't sure why he was so angry. Maybe it was because her attempt to leave before the wedding was a direct insult. Maybe it was because he had treated her roughly when he jerked her off the horse and he was feeling guilty about it. Or perhaps it was the fear for her safety that had caught up with him. Probably a combination of all three, he decided as he stared into her shadowed face.

"So that's why you were so agreeable to the shotgun wedding Ludy and Doc planned for us," he growled at her. "You were planning on hightailing it out of here without a word, weren't you? It was one big, premeditated setup!"

"You can stop yelling now," she muttered, squirming beneath him. "I can hear you just fine, thanks."

He didn't lower his voice. Couldn't. He was still fuming. "And what was I supposed to do when I discovered you were gone?"

"Thank me for resolving your problem," she said helpfully. "I braided a note of explanation into the mane on one of the horses to let you know I'd left."

"Where were you going?" he demanded sharply.

"Away."

"*Away* covers a lot of territory, angel face. Be more specific."

"You are not my husband and I do not have to answer to you," she responded as she tried to shove him off.

He didn't budge.

"Where…were…you…going?" he growled slowly and succinctly.

"None…of…your…business," she mocked defiantly.

"Damn it, Rachel. When are you going to get it through your thick skull that I am not the enemy?"

"Yes, you are. I can't trust you."

"Why not?"

"Because you are withholding the fact that you are a U.S. marshal," she spat at him. "When did you plan to tell me? After our one-year anniversary?"

Nate blew out his breath as he shifted to sit down beside her. "When did you find that out?"

She sat up, then brushed the grass and leaves off her shirt. "This morning. Phillip Dexter came by to deliver a message to the U.S. marshal about seeing—"

She clamped her mouth shut, then looked the other way. He studied her warily, wishing he could see her facial expression, but it was too dark. "That he'd seen *what?*" he prodded.

Her shoulders slumped as she expelled an agitated breath. "To tell you that some of the local businessmen had spotted the three men who attacked you. They were in town yesterday afternoon."

"And you didn't tell me?" His voice rose with each muttered word.

"No." She climbed to her feet to grab the horse's reins before it wandered off to graze.

"Why? Because you were aggravated when you found

out my present occupation? Damn it, Rachel, I ought to toss you in jail for withholding information."

"You don't know the half of it, Mr. U.S. Marshal." She scowled.

The comment provoked his wary frown. "What's that supposed to mean?"

To his surprise, she wheeled around and stamped in front of him. "It means that I saw those three men in town and I didn't tell you."

"What?" he hooted incredulously as he bolted to his feet.

"That's right. I saw them and I was concerned about your possible confrontation with them, so I mixed a potion, poured it over your food to put you in the mood so I could seduce you. I let you sleep the afternoon away and prayed those brutal bullies would leave town before you woke up." She gushed like Old Faithful.

There, she had it off her conscience and it was out in the open at last. She hadn't told him the whole truth, but enough of it for him to realize that he shouldn't want to marry her because she had deceived him and seduced him for her own selfish purposes. Now he would hate her, but at least he wouldn't feel obliged to marry her. Obligation was the very last thing she wanted from Nate.

"Let me get this straight," he growled as he loomed over her like a thundercloud. "You gave me a potion—"

"A love potion, which explains your willingness—"

"Of course," he cut in, then smirked caustically. "What other explanation could there be for a man to get mixed up with a sneaky, deceptive, fiery female like you!" he roared.

"Hey, Nate! Is everything okay down there?" Ludy called from atop the bluff.

"Just peachy!" Nate yelled back. "Rachel and I are making wedding plans!"

"That better be all," Ludy said warningly. "I told you that I'm here to keep my eye on you."

Rachel frowned, bemused. "What's he talking about?"

"Ludy has become our self-appointed chaperone. No intimacy until the honeymoon."

"Oh." Considering the way Nate was glowering at her she doubted he'd feel amorous toward her ever again.

The love potion had definitely worn off.

"Don't try to change the subject," he muttered. "We were discussing the love potion you gave me."

She bobbed her head. "The first night when you were injured, Doc mixed a sedative. When *I* tried to duplicate it, because *he'd* passed out and was of no use whatsoever as a physician, the concoction made you amorous toward me. Since we'd only met I knew some of the ingredients in my mixture must have acted as an aphrodisiac."

He made a strangled sound, but she wasn't sure what it meant. She just kept talking to get the bucket load of guilt off her chest. Well, most of it, she amended. She still couldn't bring herself to tell him that she might be wanted for murder.

"So I used the potion again yesterday, in hopes of keeping you in the room and off the street when those goons were bouncing from the bordello and saloon to the restaurant."

"You didn't think I was capable of handling those three scoundrels?" he asked in offended dignity.

"You couldn't the first time." She smirked.

"I didn't see them coming!" he all but yelled at her.

She winced when his voice boomed around her like a discharging cannon. "I was trying to protect you. Like *you* keep trying to protect *me* from harm."

She had him there and she dared him to argue.

"Fine." He flicked his wrist dismissively to concede the point. "So you were playing my guardian angel again. Then you seduced me. Quite the extreme sacrifice, sweetheart."

She smiled brightly. "Anything to spare my fellow man from agonizing pain."

"You're a real saint."

"I try to be," she insisted—but she didn't go on to say that she was a St. Raimes. He didn't need to know what name she went by these days.

The teasing comment didn't ease his bad mood. He was still glaring at her and hovering nearby, in case she tried to break and run.

"Then what was your excuse for seducing me last night? You didn't cram your love potion down my throat then."

"The potion obviously has a long-lasting effect," she explained.

"Funny thing, I'm not feeling it now," he muttered sarcastically. "In fact, I'm feeling anything but!"

She was tired of being on the defensive. "You haven't told me why you refused to confide that you are presently a federal law officer."

"I told you that I was discreetly investigating an investment as a favor for Edgar Havern and his father-in-law. It would be difficult to do if I rode into town wearing a badge. Besides, one of my deputies is handling my usual duties until the first of next month. So technically, I *am* on a leave of absence."

He took the horse's reins from her hand, then clutched her elbow. "We'll return the horse and pretend none of this happened. Ludy and Doc don't need to know you tried to run away on a stolen horse."

She grimaced at his accusing tone. She wasn't about to tell him it wasn't her first offense. He was too annoyed with her already.

"Tomorrow we'll have the wedding as planned," he decreed.

She stopped short but he uprooted her from the spot and shepherded her along beside him. *"No."*

"Yes."

"I told you it was all my fault," she protested. "You are not responsible. You are not obligated to marry me."

"Don't argue with me, Rachel," he said, and scowled. "I am not in the mood. First you left without notice and I was half out of my mind, thinking you had been kidnapped."

"I told you that I left you a note on the horse."

"Nevertheless, I was alarmed that you didn't respond when I called to you. I've had to rescue you from a wild boar, lusty cowboys and drunken drifters, so you can see why I might jump to the conclusion that you were in danger."

"I could have waited out the wild boar," she contested.

"But not those drifters who held you down," he said harshly. "You couldn't fight your way out of that alone."

She had the good sense to keep her trap shut because he was still bristling with irritation. Though she didn't know *why* he was. She had explained herself, gotten him off the hook and tried to do him a tremendous favor by leaving in the cover of darkness so he wouldn't have to marry her. She knew he didn't want a wife. He could have had the wealthy, well-connected socialite, Lenora Havern, if he'd wanted one badly enough.

Honestly, some men just didn't appreciate it when a woman did them a stupendous favor. Marrying her might alter the course of his life. He should be thanking her, not railing at her.

A U.S. marshal married to a horse-thieving murderess? How would that have worked out for him?

"As I was saying, we will be married tomorrow," Nate announced as he bustled her along at a brisk pace.

"Absolutely not," she objected strenuously. "I don't even like you that much right now."

He bared his teeth. "I'm not too fond of you at the moment, either. But, be that as it may, I've thought it over and I've decided you're right. And thank you so much for your suggestion."

"What the blazes are you talking about?" she asked, befuddled.

"If I marry you, then my manipulative father can't trot a few more potential brides past me."

Rachel could kick herself for accusing him of wanting to marry her to counter his domineering father. Now her comment had ricocheted to bite her in the fanny. Confound it, nothing about her life was working out to her satisfaction.

It was the family curse at work again, she decided. Too bad she couldn't concoct a potion to counteract her legacy of bad luck with the male of the species.

"I'm still not agreeing to this wedding," she said stubbornly. "You might have something to gain from it, but I don't."

"Sure you do. My undying love and devotion," he replied in a tone that was anything but affectionate.

"There is that." She smirked. "I'll feed you my potion every night and pretend you like me."

When they reached the tethered horses, Nate unhooked the saddle, then thrust her satchels at her. "See if you can sneak these into the back of the wagon without being seen. We wouldn't want your substitute father and big brother to think you tried to spirit off into the night without a word of explanation, now would we? After all, they worship the ground you float over, angel face."

Rachel wasn't sure she appreciated the sarcastic tone he'd attached to his pet name for her. But she decided this wasn't the time to bring that up. Already, Nate looked as if he'd bitten into a sour lemon and couldn't spit it out.

"Rachel! Damn you! Come here this instant!"

She grimaced when Doc's bellowing voice and slurred words echoed in the darkness.

"Uh-oh," she mumbled warily.

"Now what did you do?" Nate rumbled. "The joyful eve of my wedding is turning out to be a damn nightmare. Runaway bride, drunken substitute father-in-law and over-protective substitute brother-in-law."

"Get out while you can," she suggested flippantly.

"And leave all this melodrama and these misadventures behind?" he scoffed. "Wouldn't think of it. You're marrying me because you said you would this afternoon. I'm holding you to it. Besides, Doc and Ludy are demanding it and that's that."

"Damn it, Rachel!" Doc roared again.

She swallowed hard because she had a pretty good idea why Doc was furious with her. This was turning out to be a hellish night, just like the night before. Except for the part last night when she had been in Nate's arms, soaring in ecstasy, she amended as she hurried off to confront Doc.

"Calm down, Doc," Ludy coaxed.

Nate jogged around the tree while Rachel tucked her

satchels in the back of the wagon. He glanced over his shoulder to make double damn certain she didn't try to take off again. That sneaky little witch! He ought to put her in shackles to make sure she stayed put.

Love potion, seduction and withholding vital information? He huffed out an exasperated breath. All in a day's work for the mysterious Rachel Waggoner. Now she had a new agenda—scaring ten years off his life, and then infuriating him beyond words.

He shuddered to think what his wedding day would hold. If she stuck around for it—and he didn't trust her to do that. Given the opportunity, he predicted she would be long gone. Only God would know where to find her.

"Leave me alone," Doc grumbled in a slurred voice as he tried to wrest loose from Ludy's grasp. "Where's that sneaky little witch?"

Obviously, Nate and Doc were of the same opinion, but he didn't know what Rachel had done to infuriate Doc to the extreme.

"Rachel is with Nate." Ludy, who was unaware that Nate was walking up behind him, tried to steer Doc away from the edge of the cliff and back to the campfire. "How about some coffee?"

"Don't want coffee," Doc mumbled as he lurched back toward the cliff, trying to locate Rachel. "Damn it, girl, get up here this instant!"

"She's coming," Nate said as he strode up beside the inebriated doctor. "She's putting her soap and dirty clothes in the wagon after her bath." Not exactly the truth, but close enough, he mused. "Now what's the problem, Doc?"

"*She's* the problem," Doc snarled. "I took her in when she had nowhere to go and this is how she repays me!"

Nate glanced toward the wagon and frowned suspiciously as Rachel scurried toward them. He wondered what else Rachel had done to facilitate her escape attempt tonight. He knew she'd taken Ludy's horse. Had she stolen money from Doc, too?

"She had nothing but the clothes on her back—men's clothes at that—when I found her and I didn't ask prying questions!" He lurched around, then glowered when he saw Rachel walking toward him. "There you are! You devious little hellion!" Doc yelled. "Where did you put it, damn it?"

Bemused, Nate and Ludy watched Rachel halt in front of Doc. She crossed her arms over her chest and stood with her feet askance. Then she tilted her chin, refusing to cower beneath Doc's harsh tone and mutinous scowl.

"I poured it all out, and it's for your own good because this has gone on long enough. It ends tonight, Doc."

Chapter Twelve

Nate's puzzled frown became an amused smile. Ah, now he got it. She had tampered with the patented medicine Doc used as his liquor supply. He kept the fifty-proof concoctions for himself and, obviously, Rachel had disposed of it.

"You poured it out?" Doc howled in outrage. "*All* of it?"

"Every last drop," she said unrepentantly. "I replaced it with water. A few bottles at a time every evening when we made camp. You wouldn't let your patients drink that stuff. You told them to drink fresh water, so I followed your advice."

When Doc launched himself toward Rachel in a drunken fury, Nate grabbed him by the nape of his jacket to hold him at bay. Doc tried to take a swing at Nate but he couldn't land a punishing blow.

"It was my destiny to drink all those tonics," Doc railed at Rachel.

Ludy, Nate and Rachel stared at him, bemused.

"What the blazes are you talking about?" Rachel demanded. "You are *supposed* to drink yourself to death?"

He bobbed his tousled blond head, then swore color-fully.

Nate hadn't heard Doc reduce himself to foul oaths—until now. He let loose with a string of off-color epithets that turned the air black. He aimed most of them at Rachel, who defied the verbal thrashing like the strong-willed, defiant woman she was.

"You can curse me to hell and back, Doc, if it makes you feel better. But I will not allow you to kill yourself on my watch. My mother did it and once was enough. I will not have the people I care about dying on me again. I love you dearly and you need to stop downing those tonics."

"I have to!" he shouted angrily. "That's what she used because I wasn't there. It killed her. Killed *them*."

Rachel reached out to place her hand on Doc's shoulder. "You mean Margie? She took the tonics?"

Doc nodded, then swayed on his feet. Nate propped him up.

"Who was she?" Rachel asked softly. "I've heard you mention her several times before. Why did she need the tonic when you were a doctor?"

His shoulders slumped and his eyes filled with tears as he leaned heavily against Nate. "She was my wife," he said brokenly. "We had tried for years to start our family, but she was finally able to carry our first child, almost to full-term. She began having complications one night while I was away, delivering someone else's baby. Margie must have been in acute pain, and she panicked when she began losing our child prematurely. She bought tonics from the former owner of this medicine wagon and she drank too much of those quack potions to ease her pain, hoping to endure until I returned home."

His breath hitched, as if his heart had ripped wide-open

in his chest. "I should have been there. I could save everyone else but I couldn't save my wife and my unborn child," he said desolately.

"I'm so terribly sorry, Doc," Rachel whispered. "But killing yourself with those tonics won't help Margie. You know she wouldn't want that."

"I didn't want to go on without her because I felt so damn guilty about failing her," he said miserably. "Then I decided to make it my mission to put as many quacks as I could out of business, and inform the citizens in small towns of the evils of the so-called miracle cure-alls before I joined her in the Hereafter."

"You aren't joining her yet," Rachel insisted. "You still have a lot of good work to do. You have hundreds of patients to treat with authentic medications, people who will benefit from your skills and experience."

"No, I've done enough, paid enough penance." He flung himself away from Nate abruptly—and stumbled.

"Doc!" Rachel yelled in warning.

She felt as if she were moving in slow motion when Doc tripped over his own feet and teetered too near the edge of the cliff. She outstretched her hand, but she was six inches away from grabbing his arm when he fell off balance and cartwheeled over the bluff. She heard his muffled groan, heard the sounds of branches snapping as he tumbled head over heels down the steep, rock-strewn slope.

Panicky, Rachel bounded after him, clutching at every tree branch and bush along the way. She heard Nate and Ludy scrambling behind her while she watched Doc's body roll and tumble like a felled tree bouncing downhill. She heard a dull thud when his head and shoulder collided with the lopsided ring of boulders that had broken loose from the cliff long ago and rolled to the base of the hill.

"Doc?" she panted as she thrashed through the weeds to reach him.

He didn't respond, just lay motionless, his body contorted at an unnatural angle.

Rachel brushed her hand over his forehead, noting the egg-size knot. Then she slipped her hand behind his neck and felt the sticky wetness of blood seeping from the wound on his skull.

"Oh, God." Horrified, she tried to remember what Doc had instructed her to do when a patient was unconscious. She needed Doc to wake up to prescribe proper treatment.

"Let me have him, Rachel." Nate crouched beside her. "Ludy and I will carry him uphill. Go roll out a pallet beside the campfire so we can determine how much damage he's done to himself."

"I did this to him," she said shakily. "He didn't mean to fall off the cliff. He wasn't trying to kill himself."

"No, you didn't cause this," Nate contradicted. "Doc was letting the tonics and elixirs do him in. Now go, Rachel. You're the closest thing we have to a doctor right now. Go fetch Doc's black bag."

Rachel skimmed her hand over Doc's head and bit back a wail of anguish. This was her fault, despite what Nate said to the contrary. He was only trying to make her feel better. If she hadn't taken it upon herself to remove the fifty-proof tonics from the wagon, Doc wouldn't have become furious with her. He wouldn't have decomposed in front of her eyes when she forced him to reveal the torment of losing his beloved wife and his unborn child.

She might as well have shoved him off the edge of the cliff, because she had brought him to this torment.

"Rachel, *go,* damn it!" Nate barked. "Move!"

* * *

"This doesn't look good," Ludy said grimly, and then grabbed Doc's ankles.

"I know. I hope we don't cause more damage by hauling him uphill." Nate hooked his elbows under Doc's arms and hoisted him off the ground. Doc's head lolled against his shoulder as Nate sidestepped up the slope. "We can't leave him down here. He's going to need to see a doctor."

"There isn't one in thirty miles," Ludy reminded him.

Being as careful as possible, Nate and Ludy progressed slowly uphill, shouldering their way through the thicket of weeds and saplings to reach the campsite. As requested, Rachel had rolled out Doc's pallet beside the fire and lit a lantern to offer a better view of his injuries.

Nate grimaced when light flickered over Doc's scratched face. It looked as if he had scraped against every bush and twig on his way downhill. His nose looked as if it had been broken when he'd collided with the boulders. The knot on his forehead had doubled in size. Plus, the wound on the back of Doc's skull was bleeding profusely.

"Dear God," Rachel mumbled as she dipped a cloth in the bucket of water sitting beside her. She placed a cool compress over the knot on his forehead. "His face is alarmingly pale."

"I'm not sure if that is the result of his painful fall or the nostrums he consumed *before* he struck nothing but the water you put in those bottles," Nate mused aloud.

"I shouldn't have tampered with his tonic," Rachel said, tormented. "He wouldn't have become furious with me and tried to worm loose from your grasp."

"There is no reason for you to shoulder the blame for Doc's condition. This is *not* your fault," he repeated emphatically.

She tore her anguished gaze away from Doc to scoff at Nate. "You know it is. I decided it was time for him to dry out. He was furious with me. Otherwise, he'd still be conked out in the back of the wagon."

"And you'd be—" Nate slammed his mouth shut before he said *long gone* "—bathing at the creek," he finished, so Ludy wouldn't know about the attempted escape.

She stared straight at him and he stared right back. He still wondered where she had planned to go and whether or not he could have found her if he had gone looking after he'd completed his investigation for Edgar Havern and his silent partner—his father-in-law, Julian St. Raimes.

"Don't beat yourself black and blue over this, Rachel," Ludy insisted as he unbuttoned Doc's grass-stained jacket, then removed it. "You're the one who's always stuck by Doc's side while I bailed out. You're the reason he's lasted this long."

The comment suggested Doc didn't have much time left on earth. Nate knew the prospect of Doc dying, while he was so angry with Rachel, cut her to the core. Seeing all the scrapes and bruises on Doc's chest and ribs made Nate wonder just how serious Doc's condition might be. Certainly, Nate had needed several days to recover from his beating—which was the equivalent of tumbling willy-nilly downhill. In addition, Doc might have cracked a rib or punctured a lung…

"Ah, damn," Rachel muttered, dragging Nate from his pensive musings.

He watched her ease Doc's head to the side to appraise the bloody gash at the base of his skull. The cut was deep and caked with dirt. She went to work immediately, blotting the coagulated blood and cleansing the wound as best she could.

"Ludy, would you fetch my sewing kit from the wagon?" she requested without taking her eyes off the wound.

"Sure thing." He bounded off like a jackrabbit.

"We are going to have trouble figuring out the extent of internal injuries," Nate told her grimly. "We need to get him settled comfortably in the wagon and transport him to Dodge City immediately."

Her head snapped up. "We can take him somewhere else. Somewhere closer."

Nate shook his head. "You know there is no place closer that has a qualified physician. That's why Doc makes this small-town circuit to treat patients who don't have the privilege of being examined and treated by a certified doctor."

She huffed out her breath and refocused her attention on cleansing the wound.

Her behavior aroused Nate's suspicion. "What's wrong with going to Dodge, Rachel?"

She compressed her lips, shook her head, then shrugged noncommittally. "I only wish there was someplace closer."

Nate couldn't read her expression because she was good at masking her private thoughts. However, he had the uneasy feeling that Dodge City wasn't on her list of favorite places to visit. Now why was that?

"Here you go, hon." Ludy handed her the sewing basket.

"We'll make a padded bed in the wagon while you're stitching Doc back together," Nate said, rising to his feet. "You might want to give him a sedative to keep him knocked out during the ride. Maybe try out the potion you used on me while I was injured."

When Rachel looked at him sharply and frowned, he chastised himself for flinging the barb at her while she was upset. But, damn it, he was still agitated about that love potion nonsense.

What was the matter with the woman? Didn't she realize how attractive she was and that he didn't need a stimulating aphrodisiac to be aroused by her? Men lusted after her constantly—before, during and after her performances with the medicine show. Doc had hired Nate to hold the panting hounds at bay…

The epiphany that Rachel had no point of reference to distinguish the difference between his amorous pursuit and other men's pawing lust made him swear under his breath. She wrote off his response to her as the result of her potion. Rachel hadn't had caring lovers. Instead, she had fended off a string of lusty miners, gamblers, cowboys and drifters who saw her as a prize to conquer. Her concept of men was so skewered that it was only natural that she believed it required the powers of a potent love potion to bring out tender feelings in a man.

"Well, hell," he grumbled as he strode to the wagon.

"Well, hell what?" Ludy asked.

Nate jerked to attention. He'd been so immersed in thought that he'd forgotten he had company. "Just expressing my frustration with Doc's condition. Not knowing how bad off he is bothers me."

"Same here." Ludy crawled into the back of the wagon. He began pitching out dozens of bottles Rachel had filled with water so they could make more space for their injured patient. "We could drive all night to reach Dodge and it might be all for nothing. Rachel is our only hope of treating him temporarily because she's the one who works closely with Doc when he treats his patients."

"I hope she can concoct a miracle cure," Nate mumbled while he and Ludy rearranged the supplies so they could stack up the extra pallets to make a padded bedroll for Doc. Though why they bothered Nate didn't know. Doc was completely oblivious to the world around him.

Rachel cursed herself up one side and down the other while she stitched up Doc's wound, then bandaged his head. She applied the poultice her grandmother used to treat abrasions to Doc's face and chest. The deep bruise beneath his shoulder blade and the one by his rib cage worried her. If Doc suffered internal hemorrhaging, she had nothing more than Cheyenne chants to the Indian spirits to offer.

Suddenly Rachel understood the enormous burden Doc had carried after the death of his beloved wife. If Doc had suffered a deathblow because of *her,* Rachel would never forgive herself. Damn it, not only was her life cursed by loving the wrong man but she was a curse to other people's lives. Doc was seriously injured because of her. Nate felt obligated because of her. She had left Jennifer Grantham high and dry when she fled from town unexpectedly. Adolph Turner might be dead because of her—even if he *did* deserve it, she added silently.

She didn't seem to have a positive influence on anyone in white society. She should have stayed with Singing Bird and the Cheyenne tribe in Colorado. Her natural complexion was close enough in color that she didn't stand out among the members of her grandmother's people.

Perhaps she would rejoin her grandmother and follow in her footsteps to become a medicine woman and healer. She could draw upon the knowledge Doc had taught her. She could combine the best medications from the white and Indian worlds, she mused as she gently removed Doc's boots.

When Ludy and Nate returned to carry Doc to the

wagon, Rachel hesitated, wondering if this might be her last opportunity to escape. Her speculative gaze collided with Nate's. His don't-you-dare stare made her smile. She really could do him a great favor by vanishing into the night while he transported Doc to Dodge City. After all, that had been Nate's original destination before Adolph's henchmen set upon him. He didn't need her tagging along. Especially when he discovered she was a wanted criminal. He'd thank his lucky stars that he hadn't married her out of obligation.

"Hitch up the horses, angel face," Nate requested, still staring steadily at her. "I'll be over to help you in a minute."

During her brisk walk to fetch the horses she debated about telling Nate who she really was and what had happened in Dodge City that had left her running for her life. For certain, he needed to know about the three men lurking around the area.

"You'd leave Doc, not knowing how bad off he is?" Nate startled her by saying from so close behind her that she nearly jumped out of her skin.

"Stop sneaking up on me," she muttered crankily. "You're worse than a stalking Indian warrior. Every time I turn around there you are."

"Where else would I be? This morning you said I was the love of your life, or something to that effect," he mocked.

"I was being facetious." She unfastened the horses and led them toward the wagon. "Knowing how I feel about my father's shortcomings and his habit of twisting the rules to suit his needs, do you really think I'd marry a lawman and risk the possibility of history repeating itself?"

"I am not your father," he reminded her deliberately and

emphatically. He grabbed Ludy's horse and saddle. "My feelings toward you are not the least bit fatherly, either."

"How would you know for certain? You might still be suffering aftereffects from my potion," she sassed him.

"Damn it, Rachel—"

He shut up when they came within earshot of Ludy. Thank goodness, thought Rachel.

You have to tell him about Max, Bob and Warren, said the voice in her head. *He needs to know for his own protection.*

Later, she decided. She needed time to rehearse what she wanted to say. She'd tell him, then she'd leave him behind.

Leave without knowing what became of Doc? she asked herself pensively. He had saved her. He had given her a job and a place to stay, and he had befriended her. Plus, she'd nearly gotten him killed tonight. Could she walk away from Doc and never look back? Could she leave Nate when she loved the infuriating, appealing man more than life itself?

Rachel decided she was residing in her own personal hell on earth. If she stuck around long enough for Nate to discover who she was and what she had done, it would break her heart if he were the one who arrested her. She couldn't bear to see anger and disappointment claim his handsome features. Not to mention how humiliated she'd be when he put her in handcuffs and marched her to jail.

No, she mused as she inhaled a calming breath. Nothing good could come of returning to Dodge City. She knew Doc would have the best of care while he recuperated in Dr. Yeager's infirmary. The older physician had treated sundry injuries during his long years of practice.

Determined to escape before the wagon arrived in Dodge, Rachel took her seat beside Nate and bided her time.

"Well?" Adolph Turner didn't bother with pleasantries when he opened the door to the supply room to see his hired men hovering on the threshold. "Did you find her?"

Max Rother shook his shaggy brown head as he strode into the storeroom. "We made another sweep of small towns in the area, like you said."

"We checked every boutique and dry-goods store, just like you said, too," Bob Hanes spoke up as he lumbered inside.

"Rachel never applied for work at any of those places," Warren Lamont added on his way in the door. "It's like she dropped off the face of the earth."

"Maybe she died," Max suggested. "A woman alone might have a rough time of it in these parts. Especially one as attractive as that feisty chit."

"Hell, she might have been desperate enough to sell herself to some man she met along the way, if he agreed to take her with him. Happens all the time," Bob insisted. "That's how my brother took up with the woman he married."

Adolph clamped his hands behind his back and paced from wall to wall. "I suppose it's possible that she caught a train or stagecoach." After all, she had confiscated money from his wallet before she'd left so he knew she hadn't been traveling penniless.

He had refused to pass around posters and get the law involved because he wanted to choose his personal brand of punishment when he caught her. But if this unsuccessful search continued much longer he would be forced to file a formal complaint against Rachel, in hopes of getting results.

No matter what, his pride refused to let her get away from him unscathed. The deliciously wicked thought of making Rachel his slave until he tired of her still held vindictive appeal.

"Now what, boss?" Warren asked. "We've scoured the countryside south, east and west of town."

"Now you'll try the communities to the north," Adolph decided. "Four more days. If you can't locate her by then, I'll have the city marshal post a reward for her."

He bore down on his men with fierce determination. "You will swear that you saw her attack me in the storeroom and that she raced off while you were making sure I didn't suffer serious injury. I will claim that she took five thousand dollars from my safe and you are going to back me up. Understood?"

"Got it." Max lurched toward the back door. "We'll leave in the morning."

Bob thrust out his meaty hand, palm up. "But first we'll need more traveling money."

Scowling at the expense of sending his henchmen all over creation to locate Rachel, Adolph dug into his pockets. He made a mental note to extract a pound of Rachel's silky flesh to compensate. "As much as I'd like for you to be on your way immediately, I have a job for you. A local rancher has been lax in paying his loans. He needs to be reminded that payment comes due when I say it is."

After he slapped the money in each waiting hand, the scraggly trio tramped out. Dealing with those foul-smelling thugs made him wish for the perfumed skin of his new mistress. She would satisfy his lust and his need for revenge until he got hold of that dark-eyed hellion who had escaped him.

The twinge in his shoulder was an ever-present reminder that Rachel St. Raimes had gotten the best of him. He reaffirmed his vow to make her dreadfully sorry she had dared to cross him.

The closer Rachel came to Dodge City the more apprehensive she became. They had driven through the night and she had checked on Doc constantly. He hadn't regained consciousness. He just lay there without moving, his face so pale that she feared the worst. Rachel still wasn't sure if his peaked skin was the result of too much tonic or too serious an injury.

"I'm sorry, Doc," she whispered as she brushed her hand over his pallid cheek, then inched toward the wagon seat to rejoin Nate.

"How is he?" Nate kept the team of horses moving along at a slow but steady pace that would inflict the least amount of discomfort on Doc.

"The same." Rachel sank down beside him. "I don't know if that's good or bad. Maybe I gave him too much sedative. Maybe I didn't mix the right amount of each ingredient—" Her voice fizzled out when Ludy trotted up beside them.

"I was thinking of going on ahead to locate the physician and to rent our rooms," Ludy announced.

Nate cast Ludy a pointed glance. "That's fine, if that's all you're going to do."

Ludy puffed up with indignation. "It's not what you're thinking, but I'm also going to seek out the justice of the peace so you two lovebirds can get hitched as soon as possible."

Rachel resisted the urge to squirm on the seat. There

wasn't going to be a wedding, especially after Nate learned that she was a fugitive.

When she felt Nate's steady gaze on her, she forced a smile. "Can't wait. It'll be the happiest day of my life."

"Mine, too," Nate replied, never taking his eyes off her. "I'll be jumping for joy."

His voice was so unenthused that she inwardly winced.

Ludy gestured west. "I swung out to see what caused those dancing lights that I noticed in the valley. It was a drover's camp lit up with lanterns. I talked to the night guard who said his Texas outfit is bringing a large herd into Dodge this morning. There's another big herd of longhorns two miles west and three miles south of the nearby camp. Looks like Dodge will be overrun with cattle and cowboys for the next few days."

"Too bad there isn't a U.S. marshal on hand to quell any disturbance that might arise," Rachel remarked, wondering how long Nate could keep his identity a secret if hell broke loose in Dodge.

Then she wondered how long it would be before Nate knew her secret. The unsettling thought caused her to tense on the seat, wishing she could leap off and run for her life. Doc would be in capable hands soon, she reassured herself for the umpteenth time. Dr. Yeager might be getting on in years but he had earned a respected reputation with his patients. He had patched up hundreds of rowdy cowboys who'd been beaten or shot in brawls that constantly erupted on South Side.

After Rachel gave Ludy money to rent hotel rooms, he trotted off. Inhaling a steady breath, Rachel marshaled her composure then half turned on the wagon seat to stare at Nate. "There is something you need to know before you reach Dodge…"

Chapter Thirteen

"**W**hat is it?" Nate questioned caustically. "That you don't plan to hang around much longer? You probably won't believe this, but there actually are a few women who would leap at the chance to marry me."

"Then by all means, let them leap," she countered flippantly. "One would-be wife is as good as another if your intention is to put an end to your father's prearranged engagements."

"You are planning to sneak off again, aren't you?" he asked directly. "If you think you can leave Doc in good hands, you'll be gone."

She waved him off without answering his question. "This is about the three men who mauled and robbed you."

That got his attention. She figured it would.

"Go on."

She inhaled a deep breath, blew it out and said hurriedly, "Their names are Max Rother, Bob Hanes and Warren Lamont."

His eyes widened and his dark brows shot up his forehead in surprise.

"Max is fortyish with a noticeable gap in his teeth and a tall, lean build. Bob is the stocky ruffian with dark, reptilian eyes. He's about your age. Warren is somewhere around twenty-five. He has stringy brown hair and a beanpole physique. They work for a man named Adolph Turner who manages the Dodge City Freight Company."

She braced herself, knowing what Nate was going to ask before he posed the question.

"Mind telling me *how* you know all of this and *why* you're just *now* telling me?" he muttered angrily. "Damn it, Rachel! What the hell is going on?"

"You'll find out soon enough," she assured him as she turned to face straight ahead on the wagon seat.

He clutched her arm, dragging her so close that his lips were only a hairbreadth from hers. "I absolutely hate surprises," he growled. "I want answers and I want them *now!*"

"The lawman in you is bursting at the seams again," she muttered at his forceful tone.

"Get used to it. Now answer the damn question!"

She preferred to kiss him into silence because she figured this would be the last time he'd want her close to him. Once he found out about her fiasco with Adolph and the subsequent thievery, he would toss her in jail.

Despite her apprehension, the impulse to kiss him overwhelmed her. She wrapped her arms around his neck and pressed wantonly against him. She needed to feel the pleasure and excitement that he alone aroused in her. She needed one last taste of him before she flitted away to save him and herself from legal complications and personal embarrassment.

"This better not be your goodbye kiss, angel face," he mumbled huskily, then angled her across his lap to kiss her with so much hungry passion that it made her head spin.

"Don't read so much into it," she murmured evasively. "I happen to like the taste, feel and scent of you. Is there something wrong with that?"

He traced her high cheekbones with his forefinger. "No, because the feeling is mutual." He smiled wryly. "Even without the effects of your special potion."

"You don't need a potion for lust," she insisted, then held her breath, wishing he'd tell her that what he felt for her was something deeper and long lasting. She would have liked to know that he cared before he discovered she was a fugitive whom he'd have to arrest eventually.

"I'm still waiting," he prompted.

"For another kiss? Gladly." She put everything she had into the kiss and felt the pulsating hum of desire vibrating through her.

"Mmm…" he rasped. "You are very distracting, but keep in mind that this conversation is far from over. Just postponed…"

He took her lips with the ardent impatience that always assailed him when he was with Rachel. He glided his arm around her waist, then lifted her so that she was straddling his hips. He wanted her to feel what she did to him, wanted to have her legs wrapped around him, even if this wasn't the time or place to let the hot passion prowling through him run its course.

Groaning in torment, he pressed against her, wanting what he couldn't have. He held the reins in one hand and caressed Rachel's curvaceous body with the other. Desperation tried to overtake him because he was hounded by the unshakable feeling that she was going to leave him. He didn't want her to go. He wanted to know why she was apprehensive and on edge. He wanted to know how she knew the men who had attacked him. Why did she know them by name? Damn it, what else wasn't she telling him?

The questions buzzed through his mind like angry wasps but they couldn't drown out the aching demands of his body. With a growl of frustration, he brushed his cheek over the turgid peaks of her breasts, wishing the fabric of their clothes would dissolve so he could be flesh-to-flesh and heart-to-heart with her.

He suckled her nipples through her shirt and heard her quiet moan. When she arched seductively against him, seeking the ultimate intimacy with him, he growled with barely restrained need.

Damn, this mysterious, alluring woman was driving him a dozen kinds of crazy. He wanted her like hell blazing, but also he wanted to know what she was hiding from him and why she refused to trust him with the truth—

His conflicting thoughts scattered like buckshot when she stroked his erection through the fabric of his breeches. When her hand folded around him, he knew she could feel him throbbing with desire for her.

"I want you desperately," he whispered as he dipped his hand beneath the waistband of her breeches to find her hot, wet and welcoming.

When he slid his fingers inside her, caressing her gently she whispered, "I want you, too. I always have."

She kissed him as if she were dying and he was her last breath. Then she freed him from the placket of his breeches to caress him repeatedly and he swore he was going to black out.

"We need to find a room…and quickly," he said raggedly.

"As soon as Dr. Yeager checks on Doc," she agreed.

Nate's head came up quickly. He heard Rachel mutter

a curse as she climbed off his lap to readjust her clothing. He fastened himself into his breeches and swore profusely.

"You've been here before." He glared at her, daring her to deny it. "You've lived here, haven't you, Rachel?"

She refused to meet his probing gaze. "Everyone knows about Dr. Yeager. He's been here since the fort was established and he was there the day Dodge City was founded—"

"Rachel…" he snapped authoritatively. "What the hell are you hiding?"

"Stop hounding me." She scooted as far away from him as the wagon seat allowed. She crossed her arms over her breasts and thrust out her chin in that stubbornly defiant manner that amused him and exasperated him all at once.

Nate wanted to shake her until her teeth rattled, but if he touched her he predicted he'd become sidetracked again. Damnation, this woman set off so many contradicting feelings inside him that he didn't know which one to deal with first.

"Rachel, I'm trying to protect you. I can help if you tell me—"

"*Protect* me?" she scoffed sarcastically. "You couldn't defend yourself against the three men who robbed you and beat you. But I've managed to elude them for a month without suffering so much as a scratch."

Nate went completely still as he watched her shrink away from him and curse her runaway tongue. Something very dark and dangerous was going on here. Rachel, he presumed, was right smack-dab in the middle of it.

"Rother, Hanes and Lamont are chasing *you?*" he prodded.

She bobbed her head and looked the other way. Clearly, she was upset with herself for blurting out facts that she preferred to keep from him.

"Why are they chasing you?" he demanded.

She didn't answer the question, just bursted out with, "Now do you see why I have been tormented to no end?" Her voice wobbled as she dragged in a fortifying breath. "You wouldn't have been hurt if those scalawags hadn't been combing the area looking for me. I feel guilty about that because I'm indirectly responsible for the assault. Plus, I kept silent when those bastards showed up in Possum Grove. I knew that if they saw me I would be as much at risk as you were, so I detained you by seducing you, and now you're operating under the absurd notion that you are obligated to me, just because you're the first man I've known intimately. *I* refuse to be responsible for altering the course of your life because *you* feel responsible for me!"

They would debate that issue later. Right now, Nate needed facts. All of them. He vowed to be relentless in prying the truth from her.

"What do those men want with you, Rachel?" he demanded sharply.

"If I tell you, I'm not sure you'll believe me," she muttered sourly. "Adolph Turner will have his own version of our confrontation…if he's still alive."

Nate wasn't sure what he expected her to say but that wasn't it. "You've been traveling with Doc's medicine show because you're wanted for murder?" he croaked in disbelief.

She half collapsed on the seat, as if a heavy load had been lifted from her shoulders. Then she inhaled a bracing breath and shrugged noncommittally. "Maybe. I don't know for sure. I left town before I was certain if I killed him."

"We are still talking about the same Turner who manages the Dodge City Freight Company?" he asked, his mind spinning like a windmill.

She nodded jerkily. "Yes, the bastard."

He didn't think this was a good time to tell her that he was here to investigate the drop in profits at the freight company for Edgar Havern and his father-in-law, Julian St. Raimes. This placed Nate in a bit of a predicament. If he sided with Rachel about whatever had happened with Turner, then he'd be inclined to instantly suspect Turner of swindling his investors without gathering necessary evidence. Turner might accuse him of being influenced by the wiles of the very same woman who had injured him.

Unless Turner was dead already and had nothing whatsoever to say in the matter.

Hell and damnation! Nate huffed out his breath and wondered if he'd have to bend the law and pull a few strings to untangle Rachel from the treacherous web surrounding her.

"You better start at the beginning," he requested, frustrated. "Don't leave out a single detail. I need all the facts."

She glanced fretfully at him. Her hands were clenched tightly in front of her and her spine was ramrod stiff. "You can be sure my version won't coincide with Adolph's."

"So you've said. Now spit it out and quit beating around bushes," he ordered. "I'm quickly losing patience."

She didn't speak for a long moment and her gaze skittered away again. He wondered if she was going to bolt and run since they were half a mile from town.

"Rachel," he said coaxingly. "I really need to know what happened so I can help you. I *want* to help you."

She expelled an audible sigh. "I worked for Grantham Boutique. Adolph began pursuing me aggressively after his mistress went flying out the second-story window of one of the hotels."

"Was she shoved or did she take her own life?"

"According to Adolph and his three henchmen, who backed up his story, she was despondent because he called off their affair and withdrew his financial support. She supposedly jumped, but I'm not the only one in town who had a difficult time believing his version.

"Unfortunately, Adolph has enough wealth, influence and leverage with people who owe him money so he can buy loyalty," she added bitterly. "He thinks his power and connections place him above the law."

Now Nate understood why she resented men with money.

"I had been dodging Adolph's advances for a month, but he lured me into the office, claiming Jennifer Grantham had ordered a birthday gift for her ten-year-old daughter, Sophie. I wasn't sure I believed him, but he entered his dark storeroom and pretended to stumble over boxes of merchandise."

Nate swore foully. He couldn't wait to meet Adolph Turner. The bastard was going to pay for tormenting Rachel and forcing her to leave her home and her job and live in constant fear.

"Like a fool I dashed in to see if he needed help. That's when he grabbed me."

He saw her fists clench again, saw her body go rigid.

"He ripped my gown during the attack and I slugged him with my purse."

His brows elevated dubiously. "Your purse?"

"I keep a heavy metal weight from a cuckoo clock inside it for just such emergencies. No one expects to be 'clocked' by a purse. I should have had it with me last night when those drifters harassed me, but I was distracted by the events of the day."

"Then what happened?" he prompted, growing madder

by the minute. Adolph Turner was going to answer for assaulting Rachel, he promised himself resolutely. Somehow or another, despite corroboration from his hired goons, Turner would pay severely for tormenting Rachel.

"Adolph threatened to harm Jennifer and her daughter if I didn't agree to be his mistress. He told me that I wasn't a proper lady so I didn't have to be courted, only claimed."

Nate gnashed his teeth until he practically ground off the enamel. Every time he thought of the torment Rachel had endured he wanted to take Turner apart with his bare hands, then string him up by his neck. If the man wasn't dead already he sure as hell needed to be!

"Adolph grabbed me a second time and I reacted instinctively. I hit him and shoved him backward. He hit his head on the sharp corner of the shelf, then he collapsed. He was bleeding profusely, like Doc, and several heavy items from the shelves fell on him. I didn't try to treat his wound and I didn't hang around to find out if I'd killed him. Not when I knew his thugs were lurking nearby. They had stopped by the office a few minutes earlier."

Nate could understand her unease and uncertainty. The thought of Rachel wanted for murder tormented him to no end.

"I knew I couldn't remain in town, whether Adolph lived or died, because he'd want revenge and his ruthless ruffians would follow his orders. They delight in bullying everyone who gets in their way. So I stole men's clothing to disguise myself."

"The clothes I borrowed from you after I was attacked?"

"Yes. I also took money from his wallet to pay for the gown he ripped. Then I confiscated a horse to make my getaway."

Nate grimaced. For years, he had followed the laws and rules strictly. Now he was contemplating the thought of giving them a twist to suit his purposes. Even better if he could wave his arms and make all charges against her magically disappear.

"If nothing else, you'll be wanted for thievery," he speculated.

Rachel nodded grimly. "I didn't see myself as having much choice at the time. Adolph had threatened to use Jennifer and Sophie as bargaining power against me so I couldn't go to them for help or protection. The less they knew the better for them."

She twisted on the seat to stare intently at him. "I need to leave here," she insisted. "You have an investigation to conduct and I don't want you to end up in the middle of my problems. I shouldn't have confided in you. Like the Granthams, you would have been better off if you didn't know what happened and had no connection to me."

"Don't even think about leaving. I'll help you."

"I can find a way to resolve my problems," she said resolutely. "I don't expect you to be the answer."

"Damn it, Rachel—"

She pressed her index finger to his lips to shush him. "I know you'll check on Doc. I'll contact you by telegram so I can keep updated on his condition."

He removed her hand from his lips. "No. I want you here so I can protect you."

When she twisted around to launch herself off the wagon, he lunged at her. She squirmed for release but he hauled her against him—and refused to let go.

"This is what's best for you," she protested as she wiggled for freedom. "Don't make me hurt you, Nate. I know your ribs are still tender."

"You're staying with me, no matter what the conse-quen—argh!" He yelped in pain when she gouged him in the ribs.

He tried to grab her before she leaped off to dash into the underbrush that lined the dirt road. He'd known she was going to jump ship—or wagon, as the case happened to be.

"You think I won't come after you?" he growled at the darkness at large. "I will, you know. Is that what you want? For me to abandon Doc while I track you down?" He climbed off the wagon and stalked toward the place where she'd disappeared. "You choose, angel face. *You* or *him.*"

He knew she would sacrifice herself for Doc, just as she had refused to contact her friend and employer when Turner threatened her. Sure enough, she appeared from the bushes to glower at him.

"Sometimes I really hate you, Mr. U.S. Marshal," she muttered angrily.

"Yeah. I hate you, too, angel face." He gestured toward the back of the wagon. "Now crawl in the back with Doc and don't poke your head out and risk being recognized, in case worse comes to worst."

She called him a few names, half under her breath. He didn't ask her to repeat them as she stamped to the wagon. Nate climbed onto the seat, then snapped the reins over the horses. He headed to town, just as the sun rose on a city divided by a railroad track that separated the ruffians from the respectable citizens.

As soon as the physician had a chance to examine Doc, Nate planned to find out if Rachel had the notorious dis-tinction of having her sketch on a Wanted poster. Then he was going to find out what had become of Turner.

Nate hoped Turner wasn't dead already because he had a good mind to kill the conniving bastard himself.

* * *

Rachel wasn't sure what sort of reaction she would experience when they drove past the freight company. Anger and resentment bombarded her immediately. Followed by the regret of having had to leave her friends and a job she enjoyed.

She cursed Adolph for ruining her life with his attack and his threats. She cursed him a second time for forcing her to break off contact with her friends. Yet if she hadn't run for her life to escape Adolph, she might not have become intimately acquainted with Nate.

On the other hand, falling in love with Nate would cause inevitable heartbreak. And damn her runaway tongue for blurting out comments that connected her to Dodge City and aroused Nate's suspicions.

Rachel suspected her nagging conscience had seized control of her tongue. Maybe she had secretly wanted to confide in Nate so he would understand her need for another hasty departure. But nothing had worked out as she had planned. Plus, Nate had made her choose between running away and ensuring that Doc received immediate medical attention.

The wagon came to a halt, then shifted as Nate climbed down. "I'm going to find Ludy and Dr. Yeager. Sit tight," he murmured as he strode past her hiding place in the wagon.

Pensively, she studied Doc's pale features and contemplated how Nate was going to deal with her crimes when he had taken an oath to uphold the law. She cared too much about him to complicate his life and jeopardize his reputation as a lawman.

The honest truth was that she *wanted* to feel that she could trust and rely on Nate, when she hadn't allowed herself to trust any other man. She hoped that by placing her faith in Nate he didn't betray her. If he did eventually, he might as well drive a stake through her heart while he was at it.

A few minutes later she shrank back when Nate opened the canvas cover that prevented dust from rolling into the back of the wagon. "Did you find Ludy?" she asked quietly.

Nate nodded his auburn head. "He's bringing the stretcher. We'll put Doc in the infirmary behind the physician's office. Then Dr. Yeager will have a look at him." He tossed her satchel to her. "You might want to grab your cap and vest to better conceal your identity until I find out if there are Wanted posters distributed around town."

Rachel fished into her bag to retrieve the vest and cap, then tucked in her hair. Keeping her head down, she discreetly watched the gray-haired physician approach the wagon.

"What happened?" Dr. Yeager asked as Nate and Ludy carefully loaded Doc on the stretcher.

"He fell down the side of a steep hill, then slammed his head against a few boulders," Nate reported. "We stitched up the wound and gave him a sedative, but he hasn't regained consciousness since the accident."

Dr. Yeager pried open Doc's eyelids to have a closer look. "How long has he been out?"

"At least eight hours," Ludy replied. "He's a doctor. Not that it's doing him any good right now."

Dr. Yeager glanced at the wagon logo that advertised patented medicines, then he scoffed. "Right. *That* kind of doctor is no doctor at all."

Rachel wanted to leap to Doc's defense, but she clamped her mouth shut and let Nate and Ludy deal with the situation.

"Doc Grant is a certified physician," Nate explained. "He's been making it his mission to inform patients in small communities of the vices of relying on tonics and elixirs, instead of consulting a doctor. He examines injured and ailing patients in his traveling clinic."

Dr. Yeager raised his bushy gray brows, then glanced from Doc to Nate. "Truly? Glad to hear someone has taken it upon himself to spread the word."

"But he can't help patients in the outlying area until we get him back on his feet," Nate remarked.

Rachel watched the men carry Doc away. Her stomach growled so she grabbed a few crackers from the tin box. Then she poked her head around the opening—and nearly choked on her cracker when she saw none other than Adolph Turner swagger from Four Queens Hotel to enter a nearby restaurant.

"Well, that answers that question," she mumbled as the arrogant bastard disappeared from sight. "At least I'm not wanted for murder. That's a relief."

Or was it? The fact that Adolph had survived the fracas and had sent his goons in search of her indicated that he craved personal revenge. Rachel cringed. She could well imagine what sort of punishment Adolph had in mind. Lecherous, unscrupulous scoundrel that he was.

She nearly pitched from the back of the wagon when someone—she couldn't see who, since her view was blocked—led the horses around the corner. Then Ludy appeared.

"I rented rooms at the Four Queens. It's supposed to be the best accommodations in town." He retrieved her satchels, as well as his own. "Grab Nate's knapsack, will you? He's going to take a stroll through town to check for those men who attacked him before he catches a nap."

Rachel hoped Nate didn't meet up with those heartless scalawags. He couldn't use the power of his position as a federal marshal to jail his assailants if he planned to conduct a discreet investigation. She frowned when she recalled that he hadn't said which business he was investigating.

Shrugging off the curious thought, she hopped to the ground, then hunched over to ensure that no one recognized her. She glanced down the street to see that Grantham Boutique had yet to open for business. The urge to contact Jennifer tempted her, but she followed in Ludy's wake to enter the hotel. She nodded gratefully when he handed her a room key.

"We'd like hot water for our baths," Ludy requested.

The hotel keeper nodded his shiny bald head and smiled when Ludy offered him a generous tip. "Coming right up, sir."

Only when Rachel locked herself inside her room did she breathe a sigh of relief. She had vowed never to return to Dodge. Yet here she was. In the end, she hadn't been able to leave Doc behind. In addition, she hadn't been able to walk away from her fierce attraction to Nate, and she had confided the incident with Adolph, even though it placed Nate in the awkward position of harboring a fugitive.

She jumped, startled, when a loud rap resounded on the door. "Who's there?" she said in her best masculine voice.

"Water brigade."

Rachel grabbed her pistol—just in case. Thankfully, only a trio of teenage boys toted water to the brass tub, which stood behind an elegantly decorated dressing screen.

Bath and a nap. Ah, my idea of heaven, she mused as

she locked the door, then peeled off her boots and breeches.

Another knock rattled the door hinges. "Now what?"

"It's Nate. Open up."

Rachel didn't bother with breeches, just stood behind the door so no passersby would get an eyeful and realize she wasn't the young boy she pretended to be.

"Good news, I—" Nate's voice fizzled out when he noticed her bare legs protruding from the long hem of her shirt. His gaze roamed over her and desire flickered in his blue eyes.

"What's the good news?" she prompted.

"You aren't wanted for murder or thievery. Let's celebrate…"

Rachel didn't object when he scooped her up in his arms, then wheeled around to lock the door. The rakish grin on Nate's handsome face wiped all thought from her head and she forgot to ask what Dr. Yeager had to say about Doc's condition.

"There's nothing I'd like better than to finish what we started on the wagon seat before dawn," she assured him as she snuggled against his broad chest.

"You read my mind, angel face."

"Glad to hear that we're of the same mind, Mr. Marshal."

"And very soon, of the same body…if you let me have my way with you…" he growled seductively.

Chapter Fourteen

Nate couldn't control the ardent desperation that sizzled through him as he laid Rachel on the bed, then stretched out beside her. The tormenting feeling that he was going to lose her kept haunting him. It also prompted him to spend every spare minute with her. She had tried to leave him the previous night and again this morning. The feeling of emptiness that had overwhelmed him earlier still nagged at him, and all that held it at bay was losing himself in her completely.

"I swear you've become my hopeless addiction," he whispered against her satiny skin. "I can't seem to get enough of you."

She moaned softly as his hands swept over the peaks of her breasts, then down the concave curve of her belly. She strained toward his caresses, leaving him feeling all-powerful in his control over her. But only when it came to the passion that always exploded between them, he reminded himself. The rest of the time Rachel was his unfaltering, independent-minded equal. Yet when she was with him, like this, she responded without restraint, as if she were as hungry and desperate for him as he always was for her.

Lightning crackled through his bloodstream as she moved sensuously against him. When he tugged away her clothing to circle her nipples with his tongue, she whispered his name achingly. When he suckled her and kneaded her soft skin, she gasped and inched toward him again. Her wild, restless movements triggered hot, reckless sensations inside him.

His unruly body demanded instant pleasure, but he refused to be selfish. Other men had tried to make this spirited beauty their conquest, but Rachel was more than that to Nate. He couldn't be satisfied unless she was aching for him to the same mindless degree that he ached for her.

He spread a path of moist kisses from her breasts to her rib cage. He felt her shiver beneath his lips and fingertips. His hand drifted down her hip, then swirled over her inner thighs. Feeling the wet heat of her desire against his knuckles, his body clenched with barely restrained need. He ached to bury himself inside her, but he denied himself again.

His tongue swept into her mouth at the exact moment that he slid his figure inside the hot, slick channel between her legs. He groaned aloud, wanting her but waiting until she was shimmering helplessly with her need for him. When her body shuddered around his fingertip and she arched toward his hand, he felt his resistance give way. The warm rain of her desire for him was almost more temptation than he could bear.

"Nate…ahh…" she said hoarsely as she tried to pull him above her. "I need you…"

"And I need all of you," he insisted as he made his way down her shapely body, one caress and kiss at a time.

He dipped his finger inside her again and felt the honey fire of her response burning him, luring him closer.

"Stop—" her voice shattered as she shimmered around his fingertip.

"Not until I've had my fill of tasting you."

When he lowered his head to trace the dewy petals of her feminine body, he felt the last of his restraint crumble. Primal instinct sank in its sharp claws as he suckled her. She cried out his name on ragged spurts of breath and she dug her nails into his shoulders.

"Come here…please…" she whispered achingly.

When she looked at him with such wild need in those dark, hypnotic eyes, he moved on her command. He swore he'd ripped a couple of buttons off his shirt in his haste to shed his clothes so he could sink into her soft flesh.

Nate groaned when she folded her hand around his arousal and guided him to her. When she wrapped her legs around his hips, then pressed ever closer, he plunged into her, thrusting hard and deep—and tried to tell himself to be gentle. Unfortunately, his throbbing body was paying no attention whatsoever to the message sent down by his brain.

Sensual pleasure cascaded over him as Rachel matched the rhythmic strains of his body. Hot, pulsating need pounded through him as passion sent them spiraling through time and space. Brain-scrambling rapture whirled around him as sensations expanded, converged, then exploded upon him. Nate thrust against her and she clung as tightly to him as he did to her. Together they rode on the turbulent winds of ecstasy.

For a few seconds—or a few centuries, Nate wasn't sure which—he drifted in a fuzzy blur of amazing pleasure. He struggled to draw breath as he collapsed on Rachel and tried to summon the strength and the will to move.

"Are you okay?" he questioned as he nuzzled his chin against the rapid pulsations of her neck.

"Better than okay," she said with a ragged sigh. "I wanted to leave—"

"I know," he cut in. "I'm glad you didn't."

He felt her smile against his shoulder. "Me, too. For now at least. But if things don't go—"

"Sh-sh-sh," he murmured. "Let me use my authority to handle this situation. You saved my life. Let me return the favor. Okay? Just stay out of sight."

She nodded hesitantly, then asked, "How's Doc?"

"Dr. Yeager gave him some medication and said the next six to eight hours would tell the tale. He thinks there's some internal hemorrhaging and maybe a skull fracture."

"God, I hope my scheme to break him from drinking that fifty-proof elixir doesn't cost him his life."

Nate kissed her into silence, then said, "You don't have to carry the burden of whatever goes wrong in someone else's life, you know."

She gazed up at him, tormented. "No? You were injured because of me and so was Doc. I hope Jennifer and Sophie didn't suffer when Adolph tried to wrest information about me from them.

"I saw him earlier," she added, and he could feel tension coiling inside her. "He exited this hotel. After visiting his new mistress, no doubt."

Nate eased down beside her and wrapped her protectively in his arms. "I'll deal with Turner and I'll enjoy every minute of it."

"I want my turn at him," she said in a vindictive tone. "He changed the course of my life."

"I mean it, Rachel," he said intently. "You need to stay out of sight until we sort this out. Promise me that you'll stay here so I'll know you're safe."

"In this room?" She rolled her eyes at him. "I'll go crazy."

He grinned as he leaned over to kiss her, then waggled his eyebrows suggestively. "I can think of a few ways to occupy and distract you."

"I never imagined myself as a man's mistress," she grumbled.

"Think of it in terms of being my future wife," he suggested.

He felt the need to make love with her again, because the look she gave him made him wonder if she planned to duck out of town when he cleared her name. He didn't want her planning her next escape attempt, so he distracted her with heated kisses and caresses.

He predicted she would accuse him of manipulating her with sexual pleasure, but the truth was he kept feeling he was going to lose her, and he was desperate to savor the feelings and sensations she summoned from him. Rachel was fast becoming so much a part of his life that he couldn't recall what his existence had been like without her spicing it up, complicating it and satisfying a longing that only she seemed capable of fulfilling...

That was his last sane thought before she set her hands and lips upon him. The world spun off its axis, flinging him into a dizzying universe brimming with inexpressible pleasure.

It was midafternoon before Rachel woke up to find herself naked and alone in bed. She shook her head, dismayed by her complete lack of self-control where Nate was concerned. He had walked into her room and pushed her past the point of no return—not once but twice. She had barely regained enough mental capability to remember to ask about Doc's condition.

The urge to check on Doc was nearly overwhelming.

What if he didn't survive? He'd been so furious with her and he'd fallen off the cliff. No matter how much Nate tried to console her, she knew it was her fault that he was injured and unconscious.

The tormenting thought made her restless and on edge. She made use of the water left in the tub to refresh herself, then dressed. She paced the confines of the room for several minutes, pausing at regular intervals to keep surveillance on the freight office. She stopped breathing momentarily when she saw Adolph's three ruffians swagger into the office. Damn it, she had hoped the men were still wandering the countryside in search of her. The thought of the goons recognizing Nate and disposing of him before he pointed an accusing finger at them unnerved her. They must have stolen his badge, along with his clothing, so they knew he was a federal marshal.

Rachel blew out an agitated breath. Surely Nate didn't expect her to hole up in this room indefinitely. She was accustomed to activity. He knew that. And because he did, he shouldn't expect her to sit here twiddling her thumbs when she wanted to check on Doc and alert Nate that she had seen the three henchmen in town.

"Where are you, Nate?" she muttered. "If you aren't back here in five minutes, I'm gone."

Nate strode from the city marshal's office, then scowled to himself. He'd wanted to file charges against Turner's goons, but clearly Turner had Marshal Peterson in his pocket. Seth Peterson had rattled off several excuses as to why that wasn't a good idea. No doubt, the marshal was paid to look the other way when it came to Turner's underhanded dealings.

According to Rachel, the three men were hired to

strong-arm customers into paying their high-interest loans—or else. Nate had seen the tactic used dozens of times. It didn't take a genius to realize that Turner, like other businessmen in a town that had yet to establish a bank, loaned money and extended credit so he could set high-interest rates.

Nate had a pretty good idea why Edgar Havern and his parter's investments weren't paying expected dividends. Adolph Turner was embezzling money and charging high interest that he collected for himself. It was no wonder he'd become wealthy—at his investors' and his customers' expense.

After posing questions to several business owners, who didn't mind discussing their dislike for Turner's practices, Nate had a good picture of the freight manager's stranglehold on unsuspecting customers who accepted his loans. Armed with that knowledge, Nate headed for the freight office to pick up the package his brother, Ethan, had sent to him.

Nate was halfway down the street when he heard, "Psttt!" coming from the shadows of the alley. He scowled when he saw Rachel—dressed in her mannish disguise—flagging him down.

"I came to tell you that I saw the henchmen enter Turner's office," she reported.

"Didn't I make it clear to you to *wait in the room?*" he muttered irritably.

She flicked her wrist dismissively. "You know me better than that."

"Yes, I do. What was I thinking? I should have handcuffed you to the bedpost."

She frowned darkly. "Not if you know what's good for you."

He smiled roguishly. "I can think of other reasons that staking you out might be interesting."

An impish grin quirked her Cupid's-bow lips and a chunk of his heart broke off and rattled down his rib cage. He stared into that beguiling face, which was smudged with soot to conceal her identity, and felt all-too-familiar feelings and sensations channel through every part of his being.

"I can picture *you* staked out as you were when I first found you," she replied. "I'm surprised I didn't think of tying you up and making my escape. It must be because I've been distracted by the thought of Turner and his thugs scouring the countryside to have their revenge on me."

Nate curled his forefinger beneath her chin and lifted her lips to his kiss. "Revenge is the *last* thing I want from you, angel face. No matter what else happens, don't forget that."

When he lifted his head, she wiped away the smudge of soot transferred from her cheek to his during the steamy kiss. "Nate, I—" She compressed her lips for a moment, then added, "I don't want you hurt on my account so please be careful what you say and do while you're around Adolph. He is ruthless and far more intelligent than his goons."

"I will. Now, go back to the room. And one more thing."

She cast him a withering glance. "What is it this time?"

"*Stay* in your room. *Please.*"

He wasn't sure that adding *please* appeased her dislike of being ordered around. Although Nate was accustomed to giving orders and enforcing them, spouting commands at Rachel almost never worked.

She pulled a face. "You expect too much of me."

He gave her "the look" that he'd used on fugitives

dozens of times in the past. "Don't make me use the power and authority of my federal badge on you," he warned.

As expected, she thrust out her chin rebelliously. "Don't try it, Montgomery. Not unless you have that badge pinned on your chest and a warrant for my arrest in your pocket."

As if they were two gunfighters squaring off at twenty paces, they stared each other down. Nate knew he wasn't going to drag this feisty termagant to jail to keep her out of trouble. If Turner got wind of it, he would use his influence over Marshal Peterson to take the law into his own hands.

However, Nate was seriously considering handcuffs on the bedposts to keep track of Rachel. Of course, he would have to catch her and drag her, cursing, kicking and screaming, to the Four Queens Hotel. That would draw unwanted attention and word would get back to Turner.

"You could use me for bait," she suggested. "We could draw Adolph and his men out—"

He waved her off in midsentence. "No, absolutely not. I sent a telegram to my brother earlier this week, asking him to send a package of clothes and supplies. I'm on my way to Turner's office to pick it up right now."

"You can't go in there yet," she insisted. "I want to make sure the goons aren't around before you go inside."

The possibility of Rachel being recognized and overtaken made his blood run cold. "I want you to marry me right now," he blurted.

She blinked, stunned by his abrupt change of topic. "Why right now?"

He wasn't sure. It just popped out of his mouth. "Think about it, Rachel. Married to a U.S. marshal—"

"I've thought about it before and I think it would be detrimental to your position," she interrupted. "People will think I'm using you for protection and hiding behind your badge."

"Is that so bad?"

"Yes, I refuse to use manipulation."

"Even if it ensures that Turner goes down in flames and he takes his henchmen with him?" he countered.

She lifted a perfectly arched black brow. "You mean sort of like you running interference for me while I return the favor by blocking your father's marriage machinations for you?"

"Yeah, something like that. We can visit the justice of the peace and say, 'I do,' in five minutes." He didn't know why he was pushing her so hard. Maybe because she kept resisting and he took it as a personal challenge. Maybe because he didn't want her to find out that he had the kind of financial backing that she considered detestable. Hell, he made Adolph Turner look like a pauper. Nate preferred she didn't know the truth until she was legally tied to him.

What am I talking about? Nate asked himself suddenly. When had he decided that he did want to be married? He liked his freedom. Yet, the thought of having no emotional connection to Rachel when this case ended disturbed him greatly. *She* disturbed him. She made him wish for things he had never considered important to his life and his happiness—until now.

"No, absolutely not." She threw his earlier comment right back in his face. "I'm not what you need, Nate."

"That should be my decision," he countered.

She shrugged evasively, pulled her cap low on her forehead, then pivoted on her heels. He cursed her stubbornness as she disappeared into the back alley behind the barbershop.

Nate muttered in exasperation while he waited for

Rachel to return with the all-clear signal that the henchmen had left and Turner was alone. She returned a moment later to gesture toward the front of the office.

Anger roiled through him when he saw the three men, who had beaten him and stole his belongings, saunter outside. Too bad he'd taken an oath years ago to follow the law. He easily could be persuaded to make an exception when dealing with these bastards. Turner included.

When Rother, Lamont and Hanes mounted their horses and trotted off, Nate strode down the boardwalk. It was going to take considerable acting ability to confront Turner and pretend he didn't want to kill him for trying to abuse Rachel.

And damn it to hell, why would she think he would ever take the conniving scoundrel's word over hers?

Ah, yes, he mused. She believed money talked, and she had little faith and trust in men. The curse of wealth and the misuse of power and influence disgusted her. He wondered what it would take to convince Rachel that all men with money weren't the scourges of the earth.

Despite Nate's insistence that she should hide in the hotel, Rachel detoured to the back door of Dr. Yeager's infirmary. Since the physician wasn't on hand, Rachel eased down on the edge of Doc's bed. She glanced sideways, noting that another man—in his late thirties, perhaps—was asleep in the bed near the door that opened into Dr. Yeager's examination office. She noticed the man had a black eye and several cuts on his head and face. It looked as if he had taken a beating.

Rachel's attention swung back to Doc and she combed her fingers through the tuft of blond hair poking from the bandage that encircled his head. He was so pale and motionless that it tormented her beyond words.

Your fault! The accusing voice deep inside her scolded. She clutched Doc's lifeless hand in hers and gave it a comforting squeeze, willing him to respond. He didn't. She hated seeing him lying there like this. He, of course, probably wanted it this way.

"Damn you," she muttered at him. "I don't want you to rejoin Margie yet. I suppose I can't blame you for the way you feel, but I want to keep you here for a good long while. You have so much to offer the world, Doc. You're the father I never had. You've looked out for me, cared about me. And I care about you, too."

Sentimental tears trickled from her eyes as she doubled over to press a kiss to his pallid cheek. "Don't you dare give up, Doc."

When the other male patient groaned, Rachel went to check on him. He was trying to reach the glass of water sitting on the end table. Rachel held it to his lips so he could drink.

"What happened to you?" she questioned softly.

"Turner's men," he mumbled groggily. "They roughed me up when I couldn't pay on my loan."

The information made Rachel swear under her breath. When the man drifted back to sleep, she rose to her feet, then exited the same way she had entered. She lingered in the alley, wavering with indecision. She was tempted to pay a backdoor visit to the boutique to insure Jennifer hadn't suffered because of Rachel's conflict with Adolph.

Later, she promised herself as she glanced toward the Four Queens Hotel. She had another matter to attend while Nate was making Adolph's acquaintance and collecting the belongings his brother sent him.

A feeling of relief settled over Rachel as she scuttled down the alley. Having Nate believe she was innocent of wrongdoing in her conflict with Adolph endeared him to her even more than before. He had accepted her at her word. Yet, she wondered if he'd waver if Adolph offered his twisted version of the truth.

And what, she wondered, had lit a fire under Nate to start harping about marriage so suddenly? She knew he couldn't possibly love her.

She suspected his overactive sense of protectiveness was hounding him. Protecting people from harm was what he did. She was just another duty to him. That and the fact that he felt obligated because she might be carrying his child. The thought unsettled her. She had enough to deal with right now without contemplating that possibility.

Rachel cast aside her concerns to focus on her next order of business. Then she moved swiftly down the hall of the hotel.

The moment Nate clapped eyes on the fashionably dressed Adolph Turner, his fists curled reflexively. He appraised the gray-eyed man with brown wavy hair who looked to be his age, or thereabouts. Nate was itching to deliver a punishing blow that left the tall, arrogant freight manager sprawled unceremoniously on the floor.

"May I help you?" Turner asked, as he looked Nate up and down with a critical eye. "You must be new in town. I don't recall seeing you before. I make it my business to know as many people as possible."

"How friendly of you," Nate said flippantly. "My name is Montgomery. Nate Montgomery." *Remember it, you son of a bitch, because I'm coming for you very soon.* "I'm expecting a package from Kansas City."

"Montgomery," Turner murmured thoughtfully as he

turned on his well-shod heels to check the paperwork in his office. "I'll see if I have information…"

His voice trailed off when he glanced back to note that Nate was following as closely as his own shadow. Nate arched a brow in pretended innocence. In truth, he wanted a look at the bastard's office, his ledgers and the storeroom where Turner had pounced on Rachel.

The thought sent another wave of annoyance pulsating through him. It took a great deal of willpower not to double his fist and knock Turner's teeth down his throat.

Bide your time, Montgomery, he cautioned himself. *You have a case to investigate.*

"Ah, yes, here it is." Turner tapped his index finger against the official-looking paper. "The freight arrived last night on the train. I'll fetch it for you."

When Turner sauntered over to open the door to the storeroom, Nate leaned his shoulder against the doorjamb to survey the shelves lined with goods, packages and wooden crates. He could visualize the lecherous bastard mistreating Rachel and the thought made his blood boil.

"How long have you been operating this business?" Nate asked to divert his attention from the impulsive desire to ram Turner broadside and slam his head into the sharp corner of the shelf.

"Since we opened in '72," Turner replied as he searched through the merchandise.

"Do you own the business?" Nate asked conversationally, knowing damn well the scoundrel didn't.

"More or less. I have a few insignificant investors."

Insignificant? Nate silently smirked. Not hardly!

"Ah, here it is." Turner swaggered over to drop the heavy package in Nate's arms. "Are you employed in town, Mr. Montgomery?"

"I'm looking for work."

"You might try the railroad depot. Ralph Bowman is a friend of mine. I can put in a good word for you."

Probably a partner in crime, thought Nate.

"He might give you a job loading and unloading equipment and livestock in the railroad cars. Useless drifters are always walking off the job and leaving him shorthanded."

"Thanks for the tip."

Turner smiled broadly, then clamped his hand on Nate's shoulder, as if they were close friends. Nate resisted the urge to bite off the bastard's long, bony fingers.

"If you find yourself short of funds and need a loan, come see me. I can help you set up housekeeping for twenty-five percent on your loan."

Nate smirked. "The going rate at the general store is only four percent."

Turner smiled like the shark he was. "Perhaps, but I'm offering cash advances that you can't acquire at clothing stores, blacksmith shops or general stores. Money buys the primal pleasures a man needs to make working worthwhile. It also pays for room and board, don't you agree?"

"Where might I find the finer things?"

"As it happens, I own The White Elephant Saloon on South Side. Several of the barmaids rent upstairs rooms to scratch a man's itch when he's in need."

"And you get a cut of their take?" Nate presumed. "How enterprising of you. Maybe I should apply your technique to establish myself in town."

Turner's smile evaporated in one second flat. "There is one thing you should know, friend. I'm not enthusiastic about competition. This town is mine and I plan to keep it that way."

Nate flung up his hand. "No offense, Turner. I don't

want to get off on the wrong foot with you. After all, I might find myself in need of a loan to get started in town."

"Anytime, Montgomery. I look forward to doing business with you."

And I'm looking forward to seeing you behind bars, you slimy bastard, Nate replied silently.

He spun on his boot heels, then walked from the office, carrying his survival kit—of sorts—from his brother. Most of the time, he didn't make much of the fact that his family had scads of money. However, there were times, like now, when he wanted to put the cocky, pseudoelite barons of western society—like Turner—in their place.

Nate agreed wholeheartedly with Rachel. Men like Turner, who craved power and influence and flaunted their wealth turned his stomach. Turner didn't give back to society. He was the leech who sucked the life right out of it.

Chapter Fifteen

"Jennifer?" Rachel called softly from the back door of the boutique.

The moment she stepped inside, she realized how much she missed the shop and her friendship with Jen, who was as independent-minded and self-reliant as Rachel was.

She inched farther inside the back door, past the bolts of fabric shipped and delivered from the freight office. The thought reminded her of Adolph and she scowled resentfully. If life were fair—and she knew for a fact that it wasn't—that devil would receive his due. She hoped she lived to see the day Adolph answered for his corrupt business practices and his degrading treatment of women.

Rachel smiled triumphantly when she recalled the recent conversation she'd had with Adolph's present mistress. There was one woman who wouldn't be pitched out a two-story window, Rachel assured herself.

"Jen?" Rachel called out again as she tiptoed through the sewing room where she had spent countless hours working and conversing with her friend.

She craned her neck around the corner into the shop and waved her arm to call attention to herself.

"What are you doing back there, young man," Jennifer demanded when she mistook Rachel for a scruffy waif from the streets.

Rachel tugged her cap from her head and pulled the pins from her hair. Jennifer's eyes nearly popped from their sockets when Rachel's raven tresses tumbled around her shoulders in frothy disarray.

"Dear God!" Jennifer croaked as she dashed forward to bustle Rachel into the sewing room. "Where have you been all this time? What happened to you? I've been worried sick. And why the devil didn't you let me know where you were? Have you been masquerading as a boy in town all this time? *Why?*"

"Good to see you again, too." Laughter bubbled from Rachel's lips as she gave the petite blonde an affectionate hug. "Lord, I've missed you and Sophie."

"Then why did you leave?" Jen demanded. "I've tried to replace you three times, but no one can match your creativity and your work ethic. You would be surprised how many lazy women are lounging around this town!"

Rachel poked her head around the corner to ensure no one had entered the shop to overhear her. "Adolph Turner tried to attack me the night I fled from town."

"That scoundrel!" she said with an angry hiss.

"When I pushed him away, he fell and hit his head. Then several heavy objects tumbled from the shelves and landed on him. I didn't know if he survived, but either way, I had to leave town. I couldn't confide in you because he vowed he'd mistreat you and Sophie if I didn't become his mistress."

Jennifer muttered a few unladylike oaths to Adolph's

name, then said, "So that's why that ogre visited my shop last week. He came under the pretense of buying jewelry for his new lady friend."

Rachel wondered if the necklace she noticed Adolph's mistress wearing during their earlier conversation was a gift from him. Probably.

"Then he asked about you," Jen went on to say.

"I'm most grateful I had the good sense not to involve you. He might have tried to use Sophie as bargaining power to force you to tell him where I was."

Jennifer gritted her teeth. "I intensely dislike that arrogant jackal. But if he harmed one hair on Sophie's head I'd have to kill him."

"You'd have to stand in line," Rachel muttered resentfully. "I get first crack at him. Luckily, I met a federal marshal who is in town to investigate the situation. Until charges are brought against Adolph, I have to remain in disguise."

Jennifer nodded determinedly. "Adolph won't hear anything about you from me, you can count on it. When this is all over, are you coming back to the shop? I'm having difficulty keeping up with demands. Several of our customers have been asking after you."

Learning that she could return to her job and renew her friendship was a gigantic relief. She needed something to look forward to when Nate left town to resume his official duties.

"Mama? Where are you?"

Rachel glanced around the open door to see Sophie, the spitting image of her attractive mother, skipping through the shop.

"Back here, honey. I have a surprise for you."

Sophie skidded to a halt, blinked her big blue eyes

owlishly, then threw herself into Rachel's arms. "Where have you been? Mama and I didn't know what happened to you. Why are you dressed in boy's clothes? Are you coming back to work with us?"

Like mother like daughter, Rachel thought as she hugged the spirited ten-year old. "I missed you, too. I'll be back to work very soon, not to worry. I just have one minor problem to resolve first."

Adolph was a *major* problem and a *major* pain but Sophie didn't need to know that.

Sophie clutched Rachel's hand and hung on tightly. "I'm ever so glad you're coming back." She turned her attention to Jennifer. "I'm hungry, Mama. When can we have supper?"

Rachel twisted her hair into a bun, put the pins in place, then crammed her cap on her head. She knew it was Jen's practice to escort Sophie to her evening meal at one of the local restaurants. In the past, Rachel had tended the shop, but these days Jen had to close down for an hour.

"I'll be around town," Rachel promised as she turned to leave.

"You better be. If you need anything, you know you can count on me."

Impulsively, she lurched back around to give Jen and Sophie another hug. Then she strode out the back door. It was reassuring to know she could make a life for herself after Nate left. And he would, because that's what men did, she reminded herself. Even if she had agreed to marry Nate—and she had more sense than to do that—he still would be all over the countryside, tracking criminals.

At least she had discovered what heaven felt like for a short while, she consoled herself as she scurried down the alley to check on Doc again. When she darted onto the boardwalk, she saw Adolph striding toward her. Rachel's heart nearly beat her to death as she ducked her head and hunched her shoulders to shield her face. Adolph strutted past her, his nose in the air. A frown puckered his sharp features. She wondered if he'd come from the hotel to discover that his mistress had skipped town.

A wicked smile pursed her lips as she scuttled away. If she had managed to ruin Adolph's evening she would be immensely happy.

Adolph jerked open the door to the freight office, then cursed sourly. He had trotted over to the hotel during his supper break to visit his mistress. To his disbelief and outrage, she had cleaned out the room he'd rented for her and had vanished without a word of explanation. He had questioned the hotel clerk who'd informed him that the traitorous bitch had come downstairs with her luggage and caught the afternoon stage west. She hadn't left a note of explanation, either.

"How dare she!" Adolph growled as he jerked off his hat and slammed it down on the counter.

He had paid good money to have that whore at his beck and call. He had given her gifts for her to flaunt in front of her counterparts. Then she had betrayed him by leaving without so much as a by-your-leave. What the hell had gotten into her?

Still fuming, Adolph stormed into his office. Nothing was going right. His former mistress had tried to blackmail him when she'd found out he was withholding profits from the investors. He had dealt severely with her. Then Rachel St. Raimes and his present mistress had disappeared suddenly. Muttering, Adolph grabbed his ledger off the desk and tried to concentrate on business. It was impossible when he wanted to begin a search for another harlot to accommodate his voracious appetite.

Too bad he didn't have Rachel in captivity. He could take out his frustration on her. "And I *will* when I get my hands on you," he vowed to the taunting vision floating above him.

"Where the hell have you been, damn it!" Nate scowled when Rachel finally returned to her room.

"Hello to you, too, dear," she said with sticky-sweet sarcasm.

Nate huffed out an agitated breath and gestured toward the tray. "I brought supper, and you are not supposed to be gallivanting around town until I've gathered enough evidence to place Turner under arrest."

She peeled off her cap and shook out the shiny raven tendrils. Nate was tempted to comb his fingers through those rich strands, but he refrained from reaching for her because he knew he didn't have enough self-control to stop after one casual touch.

"Do you like Adolph as much as I do?" she asked.

"I hate him. Every time I thought of what he tried to do to you I wanted to strangle him, then shoot him a couple of times for good measure. Plus, the shyster offered to loan me money at twenty-five percent. That didn't set well, either."

She glanced at the large box sitting on her bed, then frowned. "Your belongings? Why didn't you put them in your room?"

"I gave up my room because I'm staying here with you." He stared her down, daring her to object. "I'm not taking any chances of Turner getting wind of your presence in town and coming after you."

She ambled over to remove the cover on the plate of food, then smiled appreciatively. "This food looks wonderful and I'm starved. Thank you, Nate."

"You're welcome. Do not leave the room again without telling me where I can find you. It makes me nervous."

"Can't have that, can we?"

All the worry and concern that had hounded him during her unexplained absence faded away when she playfully plunked down on his lap at the table. Then she showered him with smacking kisses, and he savored every moment of her unexpected display of affection.

Something about her demeanor had changed since he'd seen her earlier. He didn't know why, but he approved of her lighthearted mood and impish smiles. He should lecture her about taking unnecessary risks of being discovered. Instead, he kissed her and ran his hands over the lush curves and swells that were concealed beneath the baggy men's clothing.

"Mmm…much better than supper," he murmured between arousing kisses. "Unfortunately, I have business to conduct after dark so this will have to wait until later."

"What sort of business?" she questioned as she wiggled her hip provocatively against his arousal.

"Stop that. I can't think straight." She did it again to torment him—and he loved every minute of it. "I'm going to sneak into Turner's office to retrieve his business ledger."

"Why?" she questioned, distracted.

"Because he's the one I was sent here to investigate."

Her brows rose sharply and a pleased smile spread across her lips. "Glad to hear it. I hope he turns out to be as guilty as original sin."

"He's more than tripled the interest on customers' loans

and I suspect he's pocketing one-third for himself. Also, I wouldn't be surprised if he isn't claiming damaged merchandise as a loss to his investors, then reselling it for his own profits. All with the help of his cohort, Bowman, from the train depot. I've seen similar scams used several times before."

Rachel gave him one last lingering kiss, then eased from his lap to take the other chair. "When his business falls to pieces and he has nowhere to turn for consolation, I'll be satisfied to some extent, at least."

Nate frowned warily as he watched her munch on the tender braised beef, green peas and sweet bread he'd purchased for their meal. "What does that mean?"

"I paid a visit to his new mistress this afternoon," she said between bites. "I assured her that Adolph's former mistress had been shoved out the window and that she should leave town before the same thing happened to her."

"And she said?" he prompted.

"'I'm gone'," she reported. "I gave her money to buy a stagecoach ticket to Colorado. More accurately, I gave her some bank notes that had come from Adolph's wallet, so he was the one who put her on the stagecoach. Also, I told her to drop my name to Hubert Solomon, owner of the Golden Goose Saloon in Leadville. She tossed her belongings in her satchels and hurried off." Rachel grinned mischievously. "I passed Adolph on the street a few minutes ago while he was returning to his office so I know he knows his mistress skipped town."

"What!" Nate hooted in outrage.

She crammed a piece of sweet bread in his mouth to make him pipe down. "Relax, he didn't recognize me. He usually ignores everyone he thinks is beneath his elevated position in society."

"But what if he had?" Nate growled around the mouthful of tasty bread.

She grinned and batted her big brown eyes at him. "Then I'd run straight to you for protection, of course."

He scoffed. Rachel prided herself in resolving her own problems. And that worried the hell out of him, especially when it came to dealing with a treacherous bastard like Adolph Turner.

"You should let me retrieve Adolph's financial ledger," she suggested. "You don't have a warrant, do you?"

"No, but—"

"Then it's settled. I'll fetch it while I'm still in disguise."

"*No.*" His stern voice brooked no argument. He'd wasted his breath.

"*Yes.* I want to do what I can to help you bring a solid case against him."

"Rachel—" he said warningly.

She leaned across the small round table to kiss him into silence. Somehow, he found the willpower to clutch her shoulders and hold her an arm's length away. "I couldn't live with myself if something happened to you."

"You're sweet to say so," she murmured.

"I am not sweet." He gnashed his teeth. "I'm cautious. I expect you to be alive to marry me when this case is closed."

He noticed that she dodged his steady gaze. She was holding out on him. He could see it in her expression before she'd masked her emotions. She was going to refuse him and he wasn't sure why that aggravated him so much. Maybe it was bruised male pride. Or so he'd like to think. But deep down, he suspected that while she was generally driving him *crazy* with her secrecy, her feisty spirit and her escape attempts, he had become so crazy about *her* that returning to the life he'd known before he met her had become unacceptable.

Hell, he had sidestepped entrapments for years. Now, when he'd decided he wanted a wife, because he didn't want to live without this bewitching firebrand, she was all set to refuse him.

There was irony for you, he thought.

A light rap at the door prompted Nate to bolt to his feet and retrieve his pistol. "Who's there?"

"Ludy."

The banjo player entered, then halted to survey the twosome and the food on the table. Apparently satisfied that Nate hadn't ravished Rachel in his spare time, Ludy plunked down on the edge of the bed.

"I just checked on Doc."

"How is he?" Rachel asked anxiously.

"Awake." He reached over to help himself to a slice of bread. "Living pretty high on the hog all of a sudden, aren't you, Montgomery? Did you rob a bank without telling me?"

Nate inwardly grimaced when Rachel glanced from the expensive entrees to him, as if it just dawned on her that he suddenly had a lot of extra money to toss around.

He shrugged nonchalantly. "My brother sent me clothes, boots and extra money so I'm celebrating."

The reply seemed to satisfy his companions.

"Doc is as cranky as an old grizzly," Ludy went on to say. "Dr. Yeager came by to examine him a few minutes ago and insisted that he remain in bed for several days, just to be on the safe side."

"That should give Doc time to break the habit of ingesting those fifty-proof tonics." Rachel glanced at Ludy. "Is

Doc still cursing me for ruining his stock of patented medicine?"

"Yep," he said, and grinned widely.

"That's not good," Nate said thoughtfully. "I don't want anyone, not even Doc in the infirmary, uttering Rachel's name. It might get back to the wrong people."

Ludy frowned, bemused. "Who are the wrong people?"

Nate waved him off. "Just warn Doc that mentioning Rachel could be bad for her health."

Ludy nodded but he stared contemplatively at Rachel, who flashed him a wide-eyed innocent stare that prompted the banjo player to chuckle. "I wanted you to know that I've taken a job at one of the saloons since the medicine show has shut down temporarily. I'll be at the Long Branch Saloon if you need to contact me." He pulled the gold-plated timepiece from his pocket to check the time. "I'm due at the saloon in an hour to play the piano and sing. I'll grab a bite before I go to work."

When Ludy exited, Rachel gobbled the remainder of her meal. "I'm going to see Doc, then I'll fetch the ledger after dark."

Nate huffed out an exasperated breath. "Woman, did anyone teach you what *no* means?"

She flashed him a grin that played hell with his attempt to stay mad at her. "I forgot how to accept *no* when I started saying *yes* to you." She sank onto his lap again to plant another kiss on his lips. "Let me compensate for the pain and trouble I've caused you. I'll be careful. I promise."

When she smiled hopefully at him, Nate gave in to her, against his better judgment. Damn but he was a fool for those dark, hypnotic eyes and that beguiling smile.

Of course, he planned to be on hand, in case anything went wrong, he reminded himself. She would only be out of his sight for a few minutes.

"All right," he said, and was rewarded with another lip-blistering kiss.

"Thank you, Nate. It means a lot." She dropped another kiss to his lips. "I almost forgot. When I checked on Doc earlier, I spoke to the other patient in the infirmary. The rancher was roughed up by Adolph's goons because he didn't pay his loan on time."

"I'll interview him after I make a few more inquiries at the saloon Turner owns. I'll meet you back here in an hour."

Nodding agreeably, Rachel hopped off his lap and Nate strode toward the door.

Adolph backed into the covered portico outside his office when he saw Jennifer Grantham and her daughter returning from supper. He wondered if Rachel had contacted her by now. He was tempted to grab Mrs. Grantham when she passed by and use scare tactics to determine if she knew something she wasn't telling.

Damn it, having his mistress skip town unexpectedly put him on edge. Plus, he was having a devil of a time locating that feisty firebrand who had knocked him unconscious and escaped the previous month.

Adolph shrank deeper into the shadows when Mrs. Grantham and her daughter passed by.

"Mama? Rachel never did tell me why she's dressed like a boy," Sophie commented.

"Sh-sh-sh!" Jennifer Grantham grabbed Sophie's hand and hurried down the street.

Adolph blinked in stunned amazement. Had Rachel

been hiding in plain sight the entire time that he and his men had been searching all over creation for her?

"Damn it to hell!" he snarled when he remembered the sooty-faced brat he had pretended not to notice on the boardwalk when he was on his way back from the Four Queens Hotel. The kid reminded him of his former life as a penniless whelp, wandering the streets while his mother made her living as a second-rate prostitute.

Muttering several pithy curses to Rachel's name, Adolph stalked down the street. Rachel was skulking around town, laughing at him behind his back because she'd cleverly eluded him. But he and his men would find her, he vowed vehemently.

He spat another curse when he remembered that he'd sent his hired thugs to search the small communities north of Dodge. He could have used the extra manpower to track down Rachel. But he'd find her eventually and he'd finish what he'd started the previous month. Knowing what a scrappy fighter she was, he would be ready and waiting when she fought back.

He smiled in fiendish glee as he scanned the darkening streets in search of the elusive waif. "As it happens, the position of mistress is open. Guess who's going to fill it?"

He chuckled devilishly as he sauntered toward the boutique. He was determined to have persuasive bargaining power when he captured Rachel. Very soon, Rachel would submit to his lusty demands—and she would be wearing nothing but the choke necklace he had purchased specifically for her.

Rachel noticed that both cattle herds had arrived in town that afternoon. The pens beside the railroad depot were bulging at the seams. She predicted South Side would be jumping alive since the cowboys arrived to celebrate the end of the trail. No doubt, they would squander the ninety dollars in wages they earned for herding cattle from Texas to Kansas.

The extra noise and boisterous laughter would override any racket she might make while entering the back door of the freight office, she assured herself. Glancing every which way to make sure she wasn't noticed, Rachel scurried off the boardwalk and trotted down the side alley by the barbershop. She zigzagged around the empty crates and garbage cans that littered the alley to reach the freight office. She grumbled when she twisted the knob and found the door locked.

Couldn't anything in life be easy? she asked herself as she extracted a hairpin from beneath her cap.

"Falling in love with Nate was easy," she reminded herself as she jimmied the pin in the keyhole. The lock clicked and the door opened with little effort. "At least one thing went right tonight."

Quietly, she inched into the dark storeroom, then stood there a moment, lost to the upsetting memory of her knock-down-drag-out battle with Adolph. Composing herself, she crept along the wall, careful not to stumble over the boxes and crates that lined the storeroom.

When she reached Adolph's office, she moved immediately to the desk. She tried to pull open the bottom drawer but it was locked. She assumed that's where Adolph stashed incriminating evidence pertaining to his corrupt business practices. She retrieved the hairpin again. Within a few moments, she had the drawer open. She clutched the leather-bound ledger to her chest in triumph. Breaking and entering had been easier than expected, thank goodness.

Retracing her steps in silence, Rachel felt her way to the back door, then gasped when an unseen hand snaked from the darkness to clamp hold of her throat, cutting off her air supply. She jerked her elbow backward to level a blow but her attacker sidestepped and she connected with air.

"Imagine my pleasure at finding out you are in town, Rachel."

She stiffened when Adolph's snarling voice vibrated around her in the darkness.

"How did you know I was here?" she choked out.

"Your friends the Granthams told me."

Rachel cringed at the insinuation. "What have you done to them?"

"They will survive, *if* you come along peaceably. After all, you know we have unfinished business, you sneaky hellion."

Icy dread settled over Rachel. She knew she had only one chance to escape—a surprise launch from his choke hold to burst out the back door. If that failed, she would be at his mercy. And damn him to hell and back for terrorizing Jen and Sophie!

Hoping to distract Adolph, she pretended to choke, then slumped lifelessly against him. When she felt his grasp relax slightly she stamped on his foot, slammed the ledger upside his head, then bolted headlong toward the door…

Pain exploded against the back of her head and she staggered, determined to make it to the alley. The second blow from the butt of Adolph's pistol sent her to her knees. She felt him yank the ledger from her grasp before he shoved her face-first to the floor.

"The last woman who tried to steal my ledger and blackmail me took a flying leap out the hotel window." His voice rolled over her, as if drifting down a dark, winding tunnel. "You'll join her in hell when I'm finished using you."

Cursing Adolph up one side and down the other, Rachel collapsed on the floor…and blacked out…

Chapter Sixteen

Nate smiled politely at Dr. Yeager when he walked into the examination office, which fronted the infirmary. "I came to see my friend, Doc Grant. Is he still conscious?"

Yeager nodded his gray head, then gestured toward the closed door. "He was awake and lucid a few minutes ago when I examined him. He's been fussing a lot about someone named Rachel and someone named Margie."

"He must be feeling better."

"I think he is going to be okay. Regaining consciousness was a step in the right direction because he could tell me where he hurts. Other than his obvious broken nose." He gestured for Nate to continue on his way to the infirmary. "I'm going to fetch food for me and my patients."

Nate stepped through the door and glanced down at the battered man Rachel had mentioned. He sympathized with the patient. There was nothing pleasant about taking a beating.

He extended his hand to the rancher. "I've been sent to investigate rumors of abuse to customers who are ordered to pay loans at the freight office with only a moment's notice."

The injured man glanced around, as if to ensure he wasn't overheard. "Did that kid who stopped by this afternoon tell you about me?"

"The kid works for me," Nate replied smoothly. Then he got down to the business of interviewing the victim who identified Rother, Lamont and Hanes as his attackers. According to the victim, they had taken all the money he had, plus several household items and a bottle of whiskey.

After the interview, Nate strode over to Doc, who was sporting a black eye and swollen nose and cheek. "Doc, are you awake?"

Doc's lashes swept up. It took him a moment to recognize Nate. "Oh, it's you. I want to get my hands on Rachel."

"She hasn't been by this evening?" Nate asked in concern.

Damn it, she told him she would stop here first, and then swing back to the hotel. Hell's bells, if she had trotted off to swipe the ledger ahead of schedule he was going to strangle her. She was supposed to wait for him to come along as backup.

"Sorry I can't stay longer," Nate told Doc. "But I'll be back to visit you later. In the meantime, don't mention Rachel's name to anyone."

"That's what Ludy said when he stopped in earlier. What's going on?"

Nate doubled at the waist to pat Doc's shoulder reassuringly. "I'll be back to explain after I check on Rachel."

He hurried out the back door, cursing himself up one side and down the other. He should have known Rachel intended to fetch the ledger without having him in the vicinity. Damn it, why hadn't he said no to that woman to begin with?

The answer to that question disturbed him so he tried not to think about it. All that mattered now was making sure Rachel was unharmed.

Rachel's head pounded like a bass drum when she regained consciousness. Her vision was blurred and her stomach pitched and rolled. She sympathized with Doc and Nate. If they felt as bad as she did, there wasn't much use in getting up. Except that she *had* to, because the last thing she remembered was suffering a debilitating blow from the butt of Adolph's pistol, and she knew he planned to torment her. Plus, she had to find Jennifer and Sophie and relocate the ledger for Nate.

Rachel tried to move her arms and legs and discovered she'd been staked out. There was a pallet beneath her and she was still in the storeroom.

"Good. You're awake."

Rachel swore under her breath when Adolph's voice settled over her—all arrogance, supremacy and triumph. She had tried to be as quiet as possible, but he'd obviously been waiting for her to move so he'd know she'd come to.

"Have you been in Dodge all this time?" he demanded. "And don't you dare scream for help. If you do, Mrs. Grantham and her daughter will never be seen or heard from again."

"You're bluffing." She hoped. "It was one thing to murder your harlot for attempting to blackmail you, but people will wonder why a high-profile businesswoman like Jennifer would abandon her boutique without notice. You can't explain that away and your hired thugs can't back you up."

"I can do anything I please," he snapped cockily. His footsteps echoed on the stone floor as he came to loom over her. "I practically own this town. The part I don't own, I control."

"Ah, yes, controlled by strong-arm tactics and fear." She smirked. "How could I have forgotten? Well, you might be able to hold on to the saloon and dance halls on South Side, but your investors object to your haughty claim that you *own* the freight office. You're just the hired hand, Adolph."

He puffed up like an offended toad. "What do you know about it?"

"I've been checking up on you while I've been out of your sight," she taunted him by saying. "I even went so far as to contact one of your investors."

"You're lying!" He sneered as he gouged her hip with the toe of his polished boot.

"If you believe that, then you'll be surprised when Edgar Havern arrives from Kansas City to audit your ledgers. I will see to it that he puts you out of business. You'll rot in jail, you snake!"

"What have you done!" he roared as he sank down on top of her, forcing the air from her lungs.

She swallowed apprehensively, then realized something was draped around her neck. She remembered what Jennifer had said about Adolph purchasing two necklaces. One for his mistress—and obviously one to use as a slave collar when he'd captured her.

"You've been mocking me the whole time, haven't you?" he muttered savagely.

"Actually I was disappointed that you didn't end up dead after our last confrontation," she said with more bravado than she felt. Provoking him probably wasn't her smartest plan of action but she preferred to keep him talking to delay the inevitable. "Why didn't you contact the marshal after I bested you, Adolph? I know you have him in your pocket."

"Because I wanted to handle your punishment privately." He braced his arms on either side of her head and leaned unnervingly close. "Because I have been waiting to hear you beg when I take you as many times as I please. You'll be mine, Rachel. And you will pay dearly until I grow tired of you and discard you like the trash you are."

When he lowered his head, attempting to kiss her hard and demandingly, she turned her face away. Irate, he backhanded her and her cheek burned like fire. Rachel twisted beneath him, then screamed bloody murder, despite his threat.

She knew there were an excessive number of people on the street this evening. If one of them heard her, she might gain assistance in escaping. She was anxious to track down Jennifer and Sophie. If Adolph had harmed one hair on their heads, she'd have his scalp!

"Shut up!" he hissed viciously, then tried to cover her mouth.

She bit his hand, then shrieked again when he tugged at her shirt, attempting to rip it from her body.

"No one is going to cross me to help you," he assured her hatefully. "Your fate is sealed, hellion. Accept it—"

His voice dried up when the back door slammed open unexpectedly. Nate's big brawny frame filled the exit, and Rachel had never been so relieved to see anyone in her entire life.

Adolph's roar of outraged fury gave away his location in the darkness. Nate charged at him like a mad bull, unintentionally stepping on Rachel's outstretched arm. She didn't complain because she had the spiteful satisfaction of hearing Adolph howl in agony when Nate's doubled fist connected with his jaw and he stumbled into the wall.

In the dim light spraying through the back door, Rachel could see the two silhouettes pounding away on each other. When they rolled across the floor, she heard Nate snarling like a grizzly and Adolph swearing profusely. When Nate grabbed the front of Adolph's shirt, cocked his arm and clobbered him, Adolph flopped backward and landed on Rachel.

"Hit him good and hard for me," she encouraged Nate.

"With pleasure, angel face."

Before Adolph could get his bearings and lever himself upright, Nate jerked him to his feet. He buried his fist in Adolph's soft underbelly, forcing his breath out in a pained whoosh. Adolph staggered against the shelves.

Several items tumbled over him when he kerplopped on the floor—much the same way he had when Rachel shoved him off balance a month earlier. Only last time Adolph had kept all his teeth. She was pretty sure Nate's power-packed punch had knocked several of them down the bastard's throat tonight.

"Get up, Turner," Nate bellowed furiously. "Give me an excuse to hit you again for resisting arrest."

"Who the hell are you?" Adolph muttered, then spit blood.

"Nate Montgomery, U.S. Marshal." He retrieved his new badge from his pocket and shoved it in Adolph's battered face. "You are under arrest for assault, embezzlement and whatever else I can think to throw at you."

"Oh, hell." Adolph sighed audibly, then slumped on the floor in a crumpled heap. "All because of Rachel St. Raimes… Damn you, woman…" Then he passed out.

"St. Raimes?" Nate parroted, then stared accusingly at her. "I thought your name was Waggoner."

"I didn't want to tell you that I go by my grandfather's

last name these days, just in case you came across a Wanted poster in Possum Grove or Crossville. Thank you," she added when he untied her hands so she could sit up and pull her ripped shirt back together. "Here, use these ropes on Adolph. I'll be much happier when he's bound up like a mummy."

"Spiteful little thing, aren't you?" he teased as he brushed his lips over her forehead.

"He made me mad. *Furious* is nearer the mark." Rachel untied her feet, then bounded up to hand Nate two more lengths of rope. "Adolph said he captured my friend Jennifer and her daughter. He was going to dispose of them if I didn't submit—"

She stopped talking when she saw Nate lurch around to deliver a brain-scrambling blow to Adolph's cheek in one spectacularly graceful move.

"Hey! If you hit him too hard, he'll be unconscious for hours," she protested as she tied the hem of her torn shirt together beneath her breasts. "You're supposed to pry needed information from him."

"I'll be right back."

Frowning, bemused, Rachel watched Nate storm from the storeroom to the office. He returned with a pitcher of water, then he poured it on Adolph's head. He sputtered and gasped for breath.

The instant he was cognizant, Nate grabbed him by the hair and gave his head a hard snap against the wall. "Where did you stash Mrs. Grantham and her daughter? And keep in mind that you'll be just short of dead if you don't tell me right now," he growled ominously.

"Sewing room," he mumbled dazedly. "Don't hit me again."

"You mean *after* this time?"

Rachel bit back a smile when Nate delivered another pulverizing blow that knocked Adolph's head against the fallen crate beside him.

"Okay, I'm done here…for now. Let's go find your friends."

He grabbed her hand and headed toward the back door. He moved so quickly that Rachel's head snapped back and she stumbled against him. His arms closed around her and he nuzzled his chin against the crown of her head. "I'm sorry, I didn't mean to be rough. I should also warn you that I'm going to be mad as hell at you later, because I was afraid something awful might happen before I found you. Right now, I'm just damned relieved. And we are not doing this again!"

"Not doing what?" she murmured as she snuggled against his broad chest, ashamed to admit that she enjoyed his protectiveness.

"Not playing by your rules when apprehending criminals or gathering evidence. I'm the professional. It's what I do."

She smiled contentedly, willing to agree to anything now that she had survived. Plus, Nate had pounded Adolph flat and the Granthams were minutes away from being rescued. "Whatever you say, Mr. Marshal. You're the boss."

He scoffed. "No, I'm not. Marry me. You can be the boss if it makes you happy."

The request wiped the smile from her lips. She knew he was quivering with protectiveness and feelings of obligation. But she couldn't bear to be around when those feelings of responsibility wore off and he realized he didn't love her and never would. Watching the mild affection he felt for her dwindle away would break her heart.

She wormed loose, spun around, then headed for the

back door once again. "We can discuss this later. I have to check on Jennifer and Sophie."

"Where's the ledger?" he asked suddenly.

"I don't know. I confiscated it, but Adolph took it away from me, then he hit me on the head and knocked me unconscious."

She heard Nate's enraged growl, followed by another punch to Adolph's jaw. Well, at least Nate cared enough to be angry on her behalf, she mused as she jogged down the alley to reach the back door of the boutique. Finding the door unlocked, she hurried inside, then stumbled to a halt when she heard adolescent sobbing in the dark sewing room.

"It's okay. I'm here," Rachel said as she felt her way across the room to light the lantern.

Jennifer and Sophie were tied to chairs that were positioned in the middle of the room, away from the door and window. The instant the light illuminated Rachel's bruised face and torn shirt, Jennifer sputtered vehemently.

"Did that monster do that to you? Let me loose so I can return the favor. Why are you wearing that necklace?"

Rachel chortled as she untied the ropes. "The necklace and the bruises were part of Adolph's vengeful punishment for me," she replied. "The U.S. marshal pulverized him, so we might not get our chance at Adolph. Rest assured that Adolph is experiencing a great deal of pain at the moment."

Jennifer untied Sophie, then gave her daughter a comforting hug. "There, there, sweetheart. We are both just fine. So is Rachel, though she looks the worse for wear. But it's testament that a woman can fend for herself when necessary and don't you forget that, Sophie."

Sophie bobbed her blond head as she wrapped her arms around her mother's waist.

Rachel smiled reassuringly at the child. "We are all going to be just fine. I'll be back to work, just as soon as my new friend, Doc Grant, is back on his feet. He is going to take several days of special care." She looked hopefully at Jen. "Is that okay?"

"Take as much time as you need," Jen insisted. "Then you can tell me all about where you've been and what you've been doing the past month…"

Her voice trailed off and her gaze drifted over Rachel's head. Rachel pivoted to see what had captured Jen's rapt attention. Her heart swelled at the sight of Nate, even if he had pinned the official-looking badge on his shirt.

"Jennifer Grantham, this is Nathan Montgomery, U.S. Marshal," she introduced. "Nate, this is Sophie."

Nate bowed politely and flashed a charming smile. "It's a pleasure to meet you, ma'am. You, too, Sophie. I'll be back tomorrow to interview you about your captivity. Right now, my star witness needs to recuperate from her harrowing ordeal. Also, her friend, Doc Grant, is impatient to see her."

Rachel inwardly winced. She expected that she was going to be subjected to another tongue-lashing—like the one Doc delivered before he windmilled down the hill.

"Did you find the ledger?" Rachel asked as Nate escorted her out the back door.

"Yep. Turner was kind enough to direct me to it when he regained consciousness for a few minutes."

"I'll bet he was eager to help," she said, and smirked.

"He provided me with another opportunity to clobber him a few more times for mistreating you. He was also more than happy to tell me where I can find his three thugs."

Rachel's attention shifted to Doc when Nate held open the door to the infirmary. Dr. Yeager blinked in surprise when he recognized Rachel, who had removed her cap as she approached Doc Grant.

"Let me get a cool compress and ointment for your bruised cheek," Dr. Yeager insisted. "That blow drew blood, thanks to someone's sharp-edged ring."

Rachel inspected her cheek to feel the slice in her skin. "It's just a scratch. I can treat it myself."

"I'm taking care of it, so that's that," Dr. Yeager said as he strode off to fetch his medical supplies.

"Hello, Doc. Feeling better?" Rachel asked gently.

He scowled at her. "I feel like hell, but thank you for asking. What happened to you?"

"Someone else around here doesn't like me much." She smiled wryly. "I'm sure you understand how they feel."

He looked the other way. "Don't tell me you did what you did for my own good again. I don't want to hear it."

"Fine, I won't say it. But I think Margie will be thoroughly disappointed if you consume more tonics, and drink yourself into oblivion, just so you can rejoin her sooner rather than later." She eased down beside him and patted his hand. "You have too much to give to those of us left on earth. You're my friend so I refuse to lose you. I want you to open an office in Dodge, where I plan to stay and return to work. I'm sure Dr. Yeager would appreciate the experienced help."

Dr. Yeager nodded enthusiastically as he returned to hand Rachel the cool compress and ointment. "She's right, Joseph. We could share the office and duties, if you're willing."

"I still feel the need to administer to patients in small communities who are without a certified physician," Doc contended. "I see no reason why they should suffer just because they don't live in a larger city."

Dr. Yeager rubbed his chin thoughtfully. "I don't see why we can't work out a rotation system so we can take turns traveling to various communities a few days a week. Once we establish a routine of where we'll be on a given day, needy patients will know exactly where to find us."

"I like the idea," Doc replied agreeably. "I would be honored to work with you."

Dr. Yeager smiled at his banged-up patient—and soon-to-be partner. "Truth be told, I'm looking forward to venturing out of town for some fresh air. I'll also have the chance to talk shop with someone trained in the field of medicine."

With that settled and out of the way, Doc turned his attention to Rachel. He lifted his arm to brush his fingertips over her injured cheek. "I don't deserve you, girl."

She smiled impishly at him. "Yes, you do. Besides, I want you to be the father I never had. You can even fuss at me occasionally if that makes you happy."

He nodded wearily, then glanced at Nate. "Make sure she gets some rest. But don't have the ceremony until I can stand up without passing out. I'm still giving her away. No matter when, no matter where, no matter what."

"I'll take good care of her for you," Nate promised as he drew Rachel to her feet. "We'll be back to see you tomorrow. Count on it, Doc."

Rachel allowed Nate to escort her onto the street and into the hotel. She hoped he didn't plan to press her tonight about the arrangements for this ridiculous wedding. She was too exhausted to match wits—and iron wills—with him.

To her surprise, he escorted her as far as the door of her room, dropped a kiss to her forehead and said, "I have to wrap up my dealings with Turner and the city marshal before I call it a night. Stay out of trouble, *please*."

Rachel was sorry to say that she was disappointed when he spun on his boot heels and walked away. Maybe he had finally come to his senses and realized that his misplaced obligation to her was unnecessary. Either that or the lingering aftereffects of the love potion had finally worn off completely.

"This is what you wanted, isn't it?" she asked herself as she closed the door. "This is what is best and you know it."

Rachel peeled off her tattered clothing and donned her nightgown. Exhausted, she collapsed in bed and fell asleep, despite the headache pounding relentlessly against her skull.

Nate frog-marched Turner to jail and watched shock and wariness claim the city marshal's expression when he noticed the U.S. Marshal badge Nate was sporting. Determined to incarcerate Turner, Nate hauled him past Seth Peterson's desk to lock the prisoner in a cell.

"I don't think this is a good idea," Marshal Peterson objected.

Nate turned the lock on the cell door, stuck the key in his pocket, then rounded on Peterson. "Unless you want to find yourself arrested for obstruction of justice, you'll keep my prisoner locked up," Nate boomed.

The stocky, dark-haired marshal shrank back when Nate's voice ricocheted around the cells. He glanced apprehensively from Nate to Turner, who glared viciously at him.

"If Turner escapes, I'm coming after *you* first. Decide right now whose side you're on because I'm not giving you a second chance, Peterson."

He didn't usually throw his authoritative weight around,

but he damn well intended to do it tonight. Peterson had to choose sides or he could hand in his badge. In addition, Nate wanted Turner to rot in jail because he had abused Rachel and sent her fleeing from her home and her job. Plus, the vicious bastard had murdered his mistress, cheated his investors and tortured his customers. One of his victims was still recovering from the beating Turner had ordered his goons to deliver.

"What's it going to be?" Nate demanded impatiently.

Peterson extended his meaty hand. "I'm sticking with you, Marshal Montgomery." When Turner voiced a threat, he ignored him. "Turner will be here when you get back."

"Also, there is the matter of Turner's hired ruffians," Nate went on to say. "They paid me an unpleasant visit and I'm filing charges. I will deal with them tomorrow. It's your job to keep Turner under wraps until I transport him to federal prison—or a hanging."

Peterson nodded his bushy brown head, then said, "I recommend taking reinforcements with you to apprehend the ruffians. They enjoy breaking body parts."

Nate knew that firsthand. But he'd dealt with dozens of ruthless fugitives and he had taken a very personal interest in arresting the heartless threesome. He'd be on guard during the upcoming confrontation.

He ambled onto the street, serenaded by the guffaws and loud voices coming from the south side of the tracks. He veered into the Long Branch Saloon for a few minutes to speak with Ludy. The moment he returned to the street more racket filled the air. However, the noise didn't drown out the voice in his head warning him to get Rachel to agree to marry him—soon—or she might duck out of town to avoid him.

He *had* to marry her, he reminded himself. He couldn't

talk himself out of it, especially after enduring several hellish moments this evening when he couldn't locate her fast enough to suit himself. He'd sweated bullets. Then he'd nearly exploded in fury when he'd stepped into Turner's storeroom of horrors to see Rachel staked out like a human sacrifice to that malicious devil.

That was when Nate realized that he couldn't survive unless he knew where Rachel was, knew that she belonged to him exclusively and that she would come home to him every single night for the rest of his life.

Nate shook his head in amazement as he strode toward the hotel. How in the world had Rachel convinced herself that the effect she had on him was the direct result of a love potion?

Apparently, that little hellion had no clue how addictive and potent she was to him. The only real question was whether she cared enough about him to share *her* life with *him*.

Nate decided he'd work up the nerve to ask her— tomorrow…

Chapter Seventeen

The next morning Nate tried to ease from bed without disturbing Rachel, but she popped awake the moment he set his bare feet on the floor.

"Where are you going?" She levered herself up on her elbow and her long raven hair spilled over her shoulder.

Nate couldn't resist. He leaned over to curl the long tendrils of her hair around his fist like a rope, then drew her head to his so he could press his lips to hers. Addicted, he reminded himself. He wanted Rachel to be the last person he saw before he went to bed at night and the woman he kissed awake every morning. He just wasn't sure how to convince her to agree to that arrangement.

Promising financial security and prestige didn't seem to interest her. In fact, she was convinced most men couldn't handle power and success. She was right, of course. He ought to know, because he'd hauled a helluva lot of money-hungry rapscallions to jail for corrupt dealings.

Losing her independence also worried her, he reminded himself. Funny, it had bothered him, too, until this beguiling, maddening, high-spirited female burst into his life, making him poignantly aware that he wanted things that had never interested him before.

Apparently, this was the dawn of a new day for him.

"Don't try to distract me with kisses," she murmured against his lips. "Where are you going?"

"To round up Turner's henchmen," he said—and realized too late that *he* was completely distracted by her sensuous response.

She pulled away and bounded to her feet in nothing flat. "I'm going with you."

"*No,* you aren't. I forbid it."

He knew the instant the words were out of his mouth that he should have shut up one sentence sooner.

Hands fisted on her curvaceous hips, she glared at him. "Yes, I am and you can forbid it to your heart's content, for all the good it's going to do you."

When she scooped up her boyish attire and shed her nightgown, the sight of her lush body hopelessly sidetracked him. "Okay, you can come." Damn it, what was he saying! "On one condition," he added hastily.

She fastened her shirt, leaving her shapely legs bare to his appreciative gaze. "Is this like the 'one more thing' you're famous for?"

He bobbed his head, disappointed when she stepped into her breeches. "Yep. Same sort of thing, angel face."

"What's the condition?" she asked as she twisted her long hair into a bun, then pulled on her cap.

"That you agree to marry me and that I don't have to chase you down to get you to say 'I do.'" He snatched up his breeches and hurriedly put them on.

"That's two conditions," she grumbled.

"Take them or leave them," he said as he donned his shirt.

"You're impossible, Marshal Montgomery." She flashed him an irritated glare as she sank into the chair to pull on her boots.

He grabbed his boots, winked and waggled his eyebrows. "Part of my irresistible charm."

He almost provoked her to smile…but not quite.

"Say the word and you can ride along. Otherwise, I'm going alone," he persisted.

She huffed out her breath, then surged to her feet. "Fine. The wedding is on. Hip, hip, hooray."

He strode over to wag his forefinger in her bruised face. "I'm holding you to it, Rachel. Now, according to your dear friend Turner—"

"That bastard will never be a friend of mine," she cut in bitterly.

"—the three goons were sent to check the area north of Dodge to locate you. They were supposed to report to him this afternoon. I'm thinking a welcoming party on the outskirts of town is an excellent idea. I talked to Ludy last night on my way back to the room. He's agreed to assist."

When Rachel wheeled toward the door, Nate followed closely behind her and breathed down her neck. "No heroics," he lectured. "I'm still mad at you about last night."

"No heroics for you, either," she countered.

"Agreed." He reached around her to open the door. "Let's go arrest those thugs so they can have a well-deserved reunion with Turner…in the calaboose."

Rachel snapped to attention when she saw the three ruffians walking their horses toward the wooded area where she, Nate and Ludy were waiting on horseback.

"I don't have to shoot anybody, do I?" Ludy whispered

anxiously. "I've been shot at a time or two, but I've never shot anyone before."

Nate handed over the double-barreled shotgun. "Your job is to look threatening and authoritative." He glanced wryly at Rachel. "And make sure she doesn't blast anyone out of the saddle unless I give the word."

When Ludy grinned, his dimples creased his cheeks. "Thanks for giving me an impossible task, marshal."

When Nate glanced at her and smiled, her heart nearly melted down her ribs. She knew how her mother and grandmother had felt. *Deeply, hopelessly, completely in love.* She also knew how desolate they had become when they were forsaken.

"You're drawing deputy wages," Nate told Ludy. "You'll collect on outstanding bounties for these outlaws. I'm willing to bet they are wanted—somewhere. For something."

"Oh, good, that makes me feel better," Ludy teased.

The lighthearted mood evaporated when the threesome drew near. Rachel went on high alert. She noticed all three men looked haggard. She suspected they had been drinking heavily and had yet to recover. Good. She prayed their capture would go without a hitch. Last night's ordeal with Adolph hadn't. It would be ever so nice if *something* went according to plan.

Following Nate's lead, she and Ludy trotted from the grove of trees beside the road as the three ruffians rounded the bend. She kept both of her pistols trained on Warren Lamont while Ludy drew a bead with the shotgun on Bob Hanes. Nate bore down on Max Rother, the eldest and the self-appointed leader.

It took a moment for the men to recognize Nate without his beard and mustache. They also noticed the shiny new badge his brother had sent as a replacement. Max Rother was the first to go for his six-shooter, but he didn't clear leather before Nate blasted his shooting hand. The pistol flipped over his wrist and tumbled into the grass.

"Anyone else want to challenge me to a shooting contest?" Nate asked as he walked his horse over to snap a handcuff on Rother's wrists.

Lamont and Hanes didn't say one word, just glared murderously at Nate.

"Rachel?"

"Yes, marshal?" She never took her eyes off Lamont.

"If either of the other two thugs moves so much as a muscle, you have my permission to blow them to kingdom come. Same for you, Ludy."

Warren Lamont smirked. Clearly, he didn't think Rachel, being a woman and all, could—or would—fire at him. She decided to let all three men know she meant business. She squeezed the trigger. Lamont's Stetson flew off his head. She shot another hole in it before it hit the ground.

"The next shot will be right between your eyes, Lamont. Care to bet I can do it?" she challenged.

Lamont backed down immediately.

Nate arched a curious brow. "Dare I ask where you learned to do that?"

"My father didn't stay around long enough to teach me much, but he did teach me that," she replied.

Nate glanced at Bob Hanes. "What about you? Do you want to see how well you stand up against her pistol and Ludy's shotgun?"

Hanes shook his head. "Not now. But I will later." He glared daggers at Ludy. "All of you are fools if you think Turner is going to let you put us in jail."

"Sorry to disappoint you, boys," Nate countered. "I jailed your boss last night. He's already been charged with murder, two counts assault and embezzlement."

Rother scoffed as he cradled his bloody hand against his belly. "You won't make it stick, even if you're a federal marshal. Turner runs this town."

Nate shrugged lackadaisically. "If he did once, he doesn't now. Every bully I've arrested, who thought he owned one town or another, is serving a prison sentence. Either that or he took the short route down the gallows. Furthermore, I'm best of friends with federal and district judges so I wouldn't get my hopes up on leniency."

Nate commandeered the reins to the horses, then handed them to Ludy. He handcuffed the ruffians to their horses, then retrieved several lengths of rope to tie their feet to the stirrups.

Rachel studied Nate, duly impressed with the practiced ease with which he captured his prisoners. He was cool under pressure. She admired that about him. That and dozens of other qualities too numerous to mention. She knew there and then that he was exceptionally good at his job and she could understand why he didn't want to give it up. He derived a sense of satisfaction from ridding society of ruthless scoundrels like Turner and his thugs.

While they rode back to Dodge, Rachel made plans to flit away from town—and stay gone until Nate gave up and returned to his headquarters. Wherever that was. Only then would she circle back to resume her job at Grantham Boutique.

But damn, she was going to miss Nate like nobody's business. Yet, it was better to make a clean break now. She couldn't marry him. Wouldn't marry him if all he felt was obligation.

* * *

Nate strode from the city marshal's office, immensely pleased to have the four men—who had bullied Dodge City's citizens into submission the past several years and had made Rachel's life miserable—behind bars. Testifying against them at their upcoming trial would be tremendously gratifying, as well.

He made a mental note to request a warrant for Bowman, who ran the train depot. He had skipped town, headed for parts unknown, when he got wind that a federal marshal had arrived and that his cohort, Turner, had been arrested.

Nate veered into the infirmary to have a few words with Doc, then he returned to the street. Now for the most difficult task of his life, he mused as he strode toward the Four Queens Hotel. Convincing Rachel to stay with him wouldn't be easy, he knew. He had the unshakeable feeling that she would bolt and run if he didn't return to the room soon enough to stop her…

"Well, at least you're still in one piece, no thanks to your dangerous job. I wasn't sure how I'd find you when I got here."

Nate nearly stumbled over his own feet when his father's unexpected voice wafted toward him. He lurched around to see his father and brother—the snitch and turncoat—appear from the doorway of a nearby restaurant.

Hell and damnation, this was the last thing he needed right now!

Nate's mutinous gaze zeroed in on his brother the traitor, then he focused on his father. "What are you doing here?"

"I wanted to make sure the package Ethan sent to you arrived safely." His father looked him up and down. "Apparently it did since you're wearing some of the clothing you left behind when you scampered off to save the world."

Nate rolled his eyes at his father's melodramatics. "I'm saving my home state, not the world," he clarified. His accusing gaze landed solidly on his older brother again. "I specifically asked you not to tell Father so that he wouldn't worry."

Ethan flung up his hands in supplication. "I tried to keep him from finding out," he defended himself. "Father caught me carrying the package with your name on it."

His father flapped his arms dismissively. "Don't blame Ethan. He made an admirable attempt to stop me from discovering what was going on."

Nate sent his brother another annoyed glance. "A half-hearted attempt at best, I'm sure."

He glanced at the upstairs windows of the hotel and wondered if he was too late to overtake Rachel before she flitted off to who knew where. She was an escape artist of the highest caliber who could fend for herself, he knew. This delay could cost him valuable time in his womanhunt.

Nate called attention to himself and said, "As you can plainly see I've recovered from my minor injuries. Plus, I've locked the criminals responsible for the robbery and beating in jail. Now, if you'll excuse me, I have a very important task to attend." He spun on his heels and strode quickly down the boardwalk.

His father chased him down and latched on to his arm. "You are coming home with us. There is no need whatsoever for you to endanger your life here on this outpost of society. You need a wife and children, like your brother. It will help you settle into a nonthreatening lifestyle."

Brody hitched his thumb toward Ethan. "Look at your brother. He's happy. Aren't you, Ethan?"

On command, Ethan nodded his dark head and smiled dryly. "As a clam." When Brody gouged him in the ribs, he added, "You should come home with us. We miss you. Dozens of eligible women have been asking after you since you left. You can have your pick of the crème de la crème, little brother."

Nate gnashed his teeth while his patience grew thinner by the second. "Very well rehearsed, Ethan," he said caustically. "But as it happens, I've found a suitable match."

Brody's gray brows shot up like exclamation marks. "Here? In this godforsaken hellhole of a town on the edge of nowhere? You must be joking."

Nate glanced anxiously at the row of second-story windows again. He was running short of time—if he hadn't run completely out of time already. "I've never been more serious about anything in my life."

"Who is she?" his father quizzed him intently. "What connections does she have?"

Nate smiled wryly. "Her grandfather is a wealthy businessman in Kansas City. He moves in your elite social circle, in fact. Julian St. Raimes is Edgar Havern's father-in-law and silent business partner."

"And he allows his granddaughter to gallivant out here?" Brody hooted, then frowned suspiciously. "Is she the black sheep of her family?"

"Anything but." Nate wheeled toward the hotel. Then, in afterthought, he veered around the corner to where the medicine-show wagon was parked.

"Oh, good God!" Brody crowed in disbelief as he gaped at the logo on the wagon. "She works for a quack doctor who peddles patented medicine?"

Nate reached into the back of the wagon to grab a bottle. "She did for a while, yes. She's an exceptional sharp-shooter and survivalist. Also, she is an incredible vocalist, in addition to her other amazing talents. She puts most of the members of Kansas City's famed lyric theater to shame."

"She's a gunslinger, a singer *and* a small-time actress, too?" Brody teetered backward in shock. "Sweet mercy, the Montgomery name will be tarnished forever."

Ethan, who was biting back a chuckle, grabbed Brody when he swayed on his feet.

"Tarnish the Montgomery name? On the contrary." Nate smirked in contradiction. "She'll give our family the pizzazz it's missing. The Montgomerys have become too stuffy and full of themselves. She'll shake them up."

"Shake us up? *Phhht!* That settles it. We are taking you home on the first train out of here," Brody decreed. "You must have suffered a blow to the head that has hampered your good judgment."

Nate reversed direction and headed to the hotel. Ethan and Brody trailed a few steps behind him. Nate's future was at stake and he had no more time for his father's protests and time-consuming delays. He smiled faintly, wondering if he should turn his father loose on Rachel if she refused his request to stay with him.

Of course, Nate doubted that even the domineering, authoritative Brody P. Montgomery could convince Rachel to do something she didn't want to do. The woman had a mind of her own and she knew how to use it. That was another of the many things that endeared her to him.

"Now where are you off to in such a flaming rush?" Brody muttered as he tried to keep up with Nate's swift strides.

"To see your future daughter-in-law, if she'll have me

as a husband," he threw over his shoulder as he breezed through the hotel lobby.

"If?" Brody snorted sarcastically. "What woman wouldn't want you? You're wealthy and well-connected."

"Those are not points in my favor," Nate grumbled. "She claims men with money are self-absorbed and spoiled rotten."

"Really? How intriguing. I cannot wait to meet this multitalented misfit," Brody said, huffing and puffing his way up the staircase.

Nate took the steps two at a time in his haste to reach Rachel's room—and prayed for all he was worth that he could stop her before she made her getaway.

While Nate had been filling out official forms in Marshal Peterson's office, Rachel had stopped by her old room at the boardinghouse to pick up a few more garments and to pay her overdue rent from the previous month. Then she returned to the Four Queens Hotel to gather her belongings. Despite the ever-widening hole of emptiness that engulfed her chest, she grabbed her satchels and opened the door to make her escape from town.

She gasped in surprise when she found Nate blocking her path. "What are you doing back here so soon?" she chirped.

Nate gestured over his shoulder to call her attention to the two fashionably dressed men who bore a striking resemblance to Nate in height and hair color.

"This is my father, Brody Montgomery, and my brother, Ethan," he introduced without taking his intense azure-eyed gaze off her. "And this is Rachel in disguise."

Both men assessed her boyish attire, clearly unimpressed. Their eyes popped when Nate reached over to pull the cap from her head, allowing her raven hair to spill over her shoulders in thick shiny curls.

"Rachel is so stunningly attractive that she has to travel incognito. I, myself, have had to fight off a passel of bedeviled men with a stick to protect her."

Brody's and Ethan's expressions became more complimentary and speculative as they gave her the once-over— a second and third time. Then Brody grinned broadly and inclined his head, as if giving his silent approval.

Rachel didn't know what she'd done to earn Brody's respect, but she responded with a dazzling smile, then curtsied elegantly. She had no idea what Nate had said previously to his father, but she assumed she was supposed to play along with whatever explanation he'd dreamed up when his family arrived in town without advanced notice.

"It is an honor and pleasure to meet you, gentlemen," she said in her most sophisticated voice.

"You should book a room in the hotel," Nate advised his father and brother. "Rachel and I have arrangements to discuss. We'll see you later."

The two men bowed politely, then headed downstairs.

"Why are they here?" Rachel murmured as the men disappeared from sight.

"They came to drag me back to Kansas City, cursing and kicking, if my supposed bride-to-be bails out on me," Nate replied. He cast her a brooding glance, then strode inside the room. He paused to lock the door behind him, then glared at her again. "Where the hell do you think you're going this time? We had a *deal,* remember?"

Rachel tossed aside her satchels, then turned to face him directly. She stared up at him, committing everything about his appearance to memory so she could conjure him up in the long, lonely days ahead. "I can't marry you, Nate."

"Can't marry me or won't marry me? Which is it?" His intense gaze bore into her. "I want to know what it will take to convince you to stay."

Your love, she replied silently but she said aloud, "Nothing is going to change my mind."

"Not even if I can tell you where Julian St. Raimes is living and what he's been doing for the past forty years?"

Rachel snapped up her head. Her gaze locked with his. "I'm not sure I care to know. He left my grandmother and broke her heart so I see no need to claim him as my kinfolk."

Nate shrugged nonchalantly. "That is your decision, angel face. If and when the time comes that you want to know, I'll tell you."

She frowned, bemused, when Nate pulled an embossed bottle of tonic from his pocket. "Doc says you should take two teaspoons of this stuff."

"Why? There is nothing wrong with me."

Nate strode up in front of her and held the bottle to her lips. "I know. You're perfect. Take two swallows nonetheless."

She took a cautious sniff. It didn't smell like poison or tonic. It smelled like water. Although she was all set to refuse, she couldn't resist the engaging smile on Nate's ruggedly handsome face or the playful glint in his sky-blue eyes.

"Is this an undetectable poison?"

Nate shook his auburn head. His grin became wider as she dutifully drank from the bottle.

"It tastes exactly like the water I replaced in Doc's tonic bottles."

Nate dropped a kiss to her lips. "You're mistaken. It's a love potion. I mixed it myself."

She blinked, stunned, as she surveyed his rakish smile.

"Is it taking effect yet?" he asked as he skimmed his fingers over her mouth.

"What effect are you expecting?"

"I expect you to fall madly in love with me and agree to marry me. Doc says he'll be ready to give you away in the morning, if we hold the ceremony at the infirmary." He waggled his brows playfully. "The wedding might not be spectacular but I'll see to it that the honeymoon will be."

Lord, this was so hard, she thought. Denying what her heart wanted was the most difficult choice she had ever made. Nate was being so charming and good-humored that it was killing her to turn him down.

"Uh-oh, I don't like that look," he said. "I don't think you ingested enough of my potion. Take another big sip."

"Nate—"

"We can live in Dodge, if that's what you prefer," he cut in quickly. "I can limit the amount of time I'm away from home by hiring an extra deputy. You can keep your job and—"

She kissed him to shush him—and got lost in the overwhelming affection she felt for him. When he pulled her tightly into his arms and devoured her lips, as if he were starving for the taste of her—as she was for him—her resistance crumbled in nothing flat.

"Don't leave me, Rachel," he whispered huskily. "I need you. You make me happy… And there's one last thing you need to know…"

She tilted her head to stare at him. The expression on his face bedazzled her. "What's the last thing?"

He curled his hand beneath her chin to hold her steady gaze. "I'm in love with you, Rachel. I've never been in love before and I've tried not to be, but I can't help myself.

There's not enough willpower in the world for me to resist the way I feel about you."

She gaped at him, hardly daring to believe that he meant what he said. She simply stood in his arms, her jaw sagging wide enough for a quail to roost.

Nate nodded firmly. "This is *not* your love potion doing the talking for me. This is my heart and soul asking you to stay with me. I want to make you as happy as being with you makes me."

Rachel squealed in delight as she flung her arms around his neck and nearly squeezed the stuffing out of him. Could it be that the family curse had been broken finally? She certainly didn't feel cursed. She felt blessed. Nate loved her, just the way she was. He wanted to marry her and he hadn't said one infuriating thing about responsibility and obligation.

"I love you, too, Nate, more than words can say!" Having held back the confession for too long, it gushed from her mouth like an erupting geyser.

"You're not just saying that because you feel sorry for me after I got beat up and you felt responsible, are you?"

"*Sorry* for you?" she echoed. "Of course not." When he stared hesitantly at her, she frowned. "What's wrong?"

"I have to confess that I haven't been completely honest with you."

"I wasn't completely honest with you, until after we had the unpleasant dealings with Adolph and his henchmen all sorted out," she reminded him.

"This is different."

Now she was getting worried. "But whatever it is, you still love me…right?"

"With all my heart." Nate dragged in a deep breath that made his chest swell like an inflated balloon, then he said hurriedly, "I know you don't like rich men, but I'm wealthy. I'm sorry about that."

She blinked in stunned amazement, then blinked again when he nodded affirmatively. She'd had no clue what he'd intended to say, but that really caught her off guard. "Rich?" she squeaked, owl-eyed. "How rich?"

"Rich enough that you better drink the whole bottle of love potion. I knew I was going to upset you when I told you."

Rachel guzzled the water, then carelessly tossed aside the bottle. Her dark eyes sparkled with affection and amusement. "That is an extremely potent potion you mixed up, Mr. U.S. Marshal. Knowing that you're disgustingly wealthy isn't fazing me a bit. I promise not to hold it against you."

"All I want you to hold against me is *you*," he murmured as he wrapped her in his arms, spellbound by her impish smile and the love glittering in those dark, mystifying eyes.

The tension that had been hounding him fizzled beneath the indescribable pleasure flooding through him. Rachel loved him and all was right with his world.

"I'm absolutely crazy about you, angel face," he growled seductively as he scooped her up in his arms and wheeled toward the bed. "Now that I think on it, I believe it *must* be your powerful love potion doing the talking for me. I guess it didn't wear off, after all."

"I told you it was potent stuff."

She grinned mischievously, looking happier and more at ease than he'd ever seen her. It filled his heart with such joy that he swore it would explode.

Nate tumbled with her onto the bed, his rumbling laughter mingling with her playful giggles. In less than a heartbeat their amusement died. Passion flared hot and impatient between them, just as it always had. Just as it always would.

"*You* are my love potion, angel face," Nate assured her as he worshipped her lush body with kisses and caresses. "I'll never need anyone else but you to make my life complete."

And he never did because Rachel remained by his side, loving him as deeply and devotedly as he loved her. From that moment until long past forevermore…

* * * * *

*Fan favorite Leslie Kelly is bringing her
readers a fantasy so scandalous,
we're calling it FORBIDDEN!*

*Look for
PLAY WITH ME
Available February 2010 from Harlequin® Blaze™.*

"AREN'T YOU GOING TO SAY 'Fly me' or at least 'Welcome Aboard'?"

Amanda Bauer didn't. The softly muttered word that actually came out of her mouth was a lot less welcoming. And had fewer letters. Four, to be exact.

The man shook his head and tsked. "Not exactly the friendly skies. Haven't caught the spirit yet this morning?"

"Make one more airline-slogan crack and you'll be walking to Chicago," she said.

He nodded once, then pushed his sunglasses onto the top of his tousled hair. The move revealed blue eyes that matched the sky above. And yeah. They were twinkling. Damn it.

"Understood. Just, uh, promise me you'll say 'Coffee, tea or me' at least once, okay? Please?"

Amanda tried to glare, but that twinkle sucked the annoyance right out of her. She could only draw in a slow breath as he climbed into the plane. As she watched her passenger disappear into the small jet, she had to wonder about the trip she was about to take.

Coffee and tea they had, and he was welcome to them. But her? Well, she'd never even considered making a move on a customer before. Talk about unprofessional.

And yet…

Something inside her suddenly wanted to take a chance, to be a little outrageous.

How long since she had done indecent things—or decent ones, for that matter—with a sexy man? Not since before they'd thrown all their energies into expanding Clear-Blue Air, at the very least. She hadn't had time for a lunch date, much less the kind of lust-fest she'd enjoyed in her younger years. The kind that lasted for entire weekends and involved not leaving a bed except to grab the kind of sensuous food that could be smeared onto—and eaten off—someone else's hot, naked, sweat-tinged body.

She closed her eyes, her hand clenching tight on the railing. Her heart fluttered in her chest and she tried to make herself move. But she couldn't—not climbing up, but not backing away, either. Not physically, and not in her head.

Was she really considering this? God, she hadn't even looked at the stranger's left hand to make sure he was available. She had no idea if he was actually attracted to her or just an irrepressible flirt. Yet something inside was telling her to take a shot with this man.

It was crazy. Something she'd never considered. Yet right now, at this moment, she was definitely considering it. If he was available…could she do it? Seduce a stranger. Have an anonymous fling, like something out of a blue movie on late-night cable?

She didn't know. All she knew was that the flight to Chicago was a short one so she had to decide quickly. And as she put her foot on the bottom step and began to climb up, Amanda suddenly had to wonder if she was about to embark on the ride of her life.

The Viscount's Betrothal
LOUISE ALLEN

SWEPT OFF HER FEET!

Decima knows her family regularly remind themselves to "marry off poor dear Dessy." But who would ever want a graceless, freckled beanpole like herself? Then she encounters Adam Grantham, Viscount Weston—the first man she's ever met who's tall enough to sweep her off her feet… literally! Could such a handsome rake really find *her* attractive?

Available February
wherever you buy books.

HARLEQUIN® *Blaze*™

*It all started
with a few naughty books....*

As a member of the Red Tote Book Club,
Carol Snow has been studying works of
classic erotic literature…but Carol doesn't
believe in love…or marriage. It's going to take
another kind of classic—Charles Dickens's
A Christmas Carol—and a little otherworldly
persuasion to convince her to go after her
own sexily ever after.

Cuddle up with

Her Sexy Valentine

by STEPHANIE BOND

Available February 2010

---

red-hot reads

REQUEST YOUR FREE BOOKS!

HARLEQUIN® HISTORICAL:
Where love is timeless

2 FREE NOVELS PLUS 2 FREE GIFTS!

YES! Please send me 2 FREE Harlequin® Historical novels and my 2 FREE gifts (gifts are worth about $10). After receiving them, if I don't wish to receive any more books, I can return the shipping statement marked "cancel." If I don't cancel, I will receive 6 brand-new novels every month and be billed just $4.94 per book in the U.S. or $5.49 per book in Canada. That's a saving of 20% off the cover price! It's quite a bargain! Shipping and handling is just 50¢ per book in the U.S. and 75¢ per book in Canada.* I understand that accepting the 2 free books and gifts places me under no obligation to buy anything. I can always return a shipment and cancel at any time. Even if I never buy another book from Harlequin, the two free books and gifts are mine to keep forever.

246 HDN E4DN   349 HDN E4DY

Name _____ (PLEASE PRINT) _____

Address _____ Apt. # _____

City _____ State/Prov. _____ Zip/Postal Code _____

Signature (if under 18, a parent or guardian must sign) _____

Mail to the **Harlequin Reader Service:**
IN U.S.A.: P.O. Box 1867, Buffalo, NY 14240-1867
IN CANADA: P.O. Box 609, Fort Erie, Ontario L2A 5X3
Not valid for current subscribers to Harlequin Historical books.

Want to try two free books from another line?
Call 1-800-873-8635 or visit www.morefreebooks.com.

* Terms and prices subject to change without notice. Prices do not include applicable taxes. N.Y. residents add applicable sales tax. Canadian residents will be charged applicable provincial taxes and GST. Offer not valid in Quebec. This offer is limited to one order per household. All orders subject to approval. Credit or debit balances in a customer's account(s) may be offset by any other outstanding balance owed by or to the customer. Please allow 4 to 6 weeks for delivery. Offer available while quantities last.

Your Privacy: Harlequin Books is committed to protecting your privacy. Our Privacy Policy is available online at www.eHarlequin.com or upon request from the Reader Service. From time to time we make our lists of customers available to reputable third parties who may have a product or service of interest to you. If you would prefer we not share your name and address, please check here. ☐

Help us get it right—We strive for accurate, respectful and relevant communications. To clarify or modify your communication preferences, visit us at www.ReaderService.com/consumerschoice.

HH10